Praise for *Doña Clean*

"[Writers] have broken out of th feminism/xicanisma that can be desc tillo and others have accomplished is to demonstrate to the literary world that our stories are indeed 'rich, universal literature.' Castillo is top shelf."
 —*El Tecolote*

"The variety of voices in Castillo's collection is impressive, with characters spanning different ages, genders, nationalities, and socioeconomic backgrounds. She writes each protagonist with empathy and a convincing style."
 —*Chicago Reader*

"What a joyous, wonderful, achy collection. These stories shimmer! Ana Castillo is at her best—storytelling with compassion, clarity, and cultural wisdom."
 —Sandra Guzmán, award-winning journalist, filmmaker, and author

"Ana Castillo is back and our collective souls will be thankful for it! This rich collection is brimming over with yearning, love, and memories so visceral, I'd linger on them as if they were my own. Castillo has always birthed indelible characters, and the men and women who inhabit *Doña Cleanwell Leaves Home* prove her gift for illuminating the nuances of humanity are more lustrous than ever."
 —Xochitl Gonzalez, author of *Olga Dies Dreaming*

"Celebrated author Castillo's latest collection centers on women—their secrets and disappointments and, ultimately, their hope and freedom—via a wide variety of characters, including a geeky spinster sister whose younger brother learns of her passionate love story only after her death, and a married woman who gets unpleasantly jarred from her menopausal malaise. Throughout, Castillo uses her compassionate voice to illustrate the determination, bravery, and imagination of everyday Latina women." —*Ms.* magazine

"In the case of Castillo's story collection, the characters' worlds careen over, under, and around each other. From Chicago to Mexico City and other points south, these Mexicans, New Mexicans, Mexican immigrants, their descendants, and a few ghosts attempt to connect with varying levels of success. . . . Readers will be thrilled that Castillo has returned to fiction after her book of poetry, *My Book of the Dead* (2021)." —*Booklist*

"A new collection of stories from a grande dame of Chicana literature . . . Throughout these stories, Mexico is the source of both mystery and clarity, whether through characters' histories as immigrants or children of immigrants, or because, as happens frequently, the characters in these tales must travel there, like Dorothy to Oz, to unlock knowledge which often has the potential to alter their lives. . . . Castillo's truth-seeking characters leave an impression."
—*Kirkus Reviews*

"The seven dense and digressive stories in Ana Castillo's *Doña Cleanwell Leaves Home: Stories* breathe similar life into Chicago and Mexico City. . . . 'Tango Smoke' goes on to become the best story of the bunch. It's about a divorcée named Mártir who moves in with a much younger pot dealer who shares her love of dance. The Chicago she inhabits feels as authentically complicated and desperate as her character. Castillo deserves credit for training her gaze on working people, squarely and without sentimentality. This is a world of factories and diners, beauty schools and swing shifts; the characters struggle to make rent and look for ways to feel halfway human despite all the economic and cultural forces aligned against them."
—*New York Times Book Review*

Doña Cleanwell Leaves Home

Stories

Ana Castillo

HARPERVIA

An Imprint of HarperCollins*Publishers*

DOÑA CLEANWELL LEAVES HOME. Copyright © 2023 by Ana Castillo. All rights reserved. Printed in the United States of America. No part of this book may be used or reproduced in any manner whatsoever without written permission except in the case of brief quotations embodied in critical articles and reviews. For information, address HarperCollins Publishers, 195 Broadway, New York, NY 10007.

HarperCollins books may be purchased for educational, business, or sales promotional use. For information, please email the Special Markets Department at SPsales@harpercollins.com.

FIRST HARPERCOLLINS PAPERBACK PUBLISHED IN 2024

Designed by Terry McGrath

Library of Congress Cataloging-in-Publication Data is available upon request.

ISBN 978-0-06-325942-3

24 25 26 27 28 LBC 5 4 3 2 1

To every girl and woman who found their
voice and to all those who could not.

CONTENTS

PROLOGUE

It Starts with the Journey

IT STARTS WITH the journey; as ever, whether Quixote or Kerouac, you are in search of the Divine. In search of Light, we may find ourselves in a dark room, an abandoned building, on a long thorny road with no end. It's a pedestrian's path, no argument there, the longest trail you can fathom, a winding chain of snakes tied head to tail, the venomous and the harmless, awesome for their iridescent skins, their ability to shed and begin anew. We walk a good way on tiny legs and yet we're so insignificant, we aren't aware of being minutiae.

We think we're grand.

We think we're worlds unto ourselves.

We think we are gods—tiny gods with helmets but gods nonetheless.

Does an ant recognize the elm by the single root it so industriously scurries around?

Cuernavaca

ALTHOUGH THE REPERTOIRE was limited, he was a prodigious storyteller. A natural entertainer, some said. "Do you believe in ghosts?" my father often started. The family was all together, a grandchild on his lap, everyone around the Formica table, content after the plentiful meal my mother had prepared. Each time we shook our heads, glad to hear the story again. "Neither do I," he'd start, "but one time I had an experience . . ."

As a young man, Raymundo, "Mundo," hit Route 66 to Mexico with a few pals. It was the early sixties. They were an inseparable five who had grown up together on DeKoven Street. In their twenties, the guys put a band together. Mundo was The Heartbreakers' drummer. He said he learned to pound out a beat at the suitcase factory where he worked for a while. The leader, the band's singer and self-appointed manager, was a cool guy named Chuck. They played mostly mambos—huge fans of Pérez Prado—but Chuck's vocals also lent themselves to sensual ballads. "He thinks he's Sinatra," the crooner's younger brother and the band's bass player, Franky, used to crack. Sibling rivalry between the brothers was constant, but as the other guys saw it, regardless, either would have laid his life down for the other.

It was Chuck's idea that The Heartbreakers try their luck in Mexico. He had a contact at RCA Records who said he might get them in the studio in Mexico City, or at least that's what they told everybody. It was never clear whether The Heartbreakers got to record, but what was a fact was that they stayed in Mexico for six months. The band rented a villa in Cuernavaca just outside the capital, and the word got back that they were living the high life.

The colonial city of Cuernavaca was once home to Maximiliano, emperor of Mexico crowned by Napoleon, and to Carlota, the wife who went mad. Just outside Mexico City with year-round temperate weather, it was a popular getaway. In the early 1960s, Hollywood stars like Elizabeth Taylor and Eddie Fisher made Acapulco their playground, but private folks with means preferred charming Cuernavaca. Some had second homes, families went on weekends, and couples rendezvoused. Landlocked, the city had swimming pools throughout. The villa my father and friends leased had one. Family in Chicago resided in rented flats. The idea of a private pool was grandiose.

The Heartbreakers also had a full-time housekeeper, a girl from a village by the name of María. They were guys used to doting mothers and traditional wives picking up after them, doing laundry and cooking, so a full-time housekeeper—while also in the realm of grandiose back home—made sense there.

My parents were courting at the time. There were a few letters exchanged between them, marking that period when my mother said she called off their engagement more than once. Back then, phoning long distance was expensive and complicated. You could go weeks without hearing from someone far away, and it wasn't a big deal. Mundo's lady, my future mom, was too practical to look for him, but she mentioned he did call a couple of times—collect.

As Dad told it, a story repeated to the same captive audience over the years, that evening he and the guys were hanging out in the living room, enjoying cocktails and listening to the hi-fi stereo. Mundo made no mention of female guests, but later, in my grown-up mind, I figured them in, svelte in tight-fitting satin dresses or with cropped hair and in go-go boots. I imagined the girls doing the cha-cha solo while sipping martinis. As the night wore on, everyone got soused.

That night, someone in the group suddenly stopped and became fixated in the direction of the kitchen entrance. His face having gone pale, they all turned to see. A nude woman emerged with a glazed expression. She moved slowly, although it didn't seem she was taking steps. "It was like she was gliding above the floor," my dad said, as his gaze in the distance returned him to Cuernavaca. It seemed a faint wave of hesitation ran over his face. The figure didn't appear to be aware of anyone but continued toward the spiral travertine stairs with wrought iron banisters. She ascended not by taking steps up but floating "like an angel," Mundo recalled. Once she reached the top landing, she was out of sight.

One of the guys hurried to the landing, eyes popping and looking up, and called out, "She's not there!" She must've gone into one of the bedrooms, they all surmised. But no one volunteered to go up and check. Instead, my dad and a couple of others hurried to the kitchen. How had she gotten into the house? The back door was locked, as were the windows. The shutters were bolted from the inside.

Even as years passed, my father never failed to add one other detail, so indelibly engraved on his mind. As the mysterious lady moved from the kitchen to the staircase and ascended, each of the witnesses swore she became transparent. "I don't believe in ghosts," Dad repeated at the end of the account. "But that is what we saw."

One of us would never fail to inquire, maybe it was me, initially the smallest and youngest member of the family and most willing to show gullibility, "Did anyone ever see the lady again?" Each time my father seemed reluctant to answer, and each time the reply was the same: "Yes."

Chuck wasn't in on the evening of the apparition. When he returned, he found the story incredulous. Surely the guys had made it up as an excuse to head home. His brother, Franky, had a wife to get back to, and another worried about the job he'd taken leave from not waiting for him. Chuck didn't go as far as to call them liars but said they must have mistaken the young housekeeper for a phantom. María had come out of the kitchen and gone upstairs quietly so as not to disrupt the party. The explanation was that simple.

It was settled until something happened on another night when Chuck came home and the guys were either out or sleeping in their rooms. It was dark and quiet. The sound of cicadas and the perfume of gardenias came through the open patio doors. Chuck said he'd gone over to slide the glass doors shut when his eye caught a feminine figure coming out of the pool. He stepped outside. "Hey, who's there?" he shouted in Spanish.

"The weird thing was," Chuck told the guys over breakfast the next morning, "she didn't run off when I called out but . . ." He made a gliding motion with his hand. "She just vanished, disappeared." My father was always meticulous about his dress even in the morning: I pictured him in one of his Italian knit shirts.

"What do you mean, 'disappeared'?" Mundo asked.

"Disappeared . . ." Chuck repeated and snapped his fingers. "Poof!" The other guys winced. Whether it was the idea that the villa was haunted or a general consensus was reached, a week later the guys packed up the Cadillac and wound their way to El Norte.

My father never tired of telling the story about the phantom, and all my life I never tired of hearing it. He recalled the time he spent in Mexico so nostalgically that when, in my late thirties, I spent a summer at the villa of some friends in Cuernavaca, his stories stayed with me. For whatever reason, as if it were my own souvenir of the place, I'd brought along a postcard he'd sent to my mother. It included the address and phone number of where The Heartbreakers were staying. "Wish you were here," he added, but nothing else.

My hosts, Diego and Carolina, like me, were architects. We met at a convention in Chicago. I showed them around my hometown, and they extended an invitation to visit over the summer. They'd just redone the estate Diego inherited. He and his wife added a heated pool, tennis and basketball courts, and a beautiful art studio that nobody used, as no one in the family was an artist. We enjoyed many splendid times during that summer when I stayed in the guesthouse.

My friends often entertained. There were long formal dinners at the marble table outside in one of the gardens, and pool parties with excellent appetizers and drinks served by the full-time staff. Petra cooked and kept house; her husband, Fernando, maintained the grounds. There was a chauffeur who drove the children, dropped Diego at his office, and took Carolina on errands. The nanny was always with the children at their various activities, which were never-ending.

Just as often, my hosts had friends who dropped by casually. One frequent visitor was Enzo. He'd come from Rome years before to visit Mexico and stayed. One balmy evening, Diego was working late, as was often the case, so it was Carolina, Enzo, and me relaxing in the vast living room.

Petra and Fernando brought us gin and tonics on trays and *sopes* made with beans and shredded chicken and topped with fresh salsa. It might easily have been like the nights my father described of his extended stay there so long ago.

There was no stereo sounding out mambos, but Enzo and Carolina played a duet on the piano. It was hearing Enzo's sensitive performance that night that made me reconsider the vapid impression I'd had of him, a quickly-approaching-over-the-hill playboy.

The soft music, aromatic breeze coming in through the open windows—it was a sublime moment for me, the kind you tell yourself you'll never forget, when quickly it slipped into something else. The small talk had stopped and the only sounds in the large room were the staff's movements and the ice clinking in the tall glasses of our tart beverages with floating slivers of Mexican limes. Sensing the hour had come to say good night, Enzo took a deep swallow to finish his drink and set the glass down on the wide square coffee table.

Carolina, who always spoke with the smile of a gracious hostess, didn't ask him to stay but said, "Do drive carefully, *cariño*."

"Yes, yes, of course," Enzo said, clasping his hands together as if to indicate he was wrapping things up. The lanky Roman who'd picked up his Spanish in Mexico smiled and said, "I'll be fine. Don't worry yourself, *bella*." Then he did a little twist: "Maybe I'll go dancing."

"Ha," Carolina said, raising her glass. If her husband had been home, they might have come along, she added.

"Yes," Enzo said. "It is too bad. A pity your husband works much too much." He gave me a furtive glance, which I didn't appreciate for its implication.

Carolina brushed off any insinuation about Diego's long absences or an "us" and instead said, "Watch out that you don't run into the man with the sombrero!"

I'd never heard of the man with the sombrero. "Who is that?" I asked. Petra and Fernando both stopped their tidying up. It was like that game of Statues that I played with the kids from the block as a child. You move about until someone calls, "Statue!" You have to freeze; if you stir, you're out. The two stopped for an instant before resuming their chores and then quickly exited.

"You've never heard of the man with the sombrero?" Carolina asked, as if the thought of my ignorance on the subject was ludicrous. She gave a little laugh. Carolina's laugh sounded like what a purple hyacinth looked like, rows of fragrant little bells on a stem. It was disarming, and I immediately forgave her poking fun at me.

Enzo didn't have a sombrero on hand to perfectly illustrate but used his panama. Leaning against the wall, he imitated a drunk you might spot on the street. Thinking the man with the sombrero was meant to be a buffoon, I laughed.

Carolina's expression turned serious. "They say you run into him," she said, "when you're rolling home from a night of carousing." Enzo leaned against a wall, his back toward me but facing our hostess, hat tilted. "As you go past him, he'll call out, something like: 'Amigo, you got a cigarette?'" At this point, Enzo brought his hand up to his mouth, taking a puff from his own cigarette. "The glow shows his face," Carolina said. I started feeling tense, whether from the story they were both enjoying or Enzo's disconcerting features in the amber light cast by the wall sconces.

"That's when you see who the man in the sombrero is," Enzo said, turning and looking at me over his shoulder.

"Well, *who* is he?" I asked, doing my best not to get rattled. The pitcher of gin and tonics that we'd finished, however, had heightened my senses rather than dulling them. I was already thinking of the walk back to the guesthouse. There was a pathway through the gardens, flagstone steps up to a picturesque small bridge over the rippling pond Carolina had installed. Usually, the stroll was enchanting. Suddenly, I wasn't looking forward to it.

"They say his face is a skull," Enzo said, looking directly at me with dark eyes made darker by the night. "Others say it's half bone and half rotted flesh."

"Oh no, I hope never to run into the man with the sombrero," Carolina said, making a shuddering gesture. Her silk shawl fell over bare shoulders. There were women born to be the muse of a great and certainly tormented artist or poet. Carolina was one. That night, in a simple embroidered dress, she looked like she was sitting for a portrait to be rendered in chiaroscuro.

I shrugged, not about to let on that the pair left me unnerved. They exited through the open French doors. Carolina said she was walking Enzo to his vehicle, but I knew they were going to smoke a joint. I wasn't into weed, so they didn't invite me. I'd learned in my college years that marijuana mostly caused me paranoia. Left alone, uneasy. The Schweighofer that Carolina's father-in-law had brought from Vienna decades before now seemed like it was about to start playing on its own. I wished my friends had asked me along, even if just to take in fresh air.

The following morning, the drinks of the previous night were no doubt responsible for my sleeping in, and the family was already gone when I went down for breakfast.

I found Petra in the kitchen, preparing the ingredients for the three o'clock meal—chiles rellenos and white rice and sweet corn cakes for dessert—when everyone would be back home and would sit down together. Diego was off to work, and "The señora has gone to get her hair done," Petra informed me. "She indicated that I prepare whatever you'd like for breakfast."

Petra already knew my preferred breakfast, eggs over easy, a scoop of black beans on the side, and her handmade corn tortillas; the not-so-great American coffee; and a glass of the fresh juice of the day.

"Fernando wants to know if *usted* would like for him to heat up the pool?" Petra asked. (It was the Mexican custom to use the formal address out of respect, as we did with each other.) I nodded and thanked her. It was a treat to have it to myself in the mornings.

I went to the breakfast table just off the kitchen where Petra had already set my place. After Diego had gone through the newspaper, she'd thoughtfully refolded it and left it for me. When Petra came with my plate and as she poured my first cup of coffee, I sensed there was something she wanted to say. Looking up from my reading, I took off my glasses and waited.

"I heard you talking about the hombre with the sombrero last night," she started. I nodded. She was a small woman, and as I was sitting, my eyes met hers. "Have you ever seen him yourself?" I asked. She shook her head and promptly left the room.

Petra came back with the pot of coffee. I set the paper aside. "Well, I personally have never seen the hombre with the sombrero," she spoke up, her voice louder than usual, as if making an important announcement, or maybe it was because her bosses weren't around and she felt comfortable doing so. "I grew up on the *rancho*, you understand, early to bed, early to rise . . . with the chickens. That's our life there, the ranch life." I nodded, smiling in a way that reminded me of my hostess. Carolina practiced a smile with lips tight as if whatever you were saying was keeping her from something important.

Petra looked around. She lowered her voice and, leaning over, said, "I've never seen him, but you know who has?" I blinked and shook my head. "Many people . . . usually men. They're the ones out at night alone. *He* appears to drunks . . . That's when my husband stopped drinking."

Fernando, from what I'd seen, was a hardworking family man.

"You see, my husband used to really drink. When our children were small, he was always gone to the *pulquería* in our pueblo. *Usted* knows what *pulque* is, right?" I nodded. I'd actually tasted the potent fermented beverage once in the state of Hidalgo, where it was famous, and didn't care for it.

"Well, that is how my husband stopped drinking," Petra said. "After he had an encounter with the man with the sombrero—" Just then the kitchen door swung open, giving us a start. It was Fernando. Petra put a finger to her lips and left to resume her chores.

Later, when Diego was back, I was glad to have a chance to break the weird spell of the recent talk about a death figure in a sombrero when we went out to shoot some hoops with his kids. It was over the three o'clock meal, which that day we had outside at the large marble table so as to enjoy the summery afternoon, when Carolina brought up the night before. "You should have seen Enzo last night," she told Diego. "He was hilarious, imitating the man with the sombrero."

I'd not gotten the impression that my hostess had found anything funny about the subject, but I was curious as to what her husband might opine. Not surprisingly, like the no-nonsense guy Diego was, he said, "Yes, that Enzo is a character." Looking at the kids, he added, "You know that the man with the sombrero doesn't exist, right?"

Without comprehending myself why I did so at that moment, I blurted, "My father saw a ghost once." Carolina's eyes widened, as did her two children's. Diego looked mildly amused. It was too late to backtrack, so I decided to give my father's account. I wasn't sure if I did it justice, but the table went mum. After a long pause,

Carolina asked, "You say the villa was here in Cuernavaca. Did you ever go there yourself?"

No, I hadn't. Until that moment, I hadn't even thought of it.

Shortly after returning to Chicago, the band had broken up. While remaining friends, they gave up their musical ambitions and took factory jobs and raised families. Except for Chuck.

Dad never talked about it, but years later, my mother filled me in. When the guys were crossing the border, Chuck was detained. Rumor had it that he was caught trying to smuggle marijuana and was arrested by the Mexican authorities. According to what my dad told my mother, Chuck did five years in jail. Whether out of embarrassment or for another reason that remained unexplained, after release, he never went back to Chicago but stayed in Mexico.

Carolina said, "You say you have the address?" I nodded. "Why don't we go?" she suggested, looking at Diego. He looked at me, and after a few seconds, I nodded.

The next morning after breakfast, the children off somewhere with the nanny, Diego, Carolina, and I went to look for, as she called it, my father's "grand villa." It turned out to be nearby. Once we were on the right street, we found parking and went on foot to locate the house number. The neighborhood, heavily tree-lined and with broken sidewalks, had apparently seen better days. When we found the place, hidden behind shrubbery, it, too, was an immediate letdown.

"*This* is a villa?" Carolina said, looking around as if suddenly she'd realized she was on the wrong side of the tracks and should run. Before us and behind a tall wrought iron gate was a small pink house in bad need of a paint job. The once lush gardens, unattended. An ugly mixed-breed canine came around and began barking at us until a woman around our age stuck her head out of a side door. She pulled her sweater tight around her and hurried over with folded arms.

We explained why we'd come, and after a few minutes she said, "I don't see why you can't take a look," and opened the gate. "My father's not well and is resting upstairs."

Carolina wasted no time and headed straight for the back patio. We followed. The pool—the famous pool—was drained and filled with foliage and debris. "How sad," Carolina said, making an abrupt turn.

"My father never allowed its use," said the woman, who introduced herself as Mimi. It seemed that whenever she spoke, her words were tinged with some undefined regret. Nevertheless, she invited us inside. "Please," she said with a hand stretched out to the side entrance.

I didn't know if it was Mundo's embellishment or my imagination as he told stories about the holiday in Cuernavaca, but everything inside and out seemed shrunken. The living room still had a hi-fi stereo, although it was being used for plants and family photographs. From the living room, you could see the swinging door to the kitchen in plain view. My gaze went from the kitchen door to the spiral staircase. Even if much else about the villa was a disappointment, the path the ghost had taken, as described by Mundo, was evident.

"How long have you lived here?" Carolina asked Mimi.

"All my life," she said, and smiled. And with that, other questions and answers came that revealed who Mimi's father was—the most famous of the famous Heartbreakers, Chuck. It was he who was upstairs resting. "Your father and my father were friends . . . ?" Mimi said to me, her head cocked in surprise. After a moment, she said, "If you'd like to go up and say hello, I think he'd like that."

Diego and Carolina said they'd wait and took a seat on a settee near the door. I followed Mimi up the spiral staircase, nearly faltering after putting my hand on the loose rail. Mimi apologized. "There's no need," I said as she led me to Chuck's room.

I'd seen photographs of all the guys: The Heartbreakers onstage; Chuck at the mike was nothing short of debonair in a sharkskin suit. However, the frail man in bed in front of me held no resemblance. "Papá," Mimi said, "this gentleman says his father was in The Heartbreakers. He is from Chicago."

Of course, Chuck didn't know me. I was born after the band broke up. He lifted his nearly bald head and reached for a pair of glasses on a bedstand covered with medication bottles. "Whose son are you?" he muttered. A portable TV atop a vintage stand on rollers was on full blast. Mimi went over to lower the volume. "He doesn't hear well," she said. An older woman in modest dress sat nearby. She'd been reading aloud to her husband from the *revista ¡Alarma!* and, at my appearance, put it down with what seemed only mild curiosity.

Chuck indeed remembered Mundo—a "terrific drummer," "funny guy," and "good friend." "I never went back to Chicago," he said. "No, I never saw any of those guys again." Without prompting, he added, "After I did time in the joint, we married." He lifted one hand and pointed to the woman in the chair. "When I got arrested, María was expecting." Lifting the other hand, he pointed to Mimi. "After I got out, we stayed here and later bought the house," he said.

It wasn't any of my business—Chuck getting the maid pregnant, his time in jail, Mimi. Still, I ventured to ask my father's long-lost friend about the scene that had so long haunted him, "Do you remember anything about a ghost here? A naked lady floating around?"

No sooner had I asked than I regretted it. I realized how foolish it sounded. However, Chuck was about to heighten the drama. First, he leaned over to the nightstand on the other side of the bed. Pouring a drink from a carafe half filled with whiskey or maybe brandy, he gulped it down. He started to pour another and instead put back the glass. At this point, Mimi left the room. I also noted María's tension. Chuck gave her a look as if to say, "It's okay."

"Bluto had a crush on that girl," he said. I looked at María, who cast down her gaze. *On the ghost?* I wondered privately, but asked aloud, "Bluto?"

"Bluto—my brother, Franky," Chuck explained. "He hated to be called that . . . since we were kids. What can I say? It stuck." For the first time since I got there, Chuck smiled (the adverb "wistfully" came to mind). I was old enough to remember the Popeye cartoons. Bluto was a bully, the main character's rival for the love of Olive Oyl. Bluto, the brute with a heart. It made me chuckle a little to think of a guy called that by his best buddies. But maybe it wasn't all that funny.

Chuck's gaze went toward the window, as if he was calculating what to say next. He most certainly didn't owe me any explanation, but I took a seat on a nearby chair. "Bluto—Franky—had a thing for that girl, Gayle. She was"—Chuck sneaked a glance at his wife—"classy, pretty ... actually, gorgeous ... another Ava Gardner. So, of course, she never took a second glance at my brother."

I remembered Chuck's brother being married. I was friends with his kids.

"It was a tragedy ... for a lot of reasons," Chuck said. He was about to reach for the carafe again, then María made like she'd stop him. He gave up and resumed his story. "Gayle's father was an important judge here in Cuernavaca. She drowned ... out here." He pointed with his chin toward the window. "It was an accident. I wasn't even home that night ..." He looked at María, a plain woman in every sense, who hadn't said a word. Her face now took on a grayish pallor. Noticing her discomfort, too, her husband appeared to hesitate before deciding to continue. "María and I were seeing each other then, kind of on the sly. You know, she was employed here. Someone might have thought I was taking advantage of the situation ..."

Chuck was talking about a pretty girl who drowned there, but I only knew about the night the guys saw the ghost. What Chuck said next, however, made me a little embarrassed I'd brought up the subject at all. My dad's old friend shook his head and ran his fingers through the comb-over silver hair on top. With a deep sigh, he threw his hands up. "I did my time," he said. "What more do you want? Are you sure you're Mundo's kid from Chicago and not a reporter?"

The meeting added another veneer to my father's version, but just like the villa that turned out to be no villa, it left me to make of it what I would. Downstairs, my friends had been chatting with

Mimi. They sat drinking cold hibiscus tea. Both stood up to leave as soon as I was back. "We've invited our new friend here to our fiesta this Saturday," Diego informed me. They were having the last of their poolside gatherings for the season. It was also meant as kind of a goodbye party. I'd be flying back home the following day. I knew Diego, who in Mexico had become my unsolicited matchmaker, wanted to be sure that at least one single woman attended.

The gathering was in full swing that Saturday afternoon when Chuck's daughter arrived. I had swum earlier and was back from a shower and in fresh clothes when I saw Carolina sitting with Mimi. Her transformation took me aback: She'd made a spinsterish impression the other day, but now she was radiant. Her long hair was pulled up, strands cascading around her face and neck. Instead of the frumpy sweater and knee-length skirt, she wore a frock bright as a sunflower. I made a note—if I got to know her better, that would be my pet name for her: Girasol. Something about Cuernavaca had brought out the romantic in me, and the corny.

So, what? Back in the good ol' days, The Heartbreakers believed life was to be lived.

"I brought my bikini, too, in case . . ." She smiled when I sat down next to her. "I mean, I might go in later." The kids and a couple of their friends were currently enjoying the pool.

Carolina, who was not a swimmer, was in a silk caftan. "Of course," our hostess said. Enzo, who was there, too, was enjoying a game of checkers with one of the guests, a woman I didn't know; a man who I assumed was her companion was in deep conversation with Diego. The staff was kept busy serving appetizers and drinks in the heat. Even the nanny was recruited to help out. I surrendered to my introverted ways and grabbed a lounge chair to relax alone. It was late afternoon, the sun peeked through the jacaranda trees, and my time of languishing in Cuernavaca was coming to an end.

Shortly, Carolina signaled for me, calling out, "Listen to this!" I made my way to the women. Enzo and Diego also drew near. "*Gayle* was your father's ghost!" my hostess burst out, looking at me with large Versace sunglasses propped on the bridge of her nose. I hadn't shared what Chuck had told me, and my hostess now felt she had solved the great mystery of my father's Cuernavaca adventure.

"The beautiful socialite," I added, not about to be one-upped. I had no idea if the drowned girl was a socialite. It did add luster to the account and made up for Carolina's disappointment in my father's villa. To my surprise, Mimi nodded. "Yes, she was very rich and spoiled." Then she said, "And very much in love with my father."

Diego swirled the ice in his drink. Enzo chugged his and signaled to the nanny-turned-server to bring him another.

"No surprise," I said. "It seems Chuck was quite a ladies' man back then."

"*Every* girl fell in love with him," Mimi said. "My poor mother . . . She suffered so much from jealousy. It seems with good reason. Even until now . . ."

"Even now?" Carolina repeated.

Mimi nodded. She looked distressed. "Yes, she has to take pills for her nerves . . ."

From what I'd seen the other day, I found it hard to imagine women flocking around Chuck, but I could see him once getting into trouble. "My dad said that Chuck, your father, went to jail here in Mexico for trying to smuggle marijuana," I said.

For some reason, Enzo stood up. "The Mexican police," he said with a grunt, "all they want is this." He rubbed his thumb, index, and middle fingers together to indicate money, a bribe.

We all turned back to Mimi, who shook her head. "No," she said. "My father was never involved in drugs. He was accused of a terrible crime. He was innocent."

"Well, of course," Carolina said, although she didn't know yet of what.

"Gayle was found drowned in the pool at the house one night," Mimi said. "She was a gringa from New York, the daughter of an important judge here in Cuernavaca and an American woman."

Enzo had drawn nearer, and Diego listened with an eye on the kids splashing around. An inflated ball hit one of the guests. "Sorry! Sorry!" he called, and immediately reprimanded his children as if they could help where the ball landed. The nanny returned with a tray of drinks. I was having to rise early and fly out the next morning and declined.

Gayle, it seemed, was a bubbly young woman who liked hanging around The Heartbreakers. She came by often, Mimi said, at least according to her mother, María, who had to tolerate all the "groupies," as Mimi called the women. "When Gayle turned up dead in the pool, naked, everyone was understandably horrified. Police descended. Gayle's father, the judge, was beside himself. Although it appeared her drowning was an accident, he wanted someone to pay for his daughter's death."

"So they blamed Chuck?" I asked. If he wasn't at the villa that night, it smelled of a bogus charge.

"No," Mimi said, "they accused his brother, Franky. He was the one spending time with her."

We were all confused. Then Enzo said, "Chuck took the blame. That's what the oldest brother does." Mimi nodded. The rest of us nodded, too. It sounded like a Shakespearean tragedy.

All the while, I kept thinking of the ghost roaming around the villa. If it was Gayle, why had my father never mentioned the scandal? What secret had he kept about Chuck and Franky, loyal brothers, and their affairs in Mexico? Had Gayle's drowning been an accident? If not, why would anyone drown her?

"I think I've had too much sun," I muttered, feeling queasy, and excused myself to return to my lodging. Carolina and Diego were a little disappointed that I'd leave a party in my honor, and I promised that I'd return as soon as I felt better. Ribbons streamed across the sky with the sunset as I crossed over the small bridge, koi in the shimmering water below and gardenia scent in the air. I was sure I'd miss my own grand days in Cuernavaca as much as my father had.

The guesthouse consisted of two large rooms on top of each other. The one on the first floor, with its own bathroom, also had a kitchenette. Carolina had decided that, as a single guy, I probably wouldn't be doing any of my own cooking and had situated me on the second floor, which also had its own full bath but no kitchen. From that room, it was Diego who pointed out, you had an excellent view of all the grounds. At night, floodlights on everywhere, you could see far and wide. I lay down on the bedspread and fell into a deep sleep.

When something woke me, at first I was startled to find myself in bed fully clothed. What day was it? Had I missed my flight? It was while I was sitting up, still disoriented, that I heard something outside again.

There were muffled voices of a woman and a man below. My room was dark, and I decided to leave the lights off as I went to the window to take a look. "What are you doing?" I heard a woman say. She sounded upset, so I put my head out the window. My eyes needed to adjust to the silhouettes and shadows cast by the moonlight and electric lights.

It took no time to identify the man's voice as Enzo's. Next I heard the woman say, "Leave me alone." I ran out the door and down the stairs. They were on the bridge, Enzo trying to force himself on Mimi.

"Hey, man," I called out. Before I reached them, Enzo took off with long strides back toward the house.

Mimi was obviously shaken. I saw she was in her swimsuit, holding her things in one hand. After a swim, Carolina had suggested Mimi use the facilities on the main floor of the guesthouse to shower and dry off. Enzo had followed her.

We were still there, Mimi by then crying from the incident, when we saw Diego coming toward us. He held a flashlight, Fernando right behind him. "What's going on?" my friend asked. It occurred to me they might think I was the cause of Mimi being upset. Whatever they thought or knew, however, no one accused me of anything. Carolina showed up and took the distraught woman back to their house. I never saw Enzo again, that night or ever.

———

Back in Chicago, I went to visit my father at the senior residence home where he'd lived since my mother's passing. Recently, he'd started forgetting things, so I wasn't all that surprised when, after I said, "I saw Chuck in Cuernavaca," he replied, "Who?" It soon came back to him, though, the splendid summer when The Heart-breakers "took Mexico by storm," as he liked to say with his usual flourish. "Everyone wanted us to play at their functions," my dad said, smiling as his liver-spotted hands hit air drums.

After lunch, when he was settled again, I ventured to ask, "Was the ghost you saw at the villa Gayle?"

My father gave me a look that I found hard to decipher but which was nothing short of penetrating. For once, he was left with nothing to say. After a minute or so, I gave his shoulder a squeeze.

"Did you enjoy Cuernavaca?" he asked, changing the subject.

I nodded. "The City of Eternal Spring," I said, going to the window, a large pane that didn't have a way to open. There was an impressive view of a park and, at a distance, the lake reflecting an approaching day's end. Autumn was around the corner; leaves on the oak trees were already orange-red. Dusk always made me melancholy, kind of like the jazz tune "And soon I'll hear old winter's song . . ."

"Maybe one day I'll go back to the villa," Mundo said, clicking on the TV mounted to the wall. Picking up my jacket to leave, I nodded. "See you next Wednesday, Dad," I said.

He called out his standard parting jibe as I hit the hallway: "Not if I see you first!"

Ven

WHEN ANDY REALIZED Maggie had a love story of her own, his sister had been dead two years. She remained single all her inspired and inspiring life—"A woman of the nineties," their mother used to say in defense of an unmarried and childless daughter—when it abruptly ended in her forties in a highway collision. Their mother passed shortly after, most likely of a broken heart. There were all kinds of love stories.

It wasn't exactly true that Maggie's only brother knew nothing of an epic romance. The siblings had been the proverbial "thick as thieves." He first heard of the long-distance connection right after 9/11, when his sister returned from Peru.

Maggie met Rigo at a symposium in Lima. She came home blushing like a new bride and canceling plans just to be home to take Rigo's calls. She mailed off lovey-dovey cards and saccharine gifts: once, a handful of sand sealed in a plastic sandwich bag from a beach by Lake Michigan. Andy, ever the annoying kid brother, never missed an opportunity to rag on her about being in love. "Rico Suave," he called his sister's lover, although he didn't know whether Rigo was smooth or had just wandered onto Maggie's radar at a moment when she felt like being with somebody, which she occasionally did and would just as quickly drop them. Her research, life of travel, defined her. No *man* was going to get in the way of her independence.

The guy she met in Peru was younger than she was and, unlike Andy's "high-achiever" sister, not settled in a position but working on a doctorate in Mexico where he lived. It seemed unlikely that anything would come of them.

Andy was anxious to check out the guy. For someone who was as hard to get as his sister, he had to wonder what it was about Rico Suave that had captivated the dedicated scientist. As soon as she developed the film, an out-of-character Maggie showed off pictures the two had taken together. Her new lover, a kind of nerdy Alejandro Fernández with a beard and sporting a bomber jacket, most certainly projected potential for inciting passion. It was an affair, the brother cynically concluded at a glance, not a relationship.

Strangers in the night, do-be-do-be-do.

"Leave it at that," Andy recommended when the afterglow of their meeting faded and his sister seemed agitated over the growing sense that she wouldn't see Rigo again. He kept putting off coming to visit as promised. Maggie confessed she'd offered to fly to Mexico, and her long-distance lover had replied he was busy.

"I knew it!" Andy remembered saying back then. The siblings never held back an opportunity to say "I told you so," sometimes with unabashed delight. "I knew it was a mistake for you to take this guy seriously. Everyone has trysts at conferences . . . that's all they are." Rigo most assuredly had someone back home, maybe a live-in girlfriend, or was married with a kid already. *Something* was preventing him from seeing Maggie again. When she left numerous messages on Rigo's answering machine and at the office with no callback and her emails went unanswered, Andy just put it out there: "It's over. Chalk it up to experience, girl." When it came to breakups, he was of the "just rip off the Band-Aid" mind.

Maggie did seem to move on, and over the following years, her career, too, advanced. She bought a condo and got a cat. Maggie with the long dark hair and diamonds in her eyes, as Andy thought of her, enjoyed ballroom dancing and rock-wall climbing at the gym. Otherwise, her nose was in her work.

Maggie and Andy, scarcely two years apart, had grown up like twins. While their mother cleaned houses on weekends, they were book fiends who preferred the local library to playing outside. In sports, they were the last to be picked for a team, but regarding school, they were always at the top of their classes. Maggie won first place at the science fair all through middle school. She wanted to be an oceanographer. Andy got a kid telescope one Christmas and, never wanting to be left behind by his smart sister, told everyone he was going to be an astronomer.

She earned a scholarship and went on to UCLA but switched gears somewhat. His audacious sibling got it in her head that she'd figure out how to provide poor populations with clean water. Eventually, Maggie was conferred a PhD, held a post at a prestigious college near Chicago, and was tirelessly resolved to find the solution to the global water crisis.

Andy didn't become an astronomer. Instead, he went to school for two years and worked at a hospital as a lab technician. His greatest quest had been to find a different kind of star, which he did when he got together with Luis Ángel, now his life mate.

It was two years after Maggie's death on Valentine's Day, and a snowstorm had swept through the city the previous night. Right after an intimate breakfast in bed, stirred by the anniversary of his dear sister's untimely passing, Andy went to the den where he quietly shut himself in. Luis Ángel understood and didn't follow.

Andy put the mimosa down on the entertainment stand that held the TV set and some old DVDs and paperbacks, mostly Grisham and good ol' Stephen King, neatly lined up on a shelf.

He clicked on the television to check what time the game was coming on that day, set it to record, and clicked it off. Tightening his bathrobe sash, Andy went to the closet. On the floor was a hefty plastic tote, which he dragged out. Maggie's private papers collected from her home office. There were journals, accordion files, printed emails in manila folders, postcards, and correspondence—professional in legal size and personal letters in various groupings held together with large rubber bands.

Andy had never touched the tote's contents. Until then, his devastation over his sister's death had been too much to permit him to sift through her paper legacy—the disappointments and triumphs. Now, on this anniversary when time had lessened the shock of such a permanent loss, Andy's missing his best friend provoked him to unclasp the flat plastic lid. With the care of lifting a cover from its sarcophagus, he laid it down and stared at what remained of Maggie's life.

Where to begin? There was so much, even photo albums. Andy

held back the urge to call out to his rock, Luis Ángel—*come help me wade through this river*—and his partner would have. However, it would ruin their Valentine's Day, which was supposed to be about them and the good—great—life they'd built together. A dead sister, even as fantastic as Maggie had been—their "best" woman at the commitment ceremony, who, when in town, faithfully watched Sunday football with them and always acted a good sport even when she was the odd (wo)man out every time they insisted she join them—should be left to rest in peace. However, running fingers over his sister's journals, by turns wiping away unanticipated tears, on the day that commemorated lovers and also his sister's death, Andy wanted—needed—to know. Had Maggie ever found love?

Her driver's license: five-three, 125 pounds, forty-two when she died. Organ donor. What else did he know? PhD in something related to science and environmental studies. Two books published. Never married. Currently survived by one brother and a cat. She enjoyed socializing, but mostly she loved her profession, by which, it was known to everyone, her life was consumed. "My beautiful daughter was a career woman," their mother said. "In my day, women had to get married and raise a family . . . I was . . . am so proud of her." That day at the cemetery chapel where the body was cremated, Andy thought his mother might dissolve into a pile of ashes herself, such was her interminable sorrow.

A sip from the flute glass, and Maggie's brother gathered the strength to pick up the journal labeled 2001. Flipping the pages of the black Moleskine until he reached the entry marked "International People's Environmental Projects Symposium." He carried it over to the easy chair to make himself comfortable. When Andy went to pull off the rubber band, it broke and snapped against his fingers.

Maggie, are you here? he thought, eyes searching the room. Outside the window, the fresh snow looked like a painting. He could hear the scrape of metal against concrete, a neighbor out shoveling.

As soon as he opened the book, items fell out on his lap, photos, receipts, ticket stubs, boarding passes, and handwritten notes. The first photograph that caught his eye was of Maggie, her widemouth laugh, one leg flung up like a cancan girl in jeans, posing with a group he didn't know. He held it up, first away and then near. (He was going to have to break down and get his eyes checked, like Luis Ángel had been bugging him to do.) Upon closer inspection, he realized the bearded guy next to Maggie, arm around her waist, was most likely Rigo. Unlike the rest, who appeared to be having a good time, he looked stiff. What had Maggie seen in such a stick-in-the-mud, anyway? *Was* he a stick-in-the-mud? Maybe he just didn't like taking photographs.

Andy began to unwrap personal correspondence she'd received, wishing he had his sister's instead. Her writing was eloquent . . . *detailed*, that was the word. Maggie, in writing and when speaking, was often humorous, although it was a dry humor that a lot of people didn't appreciate. Her brother, left behind, would have to settle for a one-sided exchange from strangers. He sorted through the envelopes. It turned out nearly all were from one individual.

How many letters were there? It looked like it could be a hundred, and they were postmarked over a period of years: 2001 to 2013, the year she passed. *Rigo, Rigo, Rigo.* Later, *Prof. Rodrigo Durán.* Mail from Mexico to Chicago for twelve years. Andy thought their affair had ended in 2001, when his sister began to complain about him going MIA. But there was a Christmas postcard from him that year. And another letter postmarked *29 de diciembre, 2001*. Why had she not told her brother she'd heard from Rigo? Why never mention him again? Andy reached for the mimosa and drank it down in one swallow. "I hate you," he said to Maggie under his breath.

Luis Ángel gave a tap on the door and stepped in. "Don't forget our reservations, honey," he said cheerfully. He noticed the huge tote and that Andy seemed to be engrossed in sentimental excavation. Knowing that the death of his partner's sister brought him down sometimes, Luis Ángel added, "If you need me, just whistle, Papi. I'm gonna go up and shower."

Andy nodded, and as soon as Luis Ángel closed the study door, he pulled out the first letter from Rigo. It was one thin sheet. The handwriting was fairly legible, a kind of part-printing-and-part-cursive style. There was a *te extraño muchisimo* at the end, but otherwise it was oddly unexpressive. Andy pulled out the next letter. It was much the same stilted Spanish, some mention about what Rigo was working on and that he bought a car to travel to rural areas where he conducted investigations. In some places, *access to clean water was impossible. Sickness, especially among infants and children, rampant*, Rigo wrote. A primary objective for both Maggie and him was to implement ways to get potable water to such locations. Among the endless challenges were time constraints. He said that in the government's efforts to cut back on the smog, people had designated days of the week that they could drive their cars, which meant that he couldn't always get out. Interesting enough for a colleague, Andy thought, but it wasn't exactly the stuff of love sonnets. He wasn't convinced Rigo merited the emotions he'd seen his sister go through over him. Then again, maybe all that had come of the pair was a professional friendship, which explained the years of steady correspondence and Maggie not mentioning Rico Suave again.

There was only one way to find out. He opened the journal. Pulling up the attached black ribbon that marked the Lima symposium, he began to read. Maggie, always expressive, wrote in specifics. It seemed this was what she spent most nights doing. He pictured her in a sparse hotel room, wearing a T-shirt, curled up in bed like a teenage girl with a diary. She often wore socks to bed because her feet tended to be cold. He found the first pages not particularly interesting—details about the flight, registering upon arrival, a panel she attended, and some contacts she'd made. Maggie used her journals for all-purpose note-taking: phone numbers, ideas, and references she wanted to follow up on. Then he saw Rigo's name for the first time. Underlined twice. Nothing until the next day.

She wrote:

I'd just gotten out of the shower. The hot water felt good after an intense day. I ended up in a public argument with a guy who said we in the United States haven't a clue regarding the bureaucratic obstacles people have here.

Anyway, a group of us were supposed to meet for dinner in the hotel restaurant. Some were flying out early. A few of us have decided to stay and go to Machu Picchu—we leave tomorrow a.m. But yesterday—the Nazca Lines! I have so much to say about that.

I had rubbed on some of the hotel lotion (my skin has gotten so dry here) and then, as always, my oil (lavender for calming), when the phone rang. I wrapped a towel around me, another around my hair, and hurried over to answer. It was Rigo. "*Ven*," was all he said.

I hung up without a word. What could I say? What could any woman respond to such an invitation on the part of a near stranger? Near, I say. (Is it mere or near? What is meant by *near*—physical proximity, or does it mean someone you hardly know?) My head felt light, and I sat on the bed for a moment. We'd been around each other all day—the Nazca Lines excursion—on the small plane flying over the giant geoglyphs. I became a little sick at one point, the pilot was dipping and circling so we could get a better view and take pictures of the mysterious sand etchings. Rigo must've noticed my face because he reached over and handed me a stick of mint-flavored gum to settle my stomach. After that, I became aware that he was looking at me, not out the window on his side at the archaeological sites below. I was still shaky when we landed, and as I stepped down from the plane, he took my arm.

We'd talked here and there throughout the symposium. He told me he was going to take the same Nazca excursion that I'd signed up for, but I didn't expect it would only be the two of us. Afterward, he suggested we get something to eat, that it would make me feel better. I ordered a plain cheese sandwich. He had ceviche, a dish of fish and onions, which gave me nausea again just to look at. Waiting for our food, I started to feel tension between us.

I ordered hot tea. The water was tepid, and I had to send it back, and all the while, I felt the young professor eyeing me.

He took off his glasses, and I had no choice, nowhere to turn, but to look right at him, and I swear, for a second, I thought we

were reading each other's minds. What were they saying? Take
me! (Ha-ha. Romance-novel baloney, but there we were, living
it.) Stripped of words for what might end as an embarrassing
encounter for both, we ate in silence. I'd felt the tension before.
During the symposium, I'd walked past where he was sitting,
just before a panel got started, and I knew he was observing me.
I'd noticed him before, too, at the hotel. Once, we both got on the
same elevator and it turned out our rooms were on the same floor.
I hung back, pretending to go into my satchel looking for the key
or something that perhaps I'd left somewhere. I watched him head
down the hall, gingerly, like he knew he was being scrutinized. His
jacket accentuated his broad back and shoulders. In jeans, his legs
were slightly bowed, like a cowboy's. He was in boots for most of
the conference, which he told me today he special-ordered from
Guanajuato. He gives off a combination of Academic Meets Rodeo
Roper. He's from Mexico City. I don't know. I think I'm lost.

I slipped on the black cotton dress with pleather pockets I'd saved
for a special night, if there was to be one during the trip. I wore my
Capezios for comfort. I knew his room number, which was right
around the corner from me. We were supposed to meet people
downstairs for dinner. I thought I was hungry, but I didn't know
anymore. Yes, I'd seen how he'd been checking me out all those days.
He sounds like a predator of some sort to describe him this way,
but I was checking him out, too. It was more of a dance, the dance
of two ancient monkeys—like the geoglyph at Nazca. (The monkey
was my favorite.) Heaven knows it's not my habit to have flings at a
conference. There's always the exception. If I'm lost over this man,
all I can say—and hope—is that I'm not alone.

I went to his room; the door was ajar. He knew I'd come. I pushed the door open, and he was just coming out of the shower, a towel around him. It was like a movie. People always say that about impressionable scenes in their lives. We think that such situations when all our senses are heightened and we feel ourselves alive only happen on film, but the fact is such written scenes derive from life's preciously private moments. And then this, that I thought wasn't possible: falling for a near stranger I met on a business trip. Oh yes, this happened according to Jean-Luc Godard (or me, Anna Magnani, always cast tragically) and to all kinds of people in unexpected circumstances but never before to me, Maggie Mejía, born and raised in the Midwest and whose second language she speaks not sexily trilling Rs but like a kid lost at the fair in her grandfather's village, on the verge of tears to be at the mercy of everyone around.

I'm not going to say good-looking men never notice me because I've had my experiences, good and bad. But undefined anticipation had been building between Rigo and me, and by the time I stepped out of the aircraft, shaken as I was from the Nazca excursion, I knew something was going to happen between us.

He came out of the bathroom and walked over to me. We kissed and then he slipped my dress up right over my head. (It's kind of loose, so it thankfully came off gracefully.)

We went to the bed, me in my black bra and panties and he with the towel. The only light came from the bathroom. I think he'd done that on purpose, just like the music coming from where I didn't know at the moment, but it was soft. Then I realized it was the radio and they were playing mushy boleros by trios. I wanted to make a joke because it felt like a setup, but then I thought, *He doesn't run the radio station.* His face was buried in my neck, and I sensed he was inhaling the lavender oil. "What is that?" he whispered. *What is what?* I wondered, feeling his hand between my legs. He had more body hair than I imagined, but he was also more fit. I licked his wet shoulder, and of course it tasted of the hotel body wash, but it reminded me of the pink taffy I loved as a kid. Sometimes I spent all my lunch money on candy. All I knew at that moment was that no matter what came the next day, Rigo would always be a part of me.

Andy put the open journal facedown on his lap. Although at times Maggie had shared aspects of her relationships with him, it felt weird and intrusive reading about her sex life. Just then, a light rap, and Luis Ángel entered holding up a freshly pressed red shirt. He himself looked freshly pressed after his shower and shave. Luis Ángel gave Andy a pretty-please smile.

"I'm not wearing that," Andy said. Every holiday, his man insisted they dress for the occasion. In this case, red or pink for Valentine's Day. Luis Ángel gave in without protest, sensing it wasn't the time to pick a fight. "They're coming to plow the driveway, but if you prefer, we can cab it to the restaurant," he said.

Andy gathered up the papers strewn about and stood up. Maggie having full-on flings was no surprise. He'd never thought for a second that the one she'd had with Rico Suave was major, but too bad things hadn't worked out for them. He went to get ready for dinner. It might take a while for the cab, and in any case, the weather slowed everything down. They were now of the age when they went to early bird specials, which was what they both were calling their five o'clock reservations.

Andy and Luis Ángel had chosen sushi for Valentine's. The Japanese restaurant provided private rooms with seating on cushions on the floor. A staff person in a kimono graciously waited on the two men. Andy hadn't wanted to spoil their romantic time by bringing up his dead sister, but he found himself in a quiet mood. Luis Ángel spoke up. "One day," he said, "we should go to Mexico . . . just to trace Maggie's footsteps. She was so entrenched in her work there, and we know almost nothing about it."

Luis Ángel was right about that. But now, Andy thought, there was more to find out in Mexico than particulars regarding his sister's research. She had spent a good deal of time there, her entire sabbatical at one point. Summers. There was Christmas 2002. His first with Luis Ángel.

She didn't come home until late January. Andy and his new boyfriend went to Hawaii for the holidays, his mother in tow because Maggie was "too busy" in Mexico to come back to Chicago to spend it with them. "Well, who can blame her, staying away from the cold and snow?" their mother said, always in defense of her daughter, and Luis Ángel agreed. But Andy still found it peculiar, if not also selfish. Maggie was very close to their mother. It was fine that she was devoted to bringing clean water to needy communities and, from all indications, achieving her goals, but it was only when Maggie was back in Chicago that Andy assumed she made any time for recreation.

It began to snow again while the couple was still enjoying their meal, and it continued to come down throughout the night. By dawn the city was left at a standstill. Mayors had learned from previous years with such storms that snow trucks had to be out in full force expediently. A lot of the city stayed in gear. However, suburban neighborhoods, like where Andy and Luis Ángel lived, were half buried in snow. Both stayed home from work the next day. Sometime after lunch, Andy went back to the den to continue his quest. The quest now was strictly focused. Did Maggie ever see Rigo again? Another journal, labeled 2002. He opened it, and again a scattering of mementos spilled out. The journal was large, and his sister filled pages, but the writing went only as far as April of that year. Spring break, Maggie flew to Mexico. She was starting a new project in Campeche. There were sections detailing her findings, interrupted by notes and even doodles, but no personal entries. His eyes welled up as he remembered a sibling who wasn't only exemplary in every sense in her field but had surely left a mark on the world. And yet she'd hardly discussed it with her kid brother. Disco Duck, she sometimes called him. When had they gone their own ways such that he knew so little of how much Maggie had undertaken?

And then it was there again—*Rigo*, underlined twice.

I didn't think he'd show up. I put on some weight this past winter (too many tamales with Mami—we made about sixteen dozen for everyone this past Christmas) and overall let myself go. I didn't even know if I wanted to see him. But I did want to see him; otherwise, I'd never have let him know about my project here. He came prepared, too, with luggage and all the items I'd emailed him I'd need. Someone knocked. I knew it was him. I'd know that knock anywhere! (Ha-ha! *Of all the gin joints in all the towns in all the world.*) I know it sounds silly, but instead of swinging open the door, as I'd imagined doing for so long, and finally being face-to-face again, first I peeked through the curtain. I saw him, only partially, most likely also nervous. For a second, he was vulnerable, like we all are in the moments prior to obtaining what we've wanted at long last.

My love! my poor heart cried inside my *masa* body, but suddenly,
I feared opening the door. Why? What if he saw me now and was
disappointed? I was old, pathetic—writing, calling—and he finally
answered out of exasperation, perhaps. I shouldn't have pursued him.
I reproached myself, yes, in those seconds peeking through the plastic-
coated curtains in that motel. Maybe I should sneak out through the
bathroom window, I thought. Instead, I cautiously opened the door,
but then, seeing his bewildered expression mixed with irrefutable
longing, I threw my arms around him and he held me. All was forgiven.

Andy stopped reading. His brain, both hemispheres, welled up
with unanticipated infusions of new information. The endless
conversations he'd had with his sister, and after that first meeting,
she'd never once mentioned Rigo again. She wasn't obliged, of
course, but it had turned into a full-blown affair. She was quoting
from *Casablanca* by their second tryst. Everyone knew what that
meant. Maggie in Campeche dependent on Rico Suave was like a
bomber pilot crashed across enemy lines. Why hadn't his geeky
sister thought to ask his advice on the matter? Andy didn't have
answers to the global water crisis, but he knew men.

He tried to think back to what he was up to in those years. He
knew very well. Those were earlier times that had found him in
clubs in Boys Town every weekend, weeknights, too, when possible. It was there that he'd met Luis Ángel—a dancer. ("Before I
made an honest man out of you," Andy used to tease.) His new
lover danced at night, washed dishes at a restaurant during the
day. He hustled, but it had always been an honest hustle. Now Luis
Ángel worked maintenance at the same hospital where Andy was
employed. Yes, Luis Ángel was sexy—still sexy—and a good guy.

Before they met, he had a girl in Guatemala, and together they had a child. Even now, he sent money to family back home. In Chicago, where he'd come up to find work, first he took the dance gig, then he came out. He met Andy. Life together was right and sound. Early to bed and early to rise was their habit in recent times.

Meanwhile, Maggie was saving the world, one drop of purified water at a time. Instantly, Andy felt embarrassed that he'd let things go so adrift between him and his sister. Sure, they were adults. They each did as they pleased. The problem was, as he saw it now, that he let himself believe that what she shared at home was all she was. Everyone was complicated, but people like Maggie had sides most never even detected, like string theory, suggesting many dimensions at once.

He went back to the journal and skimmed through pages of details of the couple's fervent reunion and on to another day when Rigo's name came up again.

"Why didn't you answer my emails or any of my calls? I sent you letters," I reproached him. He said nothing. He came to the headquarters I set up, tents near the shore where we were testing waters, plant life, all the things I've been documenting. There were months of not talking. A postcard from him or a brief letter. I didn't even know if he'd show up in Campeche. But there he was. One night in bed, arms and legs wrapped around each other, I said again, "Why didn't you get back to me for so long?"

The room was dark except for a narrow sliver of light coming through the side of the curtain. Rigo stirred uncomfortably. I thought he'd pull away, but instead, he answered, "I just wanted to remember that, at least once, I was able to resist you."

Snow trucks throughout the night cleaning highways, Lake Shore Drive, and most streets, and the city was back to work the following weekday. When the guys got home that evening, after pet feeding, pulling out leftovers to reheat, and putting on flannel loungewear, they got comfortable to catch up on rerun episodes of *The X-Files*. Afterward, getting ready for bed (it was scarcely nine o'clock but they were a long way from their club days), Luis Ángel, knowing his life mate as he did, said, "We both have vacation time coming, honey. And plenty of frequent-flyer miles."

Turning off the electric toothbrush, Andy asked, "What are you getting at—we should go to Mexico?"

Yes, that was exactly what Luis Ángel meant. Maybe it was time to see what Maggie's legacy was in Mexico. She hadn't bragged about it, but it was clear that her projects had been progressing at the time of her passing. Luis Ángel thought it might help Andy with the loss that still affected him so deeply. Over the next week, Andy's husband managed to convince him that a spontaneous escape from the weather to Mexico City would do them both good. It would put a pep in their step, Luis Ángel said one night.

"I know what'll put a pep in our step," Andy said, embracing and nuzzling him. After over a dozen years, they were still an "item."

The day after the couple arrived and settled in at their hotel in Mexico City, each had a plan. Luis Ángel arranged an excursion on his own to tour the ruins of Teotihuacán. Andy was going to Coyoacán to meet "Rico Suave," who had responded to his email and invited him over to dine at his home that afternoon.

Maggie's brother had been to Mexico before, with her and their mother when he and his sister were adolescents. They'd raced each other climbing the Pyramids of the Sun and the Moon and visited other must-see sites.

He hadn't been to Coyoacán before and was immediately enchanted by its quaint and colorful atmosphere, cobblestone streets, bougainvillea everywhere, boutiques, hip young people, and older folks who looked like they thought about things. It was where Frida Kahlo had lived with her great love, Diego, *la rana*.

The driver stopped in front of Rigo's modest but picturesque residence. "Here it is," he mumbled. As soon as Andy reached the gate, a man, probably not as old as his posture seemed to indicate, opened up. Rigo emerged from the front door and walked toward Andy. He was immediately recognizable from his photographs (although his hair had gone salt-and-pepper, and perhaps his girth had thickened). He was in a denim shirt, sleeves rolled up, wearing casual trousers. Rico Suave smoked a pipe. "Dr. Livingstone, I presume?" Andy smiled, stretching out a hand. He kept smiling even when Rigo didn't acknowledge the reference. (Dour, just as he'd imagined.)

Andy hadn't quite dressed up for the occasion, either, but was appropriate in a leather jacket over his white pressed shirt and jeans. Rigo invited him to sit outside, where there were garden chairs and a table beneath a canopy of exotic vines. The man who'd met him at the gate went back to pushing the manual lawn mower. Shortly, Andy noticed a shadow; it appeared to be a woman behind the front screen door. Then she disappeared. A few minutes later, a girl of around twelve stepped out. She came over and stood behind Rigo. Kids never hid their curiosity about new people. She looked directly at Andy. "This is my daughter," Rigo said, gently tugging the girl's hand that had been on his shoulder. "Say hello, Andrea."

Andy saw the resemblance, her skin tone and wavy hair and something in her demeanor, perhaps timid but not necessarily lacking confidence. Rigo asked Andrea to let her grandmother know that they would be coming in momentarily to eat. She left, displaying utmost good manners, Andy thought, perhaps for the benefit of the stranger, the way some kids liked to do when, otherwise, they might be brats with their parents. It was perhaps not politically correct to admit, but Andy had always made it clear he didn't like being around kids. For whatever reason, he hadn't figured Rigo as a family man, but possibly inside the house, a wife and other children waited.

Instead, after they went into the small stone-and-adobe home, neat and clean but crowded with bric-a-brac, the only person besides Andrea waiting for them at the formally set dining table was Rigo's mother. Although she was introduced by name, Andy chose to refer to her simply as Señora. She was obviously the "lady of the house," just like his own mother had been, even when it was Maggie who became the official head of household. Señora was a dignified-looking woman perhaps in her sixties, short hair and dressed as if she had been out and about in that wonderful *alcaldía*—or maybe she'd dressed up for the occasion. A third thought: Unlike Luis Ángel and Andy, who could become two slobs over a weekend if they had no plans, there were people who dressed at home as if they were filming a telenovela.

Señora and Rigo sat at opposite ends of the table, and Andy was invited to sit across from Andrea. A housekeeper promptly came out of the kitchen and left a basket of warm buns on the table, along with a pitcher of cold *tamarindo* tea, and shortly after returned with bowls of chicken consommé to start the meal. There were sounds coming from the kitchen, and Andy figured someone else was in there doing the cooking and preparations.

He didn't know exactly when the right moment would be to present what he'd brought, but just before picking up the spoon, he handed Rigo the shoebox he had with him. "This is the correspondence you sent to my sister . . . over the years." Rigo held up the box as if still unsure of its contents, and Andy added, "I thought you should have them back. I don't know if you kept Maggie's letters but, well, anyway. Here are yours . . ." He looked around the table.

Andrea and Rigo's mother also had questioning expressions.

Rigo regrouped. Opening the box, he saw that, indeed, there were his letters. Still looking at the contents, he gave a slow nod with an expression that seemed reflective, even tender. Andy, unlike his verbally talented sister, wasn't good at describing what he saw, but right there, *that* face? Maggie must've fallen hard.

Rigo thanked Andy, set down the box on the floor, and they all began to eat.

Conversation seemed to be formal rather than friendly and somewhat curt, but that was to be expected. Andy asked about Maggie's studies, which Rigo seemed very familiar with, having often assisted her. "They've named a lab after her here, you know," Rigo said. In fact, Andy didn't know, and immediately, the information took him aback. He wondered if he could go visit the test site, and Rigo said he'd arrange it. He and Andrea would take him.

The entrées were served—plank-grilled chicken, pureed potato, and steamed carrot wedges—and Andy, enjoying the meal and Rigo's hospitality, and excited about the forthcoming visit to a facility named after his sister, began to relax. The subject came up as to where Rigo was currently working, and it turned out to have nothing to do with science, as once was the case; he now was a director at Andrea's private school.

It made Andy look at the quiet young girl and ask, "Is your mother a teacher there?" It was an awkward query, to be sure, but in the absence of any mention of the girl's other parent, his curiosity had gotten the best of him. Instead of replying, Andrea gave him a blank stare. She turned to her father and then her grandmother. All had the same look.

Rigo dabbed his mouth with a napkin, put it down, and excused himself from the table.

Andy watched him walk off to another part of the house, presumably a bedroom or bathroom. He looked at the two at the table, wondering what he'd said wrong. Nothing could have prepared him for what Señora was about to reveal. Utensils still in hand, she turned to Andy, then to the girl, and back to him. "Surely you know that Andrea is Maggie's daughter?" she asked in English. They'd been using mostly Spanish, but here, perhaps unsure that Andy was sufficiently fluent to get the gravity of the information, she used English.

He'd known no such thing. He was about to laugh. The suggestion was preposterous. What were they getting at? Sure, Rigo and Maggie had known each other for years, as lovers and colleagues. But if his sister had ever borne a child, he would've known about it. Their mother would've been told. The three had been loyal to one another, devoted to the others' needs and comforts all their lives. Ever since Andy and Maggie's father had walked out when they were children, they'd bonded to survive and push forward together.

Andy looked at Andrea, who'd been watching him throughout the meal. His eyes began to well with tears.

"Don't cry," the girl said. "If you cry, I'll cry." Her top lip trembled.

He felt his mouth drop ever so slightly. It was precisely what Maggie used to say to him when they were kids, when they huddled in the dark while their parents argued in another room or when Andy would experience a letdown of some sort and his sister came to comfort him. "Don't cry," she'd say. "If you cry, I'll cry."

"It's what her mother always told her," Señora said to Andy. "Every time she had to leave somewhere—on her work trips or back to Chicago . . ." The lady sighed. "But we were always here. Isn't that right, *mi reina*? Your grandmother and your father are always here for you, for whatever you need." Andrea lowered her gaze and resumed picking at her food.

Rigo returned to the table, presumably ready for the conversation that Andy would obviously want to have with the news that his sister had been a mother. Andy waited for Rigo to make eye contact, and when he didn't, Andy practically blurted, "Why didn't my sister tell me? Why didn't she let our mother know she had a grandchild? She would've helped take care of Andrea . . ." As a flood of questions arose in his head along with all the what-ifs, he found himself increasingly disconcerted.

Rigo's jaw clenched. It wasn't a far stretch to imagine the man had a temper. His combined with Maggie's combustible one had probably made a Molotov cocktail.

"Andrea," Señora said, "why don't you go see if the chickens have laid anything today? Ask Don José to help you."

Without protest, the girl reluctantly stood up, pushed in her chair, and left, obviously disappointed that she'd miss out on the ensuing conversation. Don José was the gardener. Andy hadn't spotted a roost, but he wasn't surprised the family maintained one. When they were kids, Andy and Maggie had gone to visit their grandparents in their village outside of Mexico City. They had a modest home his grandfather had built. There were chickens, a few goats, and pigs. They had a small bean farm. Every day the old grandfather put the siblings to chores.

It was Rigo who began. "We didn't hear of Maggie's accident until a week after her death," he said. "I called her university when she wasn't getting back to me, and they informed me. It was devastating news . . . especially for Andrea. We weren't even told about the funeral."

Andy felt himself sinking in the high ladder-back chair. He hadn't known that Rigo was even in his sister's life, much less that she was living a separate reality with him. Now, in view of the child they had together, he felt sick to think he had unintentionally deprived them of their right to come and say goodbye.

"Don't be unjust," Señora said to her son. "You knew that Maggie never told her people in Chicago that she had a child."

Andy shook his head. It didn't make sense. Maggie in a few words: compassionate, dedicated, reliable.

After their father had deserted them, Andy and Maggie vowed they'd never get caught up in the same predicament as their mother. She'd worked two jobs to support the family, never enjoying a day off. Later, when Maggie was in college, their mother constantly boasted about her self-sufficient daughter. It seemed there was no greater achievement for a woman than living life for herself.

After that snowy week that began with a storm on Valentine's Day, Andy had stopped going through the contents of the tote. It didn't feel right invading anyone's privacy, even if that person was already long gone. Andy wanted to know everything now. He leaned toward Rigo. "Were you married to my sister?"

"No," Rigo said. "We discussed it when she was pregnant. But we argued a lot—"

At this, Señora put her hands up with an "Ay!" She nodded as if testifying to the claim.

"It didn't seem to be the right course," Rigo said. "But for the baby's well-being, we agreed on an arrangement. She stayed in a room here with Andrea. Maggie and I got along marvelously in our—her work, in day-to-day matters and planning, always with our daughter's best interest in mind. Meanwhile . . ."

Señora finished: "Your sister was free to come and go from here as she pleased and needed. She knew her daughter was in good hands and well cared for."

Andy sat back. He felt like someone had just thrown a forty-pound sack of flour at his chest. Maggie hadn't ever abandoned her child as their father had them, he assured himself. No matter where she lived or with whom she left Andrea when her work demanded it, she always returned. She always provided. She always loved.

But why hadn't she told her brother? Had she considered Andy that judgmental, not to trust him with such a major decision—to leave her child in Mexico with the father?

He'd never thought of himself as having a double standard for his sister. A woman could be a mother and carry on a career without having to sacrifice either. A single working mother needed support. Maggie was resourceful and financially stable, so she could've figured it out in Chicago. It went without saying she had her mother, and Andy, too, would've been there. Had she doubted them? On the other hand, their mother had retired early, sick and tired of life's demands. At that time, Andy had made it no secret that his social life was everything to him.

Andy now surveyed Rigo's face; deep frown lines seemed to indicate he was serious but perhaps not necessarily stern. Apparently, Maggie's lover had no issue with being the stabilizing factor in his child's life. A lot of men had left their homes for extensive periods with the purpose or excuse of providing for families. Meanwhile, they played golf, had affairs, essentially led a separate life—even started other families—and all was justified because they were providers. "Such good men," people said. But if it was a mother doing the same thing? "What a 'bad' woman!" was the running and unfair adage. His sister had every right to design her own life.

"She never told us about Andrea" was all he found himself saying, looking at Señora.

Rigo's mother took a breath and held it momentarily, as if silently counting to ten, then she said, "Andrea has lacked for nothing here with her father. Your sister must have had her reasons not to take her daughter to the States. But she was a professional woman with many obligations. I understood. I, too, was a professional person," she continued. "I founded the school where my son works now and where Andrea attends. I ran it for a long time. Rigo and his siblings all attended there. No one ever felt neglected by my having commitments.

"Too much of the rearing of children is left to the woman who has borne them. You must give your sister—may in holy peace she rest—more credit than to think she was less of a mother because she didn't take Andrea to Chicago. Maggie knew the child was in excellent hands, in a stable home, loved dearly by her father. I suspect she didn't think her family in Chicago would approve of such an unconventional arrangement, although there was nothing wrong with it. Nothing at all." Señora stopped and reached for her glass. She, too, seemed to have been hit by a flour sack. She looked sad, worried for her son, granddaughter, dead Maggie, and perhaps the world. It was a look, Andy realized, that people of about her age had most of the time. Now he recognized, in the downturn of her mouth, it was the accumulation of life's unexpected hits. Aging didn't come just with body aches but also from flying sacks loaded with surprises that hit you right in the chest and left you gasping for air.

Knowing his sister as he had, precise in all she did, even calculating, he felt sure that becoming a mother hadn't just "happened" to her. A possible reason for Maggie keeping her child a secret in Chicago was the fact that his sister, a feminist who carried out all her goals on her own terms, had no problem arranging for her child to be left in the care of the girl's father.

But family dynamics had less to do with ideologies than with emotions. His sister and mother had always been close, but Andy had witnessed a certain pressure placed on Maggie to excel as a woman. Their mother wanted nothing to stand in the way of her daughter's success. While their mother had been exemplary in caring for her children on her own, it was apparent she was also ridden with regret that life's circumstances had minimized her own choices. The very idea that Maggie's autonomous lifestyle would be compromised by having a family was unthinkable. So as not to disappoint the woman, Andy's sister allowed herself to split like a cell into two separate identities.

Andy turned from Señora to Rigo. He was charismatic, accomplished. He could find someone, perhaps, and start a new family, plan for bright and beautiful moments, await births, holidays, and springs ahead. For that matter, Andy and Luis Ángel still had years ahead to make dreams happen, have a family of their own. His clubbing days behind him, Andy could imagine himself parenting now. Perhaps Rigo would allow them to bring the girl to the United States under their care. Maggie might have liked that.

Andrea returned and went directly to her father. She put her arms around him, and he hugged her, too, as if to assure her that everything was fine. "*Todo está bien*, Andi," Rigo whispered near his daughter's ear.

"Andy?" Andy repeated.

"Yes," Señora said, "Andrea was named after Maggie's father, Andres."

Andy, too, had been named after their father. "I'm also Andy," he said. Maggie had no fond memories of their father, but she might have actually named her child after her brother. The girl smiled and, remembering her braces, quickly put a hand over her mouth. It wasn't Maggie's smile, maybe it was Rigo's—who'd yet to smile much, so Andy wasn't sure—but in the end, it was her own. The girl reached out and put the other arm around her uncle. "You have to be strong," she said to either Andy or her father. "Like the theory of evolution, you know? Only the strong survive."

And there she was, Andy thought, the courageous sister he would miss forever, Maggie with diamonds in her eyes.

Ada and Pablo

ADA AND PABLO had a good marriage by anyone's measure. They met when he'd come from Veracruz to do graduate studies at UNAM, the national university in Mexico City, Ada's "hometown." She was finishing a nursing degree. The wedding was spectacular. "Only our closest family," Pablo said later, laughing, when about a hundred or so relations and friends came from Veracruz to attend. Ada's "closest," who were all in the capital, doubled the guest list. After the briefest of honeymoons—Cozumel—the newlyweds left for New York, where Pablo had received a research grant. Two seasons later, they were back with an infant son. The husband started a new job as a civil engineer, and Ada stayed home. She had help with family nearby and seemed content.

Ada *was* content.

It was after the birth of their second son that the young wife and mother slowly devolved into a garden slug. Gray all the time, was how she put it. Later, such a state would be identified as post-partum depression. Back then, it was decided by all concerned that perhaps she needed new interests outside the home. She signed up for an aerobics class. Attending a neighbor's embroidering circle, she converted into an old lady. Ada wanted to use her skills and eventually took a job as a nurse at a private clinic.

At work, she soon displayed remarkable administrative competence, and in a short time, Ada was no longer the assistant to Dr. Cardona, who had founded the medical facility specializing in women's health; she ran the whole kit and caboodle. Now office manager, she took pride in the confidence everyone had in her and managed the practice with impeccable efficacy.

As Dr. Cardona readied for retirement, a new physician was hired to take over patients.

The first impression the younger doctor made on everyone was that he was an outstanding choice. Dr. Almazán Robles had graduated at the top of his class, and he came with experience. If you added his modest demeanor, you couldn't hold the exceptional good looks against him, even if a couple of the women on staff complained that he'd be a distraction. Ada noticed some patients made appointments just to be attended by the new physician.

The Clinic Czar herself felt flustered around the new doctor, but then again, the reaction could just as well have been attributed to the Change, which of late gave little relief. Waking past midnight to sheets soaked with sweat provoked Pablo, who'd always been an accommodating husband, to move to the guest room.

Each day, all year round, Ada's life moved as predictably as the seasons. The couple hosted Sunday dinners. She and Pablo took two vacations a year—one to visit family in Veracruz and a second for their own mental well-being, a week at a resort or perhaps a tour abroad. She'd especially liked Florence and seeing the statue of David. While some might hold up the Louvre as the highlight of a Paris tour, it was the leisurely stroll, arms locked with Pablo on a spring day in the Tuileries, that she kept as her fondest memory.

Once a year, her husband went away on his own. Since graduating from college in Veracruz before he met Ada, he and a tight clique who'd attended with him reunited there every summer. According to Pablo, they'd studied together, partied together, and given each other a hand whenever needed. Even now, it wasn't surprising when he received a call from one or another—going through a divorce or in a career crisis—to get advice and support. Of course, there'd been a few romances among them back then, he admitted, but nothing serious, and most ended as friends after they married, or overcame life's unreasonable demands. They all met in the city of Veracruz the same time every year.

After Ada and Pablo's thirtieth anniversary—and the honeymoon-like vacation they took to celebrate: a cruise around the Caribbean—the husband left for his annual reunion. It was then that Ada first noted a certain anxiety. There were days she wanted to jump out of her very flesh and entire nights with eyeballs open with insomnia. The Gray was back. Some days it loomed over her, not like a dreary cloud but like a piano on ropes just about to drop on her head. Mostly, it slipped underneath the skin, causing shivers as if in a dank cave, even when embarrassingly drenched on the outside.

The poor woman couldn't get through the day without some discomfort or complaint. At last Sunday's dinner, for instance, after dessert was served, she turned inordinately irritated and sent everyone home. That night, Ada refused to drive Pablo to the airport, which was a first, and she had no good excuse except the sour mood. Her husband had always been an even-tempered man and, putting his wife's current state in perspective, bore it all with the stoicism often attributed to good and understanding men.

On Monday, Dr. Cardona, trusted personal physician, prescribed hormone pills.

Whenever Pablo went out of town, Ada never altered the routine. She ate at home alone. The girls who worked for the couple observed their mistress in her seat at the dining room table, pleasantly consuming the meal, reading a magazine or watching the finches that came to the feeders on the terrace, carrying on as if the whole family were there, like ghosts at their places.

Ada accepted all life's rhythms because what she hadn't elected, she had inherited. She understood the diligence her profession required. Her mother had also been a nurse with long hours at the hospital. Pablo and Ada lived in the apartment Pablo's family once owned and had passed on. There were norms and customs to recognize, and Ada—as had her siblings, as had her husband and his siblings, now all heads of families—did her best to uphold them.

Every morning Cuca, one of the girls (not a girl at all after decades of service) went to the market. Although the load was greatly reduced since the boys had grown up, Mirta, the other housekeeper, did the laundry every morning and hung it on the roof three floors up. In the past, it was boys' soiled pants, uniforms, and sports clothes. Now it was mostly towels, table napkins, and Pablo's washables. Ada's delicate undergarments were scrubbed by hand in the sink on the roof. Meanwhile, the mistress herself did nothing she didn't do when Pablo was at home. Otherwise, as if missing a stitch in an ever-growing afghan, she'd have to unravel her whole history and start anew.

This year, however, felt different.

She'd already started the hormone treatment Dr. Cardona had prescribed, but the undefined apprehension remained constant. Ada touched base by phone with Evi, her oldest friend and her youngest son's godmother. Her *comadre* agreed with the doctor. The Gray following Ada had to be part of the Change. "You know," she said, "even if a woman didn't want any more children, when you go through menopause, you experience a kind of mourning."

"Mourning who? The death of my eggs?" Ada snorted. "Did you feel that way when you went through the Change?" Her friend had never expressed wanting children and never had any.

"No," Evi said, "but I've heard of women who have."

Ada appreciated her friend's well-meaning input, but she didn't miss babies. She had an infant grandchild, the sweetest thing on Earth. He reminded her, however, how tiresome changing diapers was and how sleep-depriving being woken at all hours by a baby's hungry wail had been.

But there was something to it, the *comadre*'s suggestion of an unnamed regret. Or maybe a longing. But for what? Youth? The body she once took for granted that caught people's eyes at the beach? The surplus energy—to run the house, manage the children's schedules, her husband's needs (which had always been expressed as requests while he put in long hours at work), and on top of all that, oversee the clinic—was dissipating. She no longer had half of it to do and yet was always exhausted. Moreover, even her interest in daily activities waned.

Now, neither sons nor Pablo around, Ada took her nightly bath with mineral salts, which Mirta faithfully prepared before going up to her room to rest. It was while soaking, eyes covered with a gel eye mask and taking in the jasmine fragrance from scented candles, that the mistress of the house realized what was missing as of late. It had been months since she and Pablo had been intimate. Did men go through something like the Change, too? Like tarpons, such contemplations jumped up lately to disrupt her otherwise even-keel existence. More were to come, and by the end of that week, Ada would never be the same.

It started with coffee with the new doctor. Although coffee was always on hand, when Dr. Almazán Robles popped his full head of hair in her office to invite her out for a cup, just like that, Ada forgot the electric pot in the staff lounge, the same one she herself prepared every morning.

"They have the best cappuccino," he said, flashing his Colgate smile. "My treat?" The scruffy hair and nubby-bearded face that on another man would be taken as unkempt but on him screamed photo shoot, and his gaze directly on her, expectant of the answer, caused Ada to have a micro-blackout. Trying to recover, she turned up the corners of her mouth and forced herself to blink.

Ada found her own head—which had worn the same medium-length hairstyle for over a decade, and now the first and only pair of reading glasses she'd ever had, and neutral hypoallergenic lipstick applied once a day, by then already smudged as she'd held a pencil between her lips—nodding.

And then, of course, "there were those big hazel eyes," her assistant, Maya, said when Ada mentioned the new doctor's invitation. "Who could say no to them?"

The head administrator felt her face grow warm from the remark—or maybe it was another hot flash—and decided not to give the invitation much weight. In all likelihood, the doctor wanted to bring up a subject related to the clinic that he felt might be best discussed out of others' earshot. Coffee out, including the walk to and from, would last forty-five minutes tops, especially if they took it to go. Not time to say much, she figured.

Miraculously, they found two seats together at the busy café. Dr. Almazán Robles—Mauro, he insisted—seemed to smile all the time, maybe because his handsomeness allowed him an aura of self-assurance, or perhaps the smile was an extension of his professional persona. He was smiling when he told Ada while they waited for the cappuccinos and, upon his insistence, pastries, "That scarf is very pretty." Caught off guard by the doctor's compliment, she put her hands up to the silk *bufanda* just as he added, "It complements your complexion." Ada didn't know what to make of the doctor's flattery, but much to her horror, she found herself with eyes downcast like a daft schoolgirl.

The scarf had been a Mother's Day gift which she couldn't take any credit for, but as for the complexion . . . ? All she used was Pond's. Coming from a physician, what could a compliment on a nice complexion mean? It crossed her mind that Dr. Cardona might have mentioned to him Ada's recent health issues. The new MD must be feeling sorry for her. She was officially middle-aged. Yes, this had to be the purpose of the meeting.

If it was, nothing related to her mental or physical condition was brought up. Instead, they made small talk, enjoyed the coffee, which was very good, and desserts (wicked calories), and returned promptly to the office.

That night when Pablo called, as he always did at precisely seven, when he asked about her day and if there was anything new, she said no. She wanted to share about the new doctor's invitation or, at the very least, that the café on the corner of the clinic, which had been open for years but she'd never bothered to try, was worthwhile. Maybe they could go together sometime. But she passed on reporting on the meeting, aware that doing so put into question whether she had something to hide. She did not.

The next day, all at the office went as usual. Maya asked if Dr. Almazán Robles had spoken to Ada again. He hadn't. "Not even a 'Beautiful day, isn't it?'" Maya asked. No, nothing.

"Oh, yes," Ada said, turning around. The assistant stopped in her tracks, ready to catch office gossip. "Dr. Almazán Robles asked that we leave mail on his desk so that he doesn't have to go searching for it." Maya was disappointed, and Ada smiled as if she enjoyed teasing the younger woman. The fact was, Ada herself was disappointed.

The following morning, however, was to be different. Clouds parted and the sun shone again when Mauro stepped into Ada's tiny office. It was Wednesday, her day to work late. The drive back and forth to eat at home took too long. On Wednesday evenings, she filled in for the other nurse and locked up. It was her habit, therefore, to eat in the office, whether a bag lunch Cuca had prepared or fast food brought in by someone on staff.

"Do you have plans today—to eat?" Mauro asked. It wasn't in a voice where anyone near might hear, but personal. Ada thought about the Tupperware in her desk, Cuca's carefully prepared sandwich to which she always added sliced cucumber. It was hard to know what gave Cuca the idea that cucumber slices were added to all sandwiches, but whether ham, chicken, or fish, it was included. A pear, apple, or orange for dessert. "Yes," Ada said, "I mean, no . . . ?" She composed herself. Mauro smiled as if he knew the effect he had on her, because he had that effect on all women, and said, "Let's go eat together. I know a place down Insurgentes . . ."

"Insurgentes?" she repeated as if she, born and raised in that city, had never heard of its longest avenue.

"It's not that far, Ada," Mauro said, obviously thinking that was her hesitation. "We can walk there. I'll call ahead to make sure we have a table. You like to walk, don't you?"

She nodded, almost vigorously. As a matter of fact, Ada hated walking. Considering herself a team player, she pulled out a worn pair of cross-trainers still in the drawer from the eighties, when the boys were active in prep school with all manner of lessons and diversions; she would kill time going to Pilates before picking them up.

A reservation was being held at Mauro's place on Insurgentes when they arrived. "I enjoy coming here," he explained to Ada, "but with my work, I never have much time." The host led them through the boisterous atmosphere of the trendy locale and out to the sprawling outdoor dining area. "It's such a lovely day," Mauro told Ada as the host placed the cloth napkin on her lap. "I try to take every opportunity to be outside when I can." He sighed. She took a deep breath, too, as if they were in the Alps and not in the smog-ridden city. Yes, Ada thought, it was a nice day, quite unexpectedly bright. In fact, some might even say dazzling.

When the boys were kids, she and Pablo went to their soccer games. As a family, they played tennis. They were out in the sun every weekend. Maybe that was what she needed and not prescriptions. Sun, the amiable doctor's positivity, lunch out—it all put her in rare good humor.

It was easy to relax into Mauro's amusing, even if superficial, chatter. He asked few questions and relied on anecdotes—bumping into the president of the country right outside that very restaurant, long before he ran for president, of course, and the time Mauro was jogging and came upon a man having a heart attack. He helped him and later found out that the unexpected patient was his mother's favorite telenovela actor. "Enrique Lizalde!" Mauro said as if announcing a card at a Lotería game. Spoon filled with a superb cream-of-squash soup in midair and holding a blank smile, Ada tried her best to hide her ignorance regarding soaps.

"From *Corazón Salvaje*?" Mauro said. "What? You don't watch telenovelas? My goodness, I'm with the only woman in Mexico who didn't watch that series."

She gave an apologetic shrug and concentrated on the soup. For years, Ada's days through Sunday, when the family reunited, had been defined by managing the office and the house, and at night, a good book to fall asleep with.

The entrées arrived as her imagination took flight, conjuring up her own telenovela, a scene along the lines of: *Mauro, this between us will never work out . . . I'm a married woman, after all. And the age difference . . . Why, yes, I know it's not that much, but still, what would people say?* The plot took a turn, however, when their lunch was abruptly interrupted by an attractive passerby.

"Mauro!" Shouting and waving with effervescent excitement in the doctor's direction was a man of slight build, immaculately dressed in a cashmere button-down sweater and flashing a pair of Ray-Bans. A plastic bag of dry cleaning on hangers was swung over a shoulder.

The doctor stood up and signaled for him to come over. When the guy arrived, proper introductions were made, and Juan Felipe, as he was called, accepted the doctor's invitation to join them. "If you've already eaten, at least have coffee and dessert or a glass of wine," Mauro suggested, pulling out a seat for his friend before taking his own.

Juan Felipe sat and dragged his chair close to Mauro. Handing over the dry cleaning to the waiter who was immediately on hand, he ordered a Campari. After it arrived, Juan Felipe took a sip, swirled the liquid in the glass, and seemed to be studying Ada. "You have a very good face, *querida*. But I think if you did something with your hair—wore it shorter, let's say—you'd shed years," he said.

Mauro went pale. "Juan Felipe . . . please. This is my new boss. She looks just fine." His friend sipped his drink with unrepentant flair. Not often thrown off balance by ill-natured remarks and certainly not from a stranger, Ada self-consciously patted her hair.

It was Mauro who changed the subject. To his friend, he said, "Ada's husband is from Veracruz, like you." A few back-and-forth inquiries ensued, a little like a tennis match, or perhaps Juan Felipe was sincerely attempting a *Six Degrees of Separation* connection, and it was revealed that he indeed knew of Pablo, although not personally. "Yes, yes!" he said. Putting an arm around Mauro's chair, the other hand holding up the glass of Campari, he eyed Ada. She adjusted her collar, then her sunglasses, and finally eyed him back.

"Pablo is in Veracruz now, correct?" Juan Felipe asked. She winced.

"He and his crew are off rafting today," Mauro's friend said next, as if he'd just become Walter Mercado, the astrologist on television every evening giving zodiac forecasts, and was gazing into a crystal ball.

"How do you know all this?" Mauro asked Juan Felipe, pushing a strand of hair back over his ear. *Ave María*, Ada thought, *do his good looks never quit?* After lunch, if he suggested they meander to a nearby hotel, she might well find herself accepting. An instant later, however, the remotest possibility of such an absurd notion evaporated. Reaching down for the napkin that had dropped in the fuss of Juan Felipe's arrival, she saw Mauro's hand on the other man's knee.

"How do . . . could you know that my husband is rafting today? I spoke to him last night, and he never mentioned it," Ada said.

"Well, he is, darling," Juan Felipe said. He called everyone *darling*, in English. He pronounced it trilling the R.

After coffee and a shared slice of tres leches cake, Mauro insisted on getting the check. While they were all gathering themselves to go on with their lives, Juan Felipe said, "Maybe you should ask him."

Ada stared again. She felt like a rabbit about to be made stew.

"Ask your man, darling," Juan Felipe said. "Ask him all the questions you want. You're the wife, after all."

If you could be shrunken and pushed inside a balloon that would then be filled with helium, and—assuming you could still breathe in there—if you found yourself floating in the dark, bouncing off surfaces, wondering in which direction you were being propelled, that was what the rest of Ada's day and evening were like.

Because he knew she'd worked late, Pablo waited to call until she would already be in bed. Next to her: the chamomile tea Mirta had prepared, *La Jornada*, a notepad to scribble what she needed to get done the next day—and meanwhile, she was still in the confounding balloon. "How was *your* day?" she asked in a voice, sounding accusative rather than inquisitive, as she'd intended.

When Pablo launched into a spirited account of his rafting event, Ada came to two conclusions. Juan Felipe indeed knew the same people, and second, he was kind of a bitch. Why all the insinuations? *Her man* had been going to meet his friends for years. It was his week. What was suspicious about his where-abouts? Nevertheless, despite the Ambien she took before bed, she tossed all night.

The next day, as soon as Ada got home at the normal two thirty or so, putting off washing up to sit down to her solitary meal at the dining table, she went through an old address book kept in Pablo's desk and found the number of one of the women in his group, Juliana Short. It was suppositional, she figured, to call Pablo's longtime friend. The clique was loyal. However, as one of the few women, Juliana might be willing to reveal something to an obviously desperate wife. Ada's finger trembled as she pressed the numbers on the handset, making the direct call to Veracruz.

They'd met a few times over the years, always on special occasions. Pablo's friend hadn't attended the wedding, but she'd been at Victor's baptism. Juliana had given the baby a gift, an exquisite child's bank of pure silver from Taxco, filled with gold coins. Ada mailed a thank-you card to Juliana, but afterward Pablo said she should send flowers, too. So she did. Years later, a married Juliana turned up with her man to their tenth-anniversary dinner party at a restaurant in Polanco.

Time passed, and when Pablo turned fifty, it had been a sur-prise to see a single Juliana appear at Plaza Garibaldi. The evening was organized for the couples in Ada and Pablo's card club; they played on Friday nights and came together for such events. Most of his friends were turning fifty that year, so it wasn't all that odd, Ada thought, that one of his college friends would want to celebrate with him. Juliana flying in from Veracruz was an indication of their longtime affection.

Pablo's college chum had matured, but she still stood out in a crowd. That night Juliana's Afro hair was covered with an auburn coiffed wig, and although her figure had expanded over the years, it seemed to have been in all the right places. Whatever that meant. What it meant was that evening, during the slow dance Pablo had with his old friend, Juliana stole the show.

Ada hadn't made much of their "grind" performance. They were all outside on the Plaza, jackets and wraps on and plastic cups with tequila in hand to keep warm. Musicians for hire, a cacophony of horns, guitars, and singing all around. Their party was all tipsy, and if Ada felt any jealousy watching her husband so embraced with Juliana, she let it go for the sake of everyone's good time. Pablo's friend had divorced with no children. That's all Ada knew about her. Pablo scarcely mentioned Juliana Short.

His friend was cordial when she heard Ada's voice on the other end. Yes, she had seen Pablo recently. Yes, there was a rafting trip. No, she hadn't gone—she was too old for such adventures, she said with a low *heh-heh*. Yes, she thought in all likelihood she'd see Pablo again before he left Veracruz, at the traditional going-away party the night before everyone went their way. Juliana didn't ask the reason for the call, and the exchange was awkward. Ada struggled, trying to finesse her query. It wasn't a question that had come to her mind but for one reason: Juan Felipe and his sly allusions.

Then again, Pablo had always worried about appearances, so what if there was something to what Mauro's pal had hinted? "You've all been such good friends for so long," she said. "But surely he spends more time with—"

"You mean with his family?" Juliana interrupted. "Yes, of course. You know how he adores them."

Ada resented the insinuation that she had any trouble with her in-laws. Why would Juliana think that, anyway? As soon as Ada collected herself, she found a way to resume her intended questioning. "I mean, in the group . . ."

"In the group?" Juliana repeated.

Was Juliana playing coy or just protecting her friend? "For God's sake, Juliana," Ada muttered aloud, and sighed. "Is my husband gay?"

A few seconds had gone by, Ada looking at the receiver and wondering if the other woman was still on the line, when Juliana spoke again, "Your husband is not gay, Ada." And then: "I'm sorry, I'm getting another call. Do take care." Next a dial tone. Call waiting was the latest new thing available on home phones. People were thrilled not to miss important calls because the click-click alerted them to switch off, but just as often, perhaps, it was a good excuse to end an uncomfortable chat.

The call clarified nothing except that she now felt like an idiot for having bothered Juliana. In any case, Ada should've known that Pablo's old friend wouldn't give away confidences. Remaining at the desk, distressed over her marriage, she felt the Gray become burning charcoal. A wife who, for thirty years, hadn't the slightest suspicion about her husband's fidelity was now ridden with it. After all, he always had plenty of opportunities away from home to sneak around—late nights at the office, out with clients, and weekends on job sites.

Pablo having a fling would truly be a disaster. When they first married and a few times since, he'd been emphatic that if she were ever to step out of the marriage, even once, it would be over.

Ada began to sob, then wailed so loudly that Cuca and Mirta came running, but the distraught mistress sent them back to their duties. They looked frightened. Neither had ever seen Señora so discombobulated. Minutes later, the phone rang. It was a much disquieted Pablo. Obviously, he'd gotten the alert from the girls.

"*Por Dios*," he kept muttering as Ada sobbed on the other end. "Call Pablito to come over," he suggested of their eldest, who lived in Satélite.

Ada refused. Why force their son away from his home and family to drive through all the traffic for nothing?

"I'm going to change my flight. I'll be home tomorrow," Pablo told her.

Ada wept well into the night. Like all breakdowns, which was surely what she was having, it resulted from a series of recent perturbing irregularities, like dead-end halls in a windowless house.

First, there was the dashing Mauro's ambiguous attention. What did he want with her, anyway? She wasn't about to be made a fool. She also allowed herself to look at the possibility of dark intentions. Ada oversaw all matters related to the clinic's finances, and no one was going to pull a fast one on her, not even the persuasive doctor.

Next, Juan Felipe spoiling the otherwise fabulous lunch with his distasteful intimations.

Then she had weighed herself the other morning and seen that she'd gained five kilos. After the initial shock, she decided the decrepit scale was off. (On Saturday she was going to the Wal-Mart that recently opened in el De Efe. Everyone said they carried *everything* and at low prices.)

Finally, despite Dr. Cardona's prescriptions and expertise, all the physical discomforts of the Change continued. Was it true that women's hysterics were real? She'd always been reserved, kept her affairs to herself, and preferred others to do likewise. Would she end up getting a lobotomy like the woman in the Tennessee Williams play they once saw at the Bellas Artes?

It was a terrible night.

The next morning, Ada skipped breakfast. Then she did something else she'd never done before: She called in sick. Fifteen minutes later, the phone rang. It was a concerned Mauro. He ventured to ask, "It wasn't because of my friend the other day, was it? Juan Felipe is a sweetheart, but he can be too direct, even abrasive, for some people's taste."

Ada did feel all that about Mauro's friend, but it wasn't the doctor's fault. "No, hombre," she said in her best nonchalant voice. "Your friend was delightful. Thank you again for a splendid meal. You're very generous." She assured him that the problem lay in a bad reaction to new medication. No one's fault. These things happened. Physicians weren't God, after all.

Mauro was left to pursue the matter no further.

It was after the lonely meal at the table, which she took out of habit—first the soup, then the entrée (Sam's Club white rice, Milanese steak, *berritos* salad on the side), and she skipped dessert (packaged rice pudding again)—that she went to sit on the terrace. The finches were gone, and she felt like weeping again. Ada hadn't even noticed summer coming to an end.

A childhood memory popped into her head. When Ada was nine years old, as the Epiphany neared, she asked the Three Kings for a bicycle. She had learned to ride on her big brother's bike and wanted her own. The girl always got what she asked for, and as the holidays drew near, Ada grew more excited in anticipation. However, after mass on Christmas Eve, as they all readied for bed, she overheard a conversation between her parents (during the season, the children were always eavesdropping). The couple was apprehensive about letting Ada go out and about on a bike. Her brother might not want to go with her, and no one at home had time. She couldn't just ride around the enclosed patio.

The morning of the Epiphany, they hurried outside to see what had been left for the children, who had all dutifully placed their old shoes outside for the Three Kings. The roasted chestnuts for the Magi were gone but for the shells, and the three cups of foamy hot chocolate in terra-cotta cups were empty. Instead of the bike, however, Ada received a dollhouse. Her heart sank.

She understood her parents' fear for her safety and that their intention had been to protect her, but she wished they had discussed the matter with her. Over time, the disappointment grew to resentment. When Ada was older and starting nursing school, she took her savings and purchased an auto without consulting her parents. They hit the roof when they saw her drive up in the jalopy. But it was hers, and she insisted she'd take all responsibility. Her older siblings weighed in and defended her. In time, the parents, although never ceasing to fret, accepted and even came to appreciate her self-determination.

None of this had anything to do with what was happening now, except for one point. In always trying to protect her, they had deprived her of having any choice. Whatever Pablo thought he had protected her from, it was humiliating to think he didn't believe she could deal with the truth.

But what was the truth? Something concealed equaled deception. The unshakable sensation that their marriage had been a lie made her ill. Throughout the day, Ada stayed in nightclothes. Her unprecedented abandonment of duties was alarming to Mirta and Cuca, who went about their chores as if coexisting with the undead.

Around five o'clock, Pablito, with his wife and baby in tow, charged in as if they'd just gotten word, instead of a call the night before from Pablo asking them to check in on Ada.

"Come in, Mamá. You'll catch cold out here," her son bade her, gently taking her by the arm as if she were an invalid. The sun hid behind the trees by that hour, but she hadn't noticed the temperature dropping. "I'm fine," she mumbled, while Pablito insisted on helping her inside.

They settled in the library surrounded by the shelves of Ada's favorite books and Pablo's trophies—tennis at the club, debate team in college, "best project of the year" awards from his company, the family photographs, including a wedding portrait on the wall. Looking around, Ada no longer found comfort in what now felt like mementos of a false marriage.

"What's wrong?" Pablito repeated.

"Yes, what's going on?" asked the daughter-in-law, rocking her infant.

Anticipating the request, Cuca hurried off to put on coffee and the teapot. She was trying to recall if there were any biscuits in the tin and, in case something stronger was in order, was reaching for Pablo's Scotch when the front door opened again.

Pablo had finally returned. Mirta took his suitcase to the bedroom to unpack, and he stopped in his bathroom before heading to the family meeting. The girls informed the señor they were all gathered there and, of course, that the señora was in a very bad way.

When he appeared in the doorway, looking all the figure of authority as his status granted, he did something rather churlish. Or rather, it was what he didn't do. He didn't greet his wife with a kiss. Instead, Pablo stayed by the entrance as if he might have to make an abrupt departure. "Sit down, Father," Pablito said. For their part, Pablito and the wife, baby in arms, remained standing. While presently apprehensive about his parents' strange behavior, the older son never had a favorite parent, loving both equally. "Mensches," his father-in-law had called Ada and Pablo in a toast at their son's wedding. That was how everyone saw them, people of integrity and honor. Whatever was transpiring didn't feel like any of Pablito's business.

Ada took her place on the leather chair that once belonged to her father. Feet up on the seat, her long nightdress pulled over her knees, she gave the impression of either being snug or imitating a mummy left in a tomb in Palenque.

Matters advanced instantly.

"I called Juliana yesterday . . ." Ada started to say to her husband.

"You . . . called . . . J-*Juliana*?" Pablo asked. Before pronouncing Juliana's name, he gulped. All heads turned. With such an alarmed look on his face, she may as well have announced, "Pablo, I know you killed someone, and I've called the police."

As if throttled, Pablo dragged himself to the fireplace and sat on the hearth, hands over his face.

"Who is Juliana?" Ada's daughter-in-law asked in the most unobtrusive but clear voice, like a dinner bell.

Cuca, who had brought in a tray and set it on the desk, turned to Pablo, too.

"I'm sorry," he said to Ada, who appeared as if she might be holding her breath. "We were involved in college, Juliana and I . . ." he began.

Ada watched his mouth move but heard the words with a time lapse and in slow speed.

"I left her to come to study here at the university . . ." Pablo directed himself to no one in the room, but when he did occasionally seek a sympathetic face, it was his son's. Pablito, however, looked less sympathetic than perplexed.

For her part, the sense of a piano looming above Ada's head, which had followed her for weeks, returned. High above, like from one of those high-rises in New York, a tiny object hung outside a window. Suddenly, the ropes broke and it was plunging down fast, the piano gaining velocity with gravity. It all was becoming terrifyingly apparent. "Are you and Juliana having an affair . . . ?" she found herself blurting. As she said it aloud, it sounded outlandish. Ada and Pablo had always been the most stable couple she knew. Juliana Short? She was an old school chum.

Everyone looked first at Ada and back to Pablo, who seemed

to be weighing what his reply should be. Cuca burst out, "Oh, my Señora! How could El Señor do this to her?" She ran out without waiting for an answer.

Pablito's wife went to the divan to sit, setting the slumbering baby next to her. She pulled a pacifier from her pocket and stuck it in his mouth. Her husband remained standing, now with jaw dropped.

"It's not what you think," Pablo said, running his sweaty palms over his jeans. "Years back, I was a coward. My parents were against my getting engaged to Juliana, and I made the excuse of having to come to study at the university here."

It took no time for Ada to figure out why her in-laws had objected to Juliana as a potential wife for their son. Ada's mother-in-law kept a plaque of their family tree on the wall. Her ancestors had practically landed with Cortés. The lady never went as far as stating it, but far be it that their bloodlines held any indigenous ancestry, much less that of the slaves brought to the Port of Veracruz. As for Ada's father-in-law, how well she remembered when Pablo's parents were visiting and she had invited Dr. Cardona over to dine with the family.

Ada's new boss from Guerrero had put himself through medical school. He was magnetic and dark-skinned; people always remarked on the doctor's uncanny resemblance to Bola de Nieve, the Cuban entertainer. Dr. Cardona had worked several years at a general hospital before establishing his own clinic. But his diligence wasn't what Ada's father-in-law remarked on right after the visitor left. "Well, he's a credit to his race," Pablo's father said, taking a puff off the cigar he had started when the doctor was there. To be sure, her in-laws were courteous to him, but in truth, they looked down on the man because of his color and his humble origins.

That night in bed, Ada had a talk with her husband. Pablo apologized for his parents' obvious "prejudices," as he referred to their bigotry, but they'd been very good to him and his young family, hadn't they?

"I was ashamed of myself," Pablo said now about having rejected his black girlfriend. Whom he was talking to was unclear, since he was staring at his shoes. "I went back to Veracruz with the intention of marrying Juliana, but she turned me down."

"She turned you down?" Ada heard herself repeat.

"You were expecting at the time," Pablo said to Ada. "That's why Juliana turned me down."

Now it was Pablito who spoke up. "You were going to leave my mother knowing she was pregnant?" He glanced at his wife and infant.

"I would have provided for you," Pablo said. Realizing how it came off, he put his hands back over his face.

"So, you've been having an affair, betraying my mother-in-law all these years?" The reproach came from Pablito's wife. Ada looked at the young woman. The two had never been close, but true to physics—nothing could be disturbed without everything around also being affected—Ada sensed the room's atmosphere altered. The girl picked up the baby and left the room. After a final look at his father and then Ada, Pablito followed.

"Have you two been carrying on . . . all these years?" Ada asked. She held out hope that he might simply say no, not at all, that in fact it was a misunderstanding. They'd leave the room arm in arm, ask the girls to prepare something to eat, and everything, in other words, would go on as before.

Instead, red-faced Pablo stared at his wife. He nodded.

"Did you ever love me, Pablo?" Ada asked next. In the grand scheme of a cuckold's story, it was almost a perfunctory question. It seemed too much, and he stood up, hands out, as if about to supplicate, but Ada's expression must've caused him to stay where he was. "I was very much in love with you, always," he said softly. "When we went to New York and seeing your belly grow. Then Pablito was born. We were very happy together. Don't you remember? It was only after Victor came along and we were living here and you became so depressed that Juliana and I . . ."

"I see," Ada said. In fact, she didn't but had heard enough. All those years ago, Ada believed he'd gone home to Veracruz to speak with his parents about their getting married. Now, a lifetime later, a bulb the size of the kind on billboards turned on. He had gone home to ask Juliana to take him back.

Ada's parents both liked her new fiancé, the simpatico and promising engineer. When he went back to Veracruz, her mother asked why he hadn't invited Ada to go and meet his family. The girl, too in love or fearful of causing unnecessary drama, hadn't even questioned the lack of an invitation. As soon as he returned from that trip, they started planning the wedding. As an engagement ring, he brought a small sapphire ring with a halo of diamonds that his mother had sent to welcome her to the family. The young British Royals were engaged then, too. Diana's ring was also a sapphire. Of course, Ada's comparisons of herself with the princess, whose wedding was being lauded the world over as a fairy tale come true, were silly. Every young woman in love wanted to feel like Cinderella. What did the two young brides have in common? Well, now she knew—they'd both married two-timers.

"After Victor was born," Ada said, "that's when you went to Veracruz and started your affair with *her*?" Ada wasn't so much asking but verifying she'd gotten the time line right.

Henceforth, Juliana would no longer be his friend whom he could bring up in casual conversations. Instead, she would be referred to in the third person—*she who would not be named*. Ada felt anger toward *her*, but not as much as she felt toward Pablo.

Her thoughts were all over the place, like lottery balls in a random generator. Had Pablo's family in Veracruz been aware of his long-standing affair with his college sweetheart? Were the two seen as a couple by the rest in their crowd? Every year when they got together, it was Pablo and *her*? Teamed up for tennis matches, dancing the grind on the Malecón for the whole world to see? Did they share the same hotel room each year, coming down in the elevator, holding hands, to join the others for breakfast? Who else knew—his colleagues at the office here in Mexico City? For heaven's sake, even Juan Felipe, a total stranger, knew. Was the price to live an orderly life, respectful of proper conduct, that the wife always be duped?

Ada stood up to leave the room.

"*Mi amor . . .*" Pablo started. He took a step in her direction but hesitated. "Will you ever forgive me?"

Although she felt her head shaking, what she heard herself say aloud was "I don't know," because the truth was that she didn't. She didn't know anything anymore.

Summer ended, and as fall rolled over the city, bringing rainy weather, Mauro and she went out to eat regularly on Wednesdays, their late night at the clinic. She enjoyed his compliments and the way women, assuming they were rendezvousing, gave them side glances. Once, some ladies at a nearby table were indiscreetly watching the couple while whispering among themselves. Mauro leaned over near her ear. "Maybe they think I'm a gigolo."

"A gigo . . ." Ada started to repeat. "You mean like *The Roman Spring of Mrs. Stone*." She delicately took a bite of red snapper with a certain affectation. (Suddenly she was Vivian Leigh with Warren Beatty?)

"The Roman spring of . . . ?" Mauro was lost.

"By Tennessee Williams?" Ada said.

"Oh, yes, of course," he said, "a play." He took a swallow from the bottle of Sangría Señorial as if chugging a beer.

"The novel," Ada corrected him. "Williams's first, in fact." A rapid survey around the restaurant showed there were older men out with younger women everywhere—secretaries, mistresses, infatuations, and escorts, as it had always been. It was accepted by society and, to many, seen as a mark of a man's financial success. Times, however, were changing. So what if a married woman could also "afford" a debonair younger man to distract her from the doldrums?

Two wrongs never made a right, but such was the world, full of hypocrisies. It was the 1990s, for crying out loud, more than seventy years since Colette wrote *Chéri*.

But theirs was no tryst. Ada and Mauro were no more than friendly associates. They alternated picking up the tab at lunch until they agreed to always go Dutch. While Ada enjoyed hearing about the doctor's escapades with men (Juan Felipe was only one among Mauro's boyfriends), she didn't discuss her marriage. She found no reason to reveal what she had uncovered about Pablo in Veracruz. Instead, just as with Dr. Cardona, she preferred to be valued by the new doctor as the reliable office manager and head nurse, while keeping personal business separate.

All on the home front had returned to a calm regimen. One might be tempted to say, remarkably so, if one didn't know the ever-adept Ada. *Everything in its place*, as a needlework sampler might read. Thanks to a new prescription for antidepressants, a pill a day kept the doctor away. Or more accurately in Ada's case, the Gray.

By October, temperatures outside left the extensive apartment dank and chilly. One Saturday, the girls washed and put away all the summer bedding. Then the housekeepers brought out and washed the stored winter bedding. It was a day's project. Ada was now buying a jumbo-size jug of liquid detergent at her latest favorite place to shop, Sam's Club. "Don't use too much," Ada called out, "it's concentrated."

"The more she saves now at these new gringo stores, the cheaper she gets," Cuca whispered in Mazahua to Mirta as they loaded the washer. "These old comforters smell of mothballs."

The other housekeeper nodded but had come up with her own retaliation to the idle complaints of her mistress. On her day off when she went home, in a bag with other pantry goods, she carried a tall jar filled with laundry detergent. La Señora never noticed, and anyway, she could afford it.

Mirta and Cuca, with heavy baskets, prepared to go up to the roof to hang everything on the line. "Wait for me," Ada called. She picked up the bowl of peas she was about to shell and followed them up. It was a clear day in the city that so often grew opaque with dense smog. Ada pulled up a chair as the girls hung the bedding. When they finished and she was done shelling, they lingered, taking in the sun.

Cuca reached into her apron pocket and pulled out a crumpled pack of Delicados. Leaning against the ledge, she peered at the view of balconies and rooftops where laundry flapped in the wind, plants now withered and glum treetops losing leaves. In the distance below, there was the constant racket of ongoing traffic. That fall, there would be a presidential election. In her neighborhood of La Villita, nothing would change. The rich would get richer and the poor be further damned.

Mirta scooted down near La Señora. As she smacked a fly that landed on her forehead, she noticed her boss fanning herself with her hands. "Are you all right, Señora?" Mirta asked. Eight years before, Ada and Pablo had become godparents to her firstborn and now paid for the boy's schooling, for which Mirta and her husband were grateful, but she'd never be so familiar as to call her bosses compadres. In fact, El Señor and La Señora were more like her own godparents. She'd worked for them since her cousin Cuca had arranged it and brought the teenager from the pueblo to work there with her.

Mirta had spoken only Mazahua when she first came to the capital. She learned Spanish in the household from the señores' orders, watching *Plaza Sésamo* with the boys, going to the market with Cuca, and at night when retiring to their room up on the roof, watching telenovelas with the other girls who worked in the build-ing and also slept up there. One day, when Mirta found the time, of course, she'd learn to read and write, too.

Ada grimaced. "It's these bloody hot flashes," she said.

"Have you ever tried wild yam?" Cuca asked, taking a drag from her cigarette. "My mother used it when she went through the Change. It helped a lot. All my aunts used it."

Ada hadn't ever heard of wild yams as any cure, but she wasn't surprised at Cuca's suggestion. She was always coming up with one home remedy or another. This time, however, it turned out to be a homoeopathic salve in a jar. "I'll pick one up for you, if you'd like to try it," Cuca said, flicking the cigarette butt in the air.

At that point, with nearly a year of aggravating symptoms, Ada would have eaten wild yam raw if there'd been any chance of it helping. As soon as they were back inside, she sent the house-keeper promptly down the block to the pharmacy. They carried it, and that very night, Ada began to apply it to her skin. A month later, the hot flashes had ceased altogether.

Another development. Ada didn't need Pablo going out of town as an excuse to take an evening for herself. One day, she called her comadre Evi to see a movie together. Later, they could stop at El Moro for churros and hot chocolate, "like back in the old days," Ada suggested. And they did. Another time they went for mani-cures. Soon it wasn't unusual for one or the other to extend an invitation. Ada looked forward to their times.

Regarding Ada and Pablo's marriage, counseling helped. Pablo agreed to go only when it was presented as an alternative to di-vorce. He volunteered to quit his annual reunions back home, but neither the therapist nor Ada thought it necessary. A phone call on speaker to *her* in Veracruz sufficed. He told his longtime liaison that, while their relationship had to end, there would be friendship, if she chose it. She chose not.

That year, the youngest of the household, Victor, was coming home from Berkeley on Thanksgiving break. "He asked if he could bring a friend," Pablo relayed to his wife, who was already working on the Christmas-card list in the study. He made air bunnies with his fingers when he said "friend." Her boys had been bringing best buddies home as long as she could remember. It gave her pause to hear that he'd asked permission this time. Pablo nodded at her puzzled expression. Ada slipped the letter opener in the address book so as not to lose her place.

"He said the person used to be a *religioso* . . ." Pablo said, taking a seat across the desk. Mirta came in with the afternoon coffee on a tray. The housekeeper lingered to pick up whatever morsels she could from the couple's conversation.

"Did he say *religioso* or *religiosa*?" Ada asked.

"Well, he said *persona religiosa*," Pablo replied, meaning that the feminine noun required a feminine adjective and didn't necessarily mean the person in reference was female. The two took a few minutes to start their coffee, which Mirta insisted on pouring. Cuca had baked a batch of scrumptious cinnamon cookies. "Ay, that Cuca," Ada said, picking one up, still warm and crumbly. "She's determined to break my diet." She gave Pablo a side glance. He'd stopped going to the gym, and his trousers no longer buttoned.

"Well," Pablo started, powdered sugar on his lips from the cookie he'd just flung into his mouth, "Victor said *was*. He's almost a mystic, your son. Remember when he finished prep school and made us release him into a monastery in Hidalgo? He wanted to be a mendicant." Pablo took a sip from the cup belonging to the china set that was once his grandparents' and reached for another cookie.

"Please, Pablo," Ada said. It hurt her to think how her sons' sensitive nature was always blamed on the mother. "At least he hung in there for six months. You can't tell me our child didn't learn something from that experience about humility and to appreciate the life we gave him." Mirta decided the conversation was getting good and went to dust out the fireplace in order to eavesdrop. "*Religioso* could mean anything," Ada said. "Did he specify?"

"It was late the other night when I got back to him," Pablo said. "Maybe he said monk . . . or did he say nun?"

Ada's face looked completely lost in thought, which was almost always the case in recent times, Mirta thought, brusquely pouring ashes into a small metal bucket. Mirta remembered fondly walking little Victor home from school. The endearing cowlick, the way his knobby knees were always covered with scabs, how he managed to get Cuca and her to cover for him when he received a poor grade or talked them into dessert before dinner, all came back. Sometimes, when Victor called and his parents were out, Mirta sat down and chatted with him until Cuca came by and gave her a look.

The young woman in the pink and white uniform, which she wore day in and day out, tossed her long braid over her shoulder, picked up the bucket, and not for the first time stopped to straighten a mix-up between her bosses. "Pardon, Señor," she said, "Señora, but the person young Victor is bringing home is a girl. And she was a nun," she said, and dashed away before they could ask how she knew so much.

Victor came home from Berkeley with an affable young woman he introduced as his girlfriend. At the first meal they all sat down to, Victor's girlfriend, Ai, imparted that she had in fact been a Buddhist nun as a child. Her parents hadn't wanted a girl and had delivered her to a convent. They also had little to feed her. Once grown, she'd left and found her way to study engineering in the States, which was where, she said, she "had the great fortune of meeting Victor." Ai spoke English with a British accent, which Ada, who'd never gotten the hang of following telenovelas but had recently become addicted to a public television series about Queen Victoria, found enchanting. When Ai said, "Pass the salt, please," Ada thought she sounded like an aristocrat.

One afternoon when the young couple returned from an excursion to Chapultepec Park, and Victor's girlfriend went to their room to rest, he came to sit with his mother, who'd dozed off reading.

"You know, Ai is still a Buddhist," her son said, as if making a grave declaration that had been weighing on him.

Ada nodded. "I know," she said, giving him a gentle pat on the arm.

"They don't believe in God," Victor said.

Ada reached out and ran her hand through her son's thick hair. It was nothing short of maternal bliss having her youngest home.

"I mean, we're Catholic . . . you especially, Mamá," her son insisted. "Well, to be honest, I'm not really Catholic anymore. I don't know what I am right now . . ."

"That makes two of us, son," she said.

Victor's eyes, so much like Pablo's, which seemed to practically bulge at wonder or befuddlement, grew white around the pupils.

"I mean, of course I know who I am," Ada tried to explain. "But being who you are isn't static." She sat up, putting both hands to her lower back as if needing to stretch. "Come," she added, "let's go to the table."

Victor offered his mother a hand up. It was true, how you were always changing even when you thought you were in a rut. Ai and he often talked about such paradoxes. Changes offered an aperture toward self-awareness, or you could choose to regress into ignorance.

Regress into ignorance? Was that what his beloved had said? Or had Ai said, "Or you can remain in your stupor even after many lifetimes of lessons"? Then again, Buddhists didn't believe in reincarnation. It was called *anattā*—no soul, no self. Was he simply getting thoughts and ideas muddled the way he did when he was hungry? His nostrils swelled with the aromas of Cuca's roasted turkey, stuffing with chicken livers, and sweet potato enchiladas in honor of the special guest.

Ada was stepping quickly toward the kitchen to give the girls serving instructions when her son reached to catch her hand. She turned with the look of immediate concern that she always had when one of her loved ones needed attention. Victor offered a smile to reassure her it was nothing, really, just a thought, a question. "How is it that you and my father have kept it together for so many years, Mamá?" he asked. "I hope my marriage—when I marry—will be as successful as yours."

His mother looked somewhat surprised or perhaps embarrassed

by Victor's admiration. Just then, Pablo came in from another room and caught his son's query. "No marriage is perfect," he said cheerfully, "but Cuca's cooking is close to it." The others in the household were drawing near the dining room, too.

"Men are so simple." It was Pablito's wife who lately seemed to have found her voice. "Full stomachs, sports, and, oh yes, sex."

"Sex is important for women, too," Ada found herself saying. She looked around as if challenging someone to contradict her. No one did. Philosophizing so generally about the inherent differences between men's and women's needs had become abhorrent to her. *Abhorrent* might have been too strong a word; nevertheless, it would have to do for now.

Tango Smoke

WHAT WAS IT about holidays that in the midst of gaiety and song, feasting and remembrances, family members turned rabidly against one another, made lovers and friends reach a point of no return, and cast others off to an isolated island wrought with remorse? Not every year, fortunately, but this year, for one. An emotional eruption occurred like tectonic plates about to decompress with an eruption. It seemed like a loss of seismic proportions, but in fact, release was necessary. The pent-up anguish had been too much. Change was inevitable. Once the shock subsided, everyone would have to adjust . . . or not.

The slow push to change may have started when Mártir reached a new phase in life and figured she'd never been so wise. It had happened before—in her teens and then around twenty-one. She thought she knew firsthand everything about human existence. Then, as confidence waned after thirty, she reached the pinnacle of waxed acumen: forty. Henceforth, no one would surprise her with their actions or failure to act. Now, sharp and observant, she was aware that humanity was frail and mostly selfish. Disappointments and even another broken heart were expected. These were among the musings that had begun to consume Mártir since last New Year's Eve, 2010.

The new decade shouldn't have felt so foreboding for a woman of a certain age. All that talk in magazines, the Sunday paper's fashion section, and in Lifetime movies about forty being the new twenty. Usually, they were long-legged Anglo women in Chanel suits. A lead picture in the article would show a shirtless beefcake mixing up a martini in the background or a woman, presumably a CEO or president, at her desk surrounded by a staff of cute guys in suits and sexy five-o'clock shadows, all reaching out to serve the boss in some way.

Was Mártir, who wasn't represented by any of the glossy images, truly a woman of the times? Or had life just passed her by, the same way it did with her mother, an émigré who spent her life in Chicago as a seamstress and homemaker, dedicated wife and mother?

The media now said it was okay to be divorced (check), raise children on your own (check), be financially independent (check, although on this count, the bills were barely met). Cougars called the shots on their sex lives (Mártir didn't like the predatory sound of the word for fortyish-year-old women with younger men, but *check*). You weren't embarrassed if people smirked behind your back because your marriage failed or your outfit was too *jeune* for your age. At forty-seven, perimenopause reared its ugly head with hot flashes, but you could still aspire.

She'd been studying dance on and off since the age of thirteen in after-school classes at the Chicago Park District. Now, with her children on their own, Mártir, who'd previously worked part-time in retail, looked into doing something to revive her left-behind ambitions. It started with her and Esteban giving dance lessons at assorted venues.

Esteban, exactly sixteen years her junior, and she were living together. He sold weed and produced emo music. People Mártir didn't know, and didn't necessarily care to meet, came in and out of the apartment. A stale waft of smoke from beneath Esteban's studio door assailed her whenever she passed through the hall on the way to the bathroom.

On Wednesday and Thursday evenings, Mártir took the L to Wells Street, then walked three blocks to a snazzy Latin nightclub where she offered a quick salsa dance lesson during happy hour to get the growing crowd in the mood. As part of her compensation, dinner was the free hors d'oeuvres—chicken wings in chipotle sauce, chips and salsa, and celery sticks with ranch dressing on the side.

At such venues, she wore a silver shimmery dress, just above the knee, or, if it was at the cleaners, the chiffon chemise with sequins bought at Filene's Basement last holiday season. On her ever-widening feet, Nine West pumps with a strap, not proper tango shoes but they had to do when at a milonga. (She and Esteban didn't give lessons then but practiced their tango.) The time had come, at least on the dance floor, when petite Mártir, once (and, perhaps arguably, still) the unpretentious daughter of Andalusians, now, beneath the flashy costumes, wore a push-up bra and a *pompis*-lift undergarment ordered from an 800 number off a late-night infomercial.

Above all, Mártir was her own woman.

At this stage what most required her attention was caring for her aging parents and ongoing anxiety over her now grown children. Her father had retired after a stroke. He was cared for by her mother. Besides the occasional joint swelling, Doña Cuca was gratefully capable. The daughter, Lucinda, twenty-one, was away at college. The first in the family to pursue a degree. She excelled in academics, but you always worried about a daughter's safety and well-being. Teo, nineteen, hadn't quite found himself. He stayed with his father on the South Side.

When at home, which was most of the time, Mártir remained in the bedroom. From behind the closed door, she heard Esteban moving about and the occasional voices of strangers passing through. He came to her at bedtime. "Would you like a snack? A glass of cabernet?" he might ask, dropping his jeans on the floor, pulling the black hoodie over his head, going back and forth, in and out of the bedroom, to brush his teeth, make sure doors were locked, check phone messages on the machine in the living room. Finally, tucked under the covers, they made love or watched whatever was on local channels until they fell asleep to the rattle of the L train nearby.

It was just before Lucinda's midterms, which would be followed by a school break, when one evening Esteban came to bed and said, "Your daughter is here." Mártir had gone to sleep waiting for her lover to come home from his gig at El Mediterraneo, where he played guitar for tips. The news made her sit up. "What?" She climbed out from under the pile of blankets and reached for the robe at the foot of the bed. The floor was cold, but she didn't bother searching for slippers.

Mártir had stopped waiting up for her lover on nights when

he was out. Worrying was of no consequence. He called only if it passed through his mind, and returned when it suited him. She'd go to bed anguished. Their car wasn't in the best shape, it could stall or worse, he could get into an accident. She reminded herself she wasn't his mother to worry so much and not his wife. If the reason for his staying out late was another woman, what could she do about it?

Mártir hadn't heard her daughter, who had a key, come into the apartment. The young woman was curled up on the love seat that served as a couch in the tight living room; she was using her winter coat as a blanket. "Lucinda?" her mother said, reaching out to gently nudge the girl's shoulder. "*¿Qué pasa?*" Her daughter was studying hard to stay on the dean's list. It seemed unlikely that she'd have driven three hours up to Chicago at night without a call if it weren't *something*.

The two went to the kitchen to put the pot on for tea and talk. It was about a former boyfriend. Lucinda had no confusion or mixed feelings about the breakup. It was he, she said, who must be having difficulty letting go.

"My friend Belkis said she saw Adán hanging around outside my dorm," Lucinda relayed. Unlike her mother or perhaps because, as a student, she'd put aside care to grooming, Lucinda's nail polish was mostly peeled off of bitten nails. Her long hair was held up by a claw clasp. She wore the same sweatshirt she'd had on the last time her mother saw her.

"Who is Belkis again, *mija*?" Mártir asked. It was hard keeping up with the new crowd her daughter had at college.

"Belkis?" Lucinda said. "She works at Jack in the Box. Remember, I told you we met at the drive-through window."

Her mother nodded, then got that frown she often had on her face. "She doesn't go to your school?"

Lucinda sipped from her mug and grunted. "Just because my friend isn't in college, Mom . . ."

It hadn't taken much, but already mother and daughter were at odds. Mártir found it difficult to hide her hopes for her only daughter to become a professional, lead a different life from her own, have friends who talked about poetry or dressed up and went to the opera. It was a fantasy, of course, right out of a black-and-white Hollywood movie. Lucinda wasn't Ingrid Bergman. It was a chimera passed on from Mártir's mother, who watched classics alone at night, waiting for her own kids to get home in time for curfew on weekends, sneaking a hand-rolled cigarette from her snoring husband, with the window open and city sounds of a night teeming with life in Chicago that Doña Cuca herself had not experienced.

Now Mártir, who never wore a formal dress or even cared about *Figaro*, was passing it on to Lucinda. She wanted everything shiny and new for her daughter. When the girl dismissed those wishes, she was set adrift.

The conversation got derailed because of their friction, but the mention of a guy from Chicago, who had no business on her daughter's campus, was noted and initiated new apprehension.

"Lucinda says that her ex is stalking her." Mártir spoke in such a low voice that Esteban propped himself on elbows on the bed to hear.

The girl had broken up with her boyfriend, who worked doing heating and air-conditioning repairs at the dad's shop in Chicago. How—why—would he be stalking Lucinda? What did she mean by stalking, anyway? One night, Lucinda said she thought she'd seen his car go by when she was walking back to her dorm. The girl was terribly nearsighted, but would she mistake Adán's car?

"A friend of hers says she saw him hanging around Lucinda's dorm last night," Mártir said. "I don't know why my daughter didn't call me. I was up late waiting for you ..." Esteban hadn't come home until almost three in the morning. His clothes and hair always smelled of pot, but last night he'd smelled of drinking, too.

"Who saw him ...? Adán, right? We're talking about *that* ex?" Esteban brought the conversation back to the current topic before ending up in the argument of the night before when he'd come home so late.

"Of course it's Adán, Esteban." Mártir ran a hand through her long hair, starting at the scalp. Roots were going white and she was due for a touch-up, but lately, expenses like the beauty salon were being bypassed so as to get things like the rent and heat paid on time. "Adán is the only boyfriend my daughter has had. They met in high school. He got so possessive. And then when she left Chicago ..." Mártir's tone became pitchy. "I think he couldn't stand the fact that his girlfriend was going to college and would become too educated for him."

Esteban stroked his sparse goatee to show Mártir that he, too, was preoccupied with the matter. In truth, he wanted to sleep.

Mártir gave a deep sigh, got out of her bathrobe, and went to bed. The next day she'd get more information from her daughter.

If they had to report Adán for being on campus grounds, that's what they'd do. It was important that Lucinda not engage with such a guy anymore. Nothing should stand in her way to success.

But maybe there'd been some kind of confusion. Lucinda hadn't seen the boy herself.

"Belkis from Jack in the Box?" Mártir had repeated earlier when her daughter told her. She may have rolled her eyes.

"Mom," Lucinda said. "I like my new friend. Just because she doesn't go to college, it doesn't mean, like, she's not intelligent or good enough to hang out with me." It frustrated Lucinda how both parents placed such high expectations on her. She'd always been an honor student, perhaps that was why. On the other hand, her kid brother got away with everything. He was working as a food carrier in a restaurant, and his parents both seemed thrilled he was getting a paycheck. Her father even bought him a car, a used one, but it was a dope ride. No car payments and living rent-free with his dad, Teo had it made. What else could the kid ask for? But Lucinda had to work doubly hard to please everyone.

"Belkis said when she was coming over last night to borrow my cashmere dress that Adán was standing right under a lamppost nearby. She said he turned his back when he saw her, but she knew it was him."

"You're lending out your nice clothes now?" Mártir asked, dropping a hand down on her lap for emphasis. The cashmere dress was a special birthday gift.

"Ma!" Lucinda said. She started crying.

"What a bum that Adán is. What's he doing down there at your school, anyway?"

Lucinda covered her face, shoulders trembling. When she got

hold of herself again, she said, "I don't answer his calls anymore. That's probably why he showed up. And I didn't see him, Belkis did."

While Mártir was doubtful the school would do anything about a guy who hadn't approached her, Lucinda seemed comforted when her mother promised to call the next day and complain about security there.

A week before Thanksgiving, Mártir and Esteban were busy with their various side hustles, trying to keep up and to have a little extra for the holidays, when she got a visit from her son. "I'm worried about Lucinda," he said as soon as he'd taken the glass of juice his mother offered. The apartment was far from the comfortable one-family home where he and his sister had been raised in the burbs. As if the American Dream had folded its tent and moved on to the next town, as soon as he graduated, his parents sold the house and took separate residences. Gone was the backyard with memories of barbecues, birthday parties, and his mother's manicured garden. Vacations to Orlando and family road trips to the Grand Canyon and Canada rendered into the archives. Each (wo)man for himself seemed to be the most recent memo.

"What's happened? Why didn't she call me?" Mártir grew immediately distressed. She had no gigs that day, and she was in pajamas watching daytime TV.

Teo shrugged, unzipped his insulated jacket, and sat down. "I dunno," he said. "But she says that someone saw her ex-boyfriend on campus again, that guy Adán. I think she's getting scared about what he might be doing there."

Mártir took a seat, her hands clenched against her chest. On the surface, Adán always seemed pleasant enough, courteous, soft-spoken. She'd never been witness to any of the couple's fights. Who could predict how people reacted to rejection? "That's it," Mártir said. She went straight to the closet to get out her coat before remembering that she had to change clothes. "I'm—we're going down there. Obviously, they didn't take my phone call seriously."

Teo looked surprised. "How are you getting down there? Where's Esteban?" His mother and boyfriend shared a car.

She hadn't seen her live-in companion, in fact, since the night before. He'd called around midnight to say he was going to a friend's to do some music. If he felt he'd had too much to drink, was too tired to drive home, or the weather was bad, he had no problem crashing at the friend's apartment. She didn't feel like giving her son an explanation and simply said, "I'll leave him a note on the kitchen counter. I'll put gas in your car, *hijo*. Just let's get down there. God forbid your sister needs us and we are here, all oblivious."

It was a long drive down to Lucinda's campus, and most of the way, mother and son debated how they would handle their unannounced appearance once they got there. It would be after business hours, so there wouldn't be anyone in administration to handle their worries. They could go to the campus police to issue a complaint, but on what grounds? All they knew was that a girl who didn't go to school there had claimed she'd seen Lucinda's ex-boyfriend from Chicago by the dorm.

Moreover, what would Lucinda say about her mother and brother's sudden appearance? She was in the midst of turning in papers and tests, so she wouldn't be able to return to Chicago with them. Mártir wished she hadn't fretted about her daughter's new BFF rather than focusing on Adán's unacceptable behavior. Now Lucinda wasn't confiding in her.

By the time the two reached campus, they had exhausted any practical idea for addressing the matter and sat in Teo's car, engine running with heat on to stay warm. Adán had never threatened Lucinda. Except for a secondhand account, Lucinda had made no other claim. But if the young woman was afraid, that was enough for her family to look into it, unlike the college administration.

The two stayed in the car. Mártir's son, tall like his dad but puffy like a kid with baby fat in his down-filled jacket, took up most of the space. He reached in the backseat and produced a family-size bag of Doritos. Mártir let herself slump down, wool collar up to her chin. "We could check in to a nearby motel and go to the dean's office tomorrow morning," she suggested.

Without looking at his anxious mother, Teo shook his head. "You know I got work tomorrow, Ma," he said. "Anyway, I'm not checking into a motel with a lady who looks like my mother."

"Teo, I don't look like your mother. I *am* your mother." Mártir heard the crack as a dig aimed at her relationship with her young lover. Esteban's long hair and dingy jeans gave him an even younger demeanor. Lucinda seemed somewhat less resentful of her mother's boyfriend choice, but whenever addressing the subject, she, too, had little to say in support.

Teo straightened up to start the car. "Let's just go back to Chicago," he said. "If you want, call Lucinda from a pay phone. If she's not all right, at least we're here."

They found one at a gas station. Mártir was shivering outside as she spoke to her daughter. Lucinda had answered with a sleepy voice. After an exam that afternoon, she'd been studying all evening. Their exchange was snappish, and it seemed best not to mention Teo and she were there.

When Mártir was back in the car, fastening the seat belt, Teo said, "I could just go to Lucinda's building to see if I see Adán hanging around. You wait in the car, Ma." Although they didn't have a permit, they parked in a lot close to Lucinda's dorm to facilitate the jaunt to the building. Mártir had closed her eyes when a hard rap on the window startled her. It was Teo with a security guard. Mártir pressed the button to let the window down. She and the security guard eyed each other. "Do you know this young man?" he asked her. After a taut exchange in which she was able to clarify that her daughter was a student and they were there to check on her safety, the security guard gave Teo back his license and let them go.

"You'd think they'd be on the case like that when someone really was there stalking the girls' dorm," Teo said, face reddened, understandably rattled by the incident.

"It's not a girls' dorm," Mártir said. "It's coed, but yes, I know, *hijo*." She already regretted bringing him down on such a useless mission, and they rode back to the city with few words between them.

Angst over her daughter's safety had only increased as the girl developed into the young woman she was now and men seemed to pop up everywhere eyeing her. *Lustful*, yes, that was what those looks meant. Mártir, when she was younger, also experienced unwanted attention.

Before marrying Teodoro, she worked at a family-owned jewelry business downtown on Wabash. The patriarch was an old man who, to the young woman, looked to be a hundred. Every day he went to work in suit and tie and sat behind the counter observing everyone and everything. His son, a boisterous and talented goldsmith, and his two sons, also skilled, promoted their unique designs. Mártir thoroughly loved the atmosphere. It felt posh, although it was a tiny place on the fourteenth floor of a very old high-rise. The son of Señor Lepe, the patriarch, was a friend of her father's. The men had a small group of friends from Spain and met once a month for cards and cigars. Señor Lepe promised Mártir's father that he would sponsor the girl through an accounting course. She was clever with numbers, and one day, perhaps, she'd handle the books when his current bookkeeper retired, which, like his own father, he should have done long ago.

However, before she started any such course, Mártir's boss, Lepe Jr., was becoming increasingly touchy-feely with her. He'd have a hand rubbing her lower back when they were both talking to a customer, whispering close to her ear instead of addressing her face-to-face, and finally, one day in the back, he tried to kiss her on the mouth. She grabbed her purse and sweater, ran out, and never returned. Since she had no other financial support, it ended her potential career as an accountant, something her father reacted to with more disappointment than her reasons for leaving the place.

In retrospect, as a mother who would give her last dime to help with either of her children's goals, she found it difficult to understand that her parents had made different decisions. As each of the kids turned the legal adult age of eighteen, Mártir and her brother had been expected to seek their own means. Her brother joined the army and she moved out.

An experience that she'd actually found frightening was seen by both her parents as incidental. "Did Papá really want me to ignore Señor Lepe's advances?" she asked her mother once before the whole matter was dropped and never mentioned again.

"No, *cariño*," her mother said, smiling, "but you also couldn't blame Lepe. You're young and so pretty . . . And after all, you know men will always try. Once he saw you weren't going to lend yourself to all that, he would have stopped. Men only do what they want when you let them."

From that day on, not only was the prospect of her becoming a well-earning accountant never brought up again, but neither did she turn to her mother regarding any matters to do with the opposite sex. The first time her parents met her future husband was the same day he asked for their daughter's hand. It was a formality. She and her fiancé were already planning the wedding.

Now, a lifetime later, Mártir's daughter might be dealing with a man who also didn't respect boundaries. Doña Cuca's opinion was way off. Some men didn't just go away because you said *stop*.

She glanced at her son, his eyes fixed on the road. Did her adult offspring think that, in being with a younger man, she had become the predator? *Cougar*—a savage beast with deadly fangs and daggerlike claws? Well, in the urban jungle, where sexual pursuits might end after a night, it was Esteban who persisted with the chase. Neither made much money and both split expenses. Although Esteban was younger, Mártir knew he had more confidence than she in the romance department.

It was Pilar, a casual friend in the tango practice circle, who told her about the milonga held once a month in a dance studio upstairs from an Italian restaurant. On that night, they called it

Salón Río de la Plata. Pilar said, "They have a cover charge. It helps keep the place going." Mártir didn't consider herself very good and, in any case, had no dance partner. "Oh, that's fine," Pilar assured her. "At the milonga, men sit at their own tables and women at theirs across the room. When the music starts, they come over to ask you out to dance. Even couples do it like that."

It sounded *très* retro, Mártir thought, and for the sake of allowing herself new opportunities, she went with Pilar. As soon as the DJ started "La Puñalada," a young man, his gaze intently on her, aimed straight in her direction. "What do I do?" she whispered. "Dance!" Pilar said, and laughed, giving her older friend an elbow. Mártir was bashful and blushing, for heaven's sake. The guy had on dancing shoes, so he had to be decent on the floor.

As it turned out, the two tangoed well together. Esteban was patient as Mártir's partner, and before the early night ended, they exchanged numbers. "Don't forget," Mártir said, making a gesture with her hand to her ear indicating she'd expect a call as she and her friend left the event. He smiled, white even teeth against dark skin, something he'd done nonstop that evening. He seemed calm and charismatic, and unlike with other men since her divorce, she felt relaxed with him.

Mártir missed his call a few days later, but he left a detailed message in Spanish, his first language, of another milonga. This time Mártir went on her own. Now she knew the protocol and took a table near the dance floor. She noticed Esteban chatting with another man by the refreshments. The *Porteño* couple struggling to keep their studio open sold homemade empanadas and malbec in plastic cups. The pair made every effort to re-create the atmosphere of a traditional tango bar, low lights, miniature gas lamps (battery-run) on the small tables. The music was selected by a DJ, but the hosts took a mike to introduce the various numbers. Each went around giving dance instructions, trying to drum up business.

As the second song began, Esteban came right over. It was fun and flirty, and perhaps it would be a whirlwind affair. Not long after he came over for dinner (Mártir hadn't been able to resist the impulse to boast about the skewers she knew how to make), they became exclusive. One morning after he'd stayed over, Esteban announced, "My roommate wants me out."

They were having *café con leche* in bed. Mártir had stopped by Esteban's place only once, when they were on their way to a movie. She'd liked how it was furnished, especially the living room, with a few original paintings on the walls and a plush leather couch. Now she realized Esteban was only renting a room there. "Yeah, he just got engaged, and his fiancée is moving in," her new beau added. There was a silence heavy with the fact that Mártir had an extra room in her place. Finally, she said, "Do you want to live here . . . I mean, with me?"

That was nine months ago.

The cohabiting-lovers adjustment was fairly easy. Now, however, as quickly as it had started, it seemed to be going up in smoke, like gauze spiraling upward into the clouds. But who would say it first?

Back in Chicago, when they reached Mártir's building, Teo double-parked and waited until his mother got inside and gave the okay signal—flashing the living room light on and off a couple of times and only after a quick check around the place.

No intruder but also no Esteban. The note left on the counter was still there. She stared at the paper with her scribbling as if it had something to report about Esteban's absence. Had he been home, read it, and gone back out? Had he not returned at all? The answering machine light was blinking, and she pressed play to listen while pulling off snow boots, coat, scarf, and other items to hang in the coat closet. Beep, hang-up, beep, hang-up, beep, her ex-husband's voice, looking for Teo. They should have let him know, Mártir thought. Teodoro Senior was sure to be upset because they'd left him worrying. She shouldn't have corralled their son on such a long drive knowing he had to work the next day. But what if Lucinda was in danger? If so, the trip had revealed nothing.

Just then a key turned in the lock, and seconds later, Esteban was inside. He looked cold but also flustered—no, not flustered, drenched in some undefined guilt. They stared at each other.

"Are you just getting home now?" Mártir asked. She pressed stop on the machine. In the narrow space of the room, she was squarely in front of the young man. He smelled of weed and the street. "I tried calling, but you didn't pick up," he said, and began pulling off outer garments. He was flushed, whether red from the cold, intoxicated, being surprised by an alert woman whom he'd expected to be fast asleep, or perhaps all three, was uncertain. Down to jeans and hoodie, pulling off a belt which he tossed in the direction of the bedroom and grimy wet socks, Esteban escaped to the bathroom and closed the door behind him. Minutes later, she heard the shower. *Well, that's that*, she thought. You didn't have to be a private eye to figure the man had something to wash off, even if it was a spotty conscience.

In the days and nights that followed, the couple's exchanges were perfunctory. She didn't hear from her daughter or son and was left to assume there were no updates. Thanksgiving Thursday was coming up, and everyone in Mártir's small family agreed to meet at her parents' apartment. Cooking the family feast had been left mostly to her for years, except the dishes that her mother insisted on preparing, rice with saffron, *patatas alioli*, and anchovies in vinegar. To be sure, they weren't dishes that the English Pilgrims had shared, but in Mártir's home they'd been staples, and her father refused to sit down without the delicacies and aromas of his upbringing.

Mártir was starting her preparations when Esteban stepped into the kitchen and made an announcement: He was going to sign up at a cooking school. That was how he put it, "I'm signing up at a cooking school." Music, dance lessons, even dealing marijuana, all together had taken their toll, he said. In its own way, a culinary career would allow for his creativity. There were plenty of jobs out there for such skills. "Maybe one day, we'll own our own restaurant," he said, smiling broadly, hoping to bring Mártir around to his thinking where, just maybe, she might offer to financially support his new project. When his comments elicited no response, he made an unprecedented offer. He would cook the Thanksgiving turkey to demonstrate the seriousness of his intentions as well as his gastronomy talents. "I know I have *el sazón*," he said, "to become an excellent chef."

The pronouncement actually caused Mártir to take a step back. Making coffee was the extent of Esteban's time in the kitchen.

"Teodoro always prepares the turkey," she said, referring to her ex-husband, who customarily joined the family for the holiday.

"I'll make a second one," Esteban said. "The way your ex and Teo eat, we need two, anyway. Mine will be Guatemalan-style." *Whatever that means*, she thought.

Mártir's stare clearly made him uneasy. She was having a hard time recognizing him. Such ambition, which would involve commitment and determination, was unprecedented. As she studied his face, she noticed Esteban's complexion was ashy from the bitter winds outside. "Why don't you put on some of my Olay?" she suggested.

Talking about his looks threw him off. He'd hoped to start winning her back. Ever since he'd stayed out all night, she had turned her back on him in bed. "I'm not putting women's products on my face," he said.

"Come on, babe. It's just cold cream," Mártir said. She wasn't going to push, but it was funny how sensitive he was. "I'm not suggesting you splash on Summer's Eve!" She laughed at her reference to a douche product, and that was enough for Esteban, who left the room.

In the end, there was a lot to carry over to her parents' modest home: a large roasted turkey in a pan and various casseroles covered with aluminum foil. Esteban had combed his hair for once. Mártir was in the shimmery dress.

It was the family's custom to dress up on such occasions, as if going to a party. It *was* a party. After they ate, Mártir's father would go to the stereo and put on LPs. His grandson had given him Paco de Lucía's recent album. He'd insist that Mártir, Lucinda, and his wife, despite her chronic *reumas*, get up and dance for them. It was she who had taught Mártir *compás*, how to mark rhythm with her feet and hands, and the living room session brought tender nostalgia to everyone for their own reasons. Afterward, the grandmother would sit out of breath, fanning herself with the silk folding fan she'd brought with her from across the ocean. There'd be vino all around and cognac for the men, and when eight o'clock struck, her father would announce it was time for bed and for the others to go home.

One year it had begun to snow steadily, a sure snowstorm. "*¡Basta!*" the old man said at the strike of eight on the wall cuckoo clock, clapping his hands and then waving them around as if doing away with a bad spell. He went to bed and let his wife figure out the sleeping arrangements when she insisted they not try to drive in such weather. The next morning when Mártir woke, she quickly dressed and left before her mother rose and recruited her to help cook breakfast for everyone.

That afternoon, when Teodoro arrived with their son, carrying in his turkey through the kitchen door, and saw a roasted turkey already on the table, he looked like he was seeing an illusion. The two birds were set side by side on the table too small for much else. Dishes were set on either side of the sink and on the cart that also held the microwave.

Mártir's father, in the same plaid newsboy cap since how long, never moved from his chair, both hands clasping a cane. He was five years retired from the tanning factory job he took decades before when arriving in the Midwest. Don Salomón, seventy-four on his last birthday and afflicted by varicose veins, was resigned to exerting himself as little as possible while his stout wife moved around, squeezing past this person and that one, trying to accommodate the situation that was less festive than obligatory.

"How did your exams go, honey?" Teodoro asked his daughter as soon as everyone had fixed a plate. The apartment held no dining room, and under such circumstances, there was hardly sitting room left in the kitchen.

Lucinda, not in the cashmere dress her mother had requested her to wear but in flannel pajamas and a stained sweatshirt, hood partially covering her face, seemed put out to be asked anything. She shoved forkfuls in her mouth and sniggered between bites at random things people said. Her eyes seemed glazed, perhaps from mental exhaustion. Teodoro and Mártir made sure their daughter didn't have to work so as to concentrate fully on her studies. If Mártir didn't know her daughter better, she'd have suspected the girl was on drugs. She claimed not to even take aspirin for a headache. What happened to the manners she was raised with? "Slow down," Mártir blurted, "you're acting like you just got released from the gulag."

"Whatever, Ma," Lucinda snapped back, and gulped down a glass of her grandfather's red wine from a juice glass, then poured herself a second.

"Did you get your new tire put on?" It was the grandfather shouting across the table at the girl. His cigar was out (upon strict orders from his wife and doctor), but he kept it clenched between dentures, a symbol of past times, repressed urges, or ongoing defiance.

"Tire?" Mártir asked, as if the mere word were cause for alarm. She made sure to take slices from Esteban's turkey and her children's father's traditional turkey, and not much else fit on her plate.

An account rolled out reluctantly between Lucinda, Teo, and their father that, weeks before, the girl had gotten a flat. Having no idea how to fix it, she'd called her father in Chicago. He and Teo made their way down and changed the tire, but the spare wasn't in good shape. On the way out of town, Teodoro stopped at a tire shop and put one aside for her. As soon as she had a chance, Lucinda was able to get the spare replaced.

"Wow," Mártir said, mouth wide, as if an entire crisis had occurred without her knowledge. She looked at Esteban and he shrugged. No one had commented on his turkey, and he was brooding.

"Anyway," Teodoro said, pointing at Mártir with his fork, "what's this that you and Teo went down there to see about Adán stalking Lucinda?"

"What? Is that guy bothering you, *chiquitina*?" the grandfather asked. His wife said nothing, but her small hands pressed against her powdered cheeks. Since she applied face powder only on special occasions, Doña Cuca had owned the same Max Factor compact since Mártir was a girl. It lay on the dresser next to the sable hairbrush, hand mirror, and varnished jewelry box her army-officer son had brought her from his first tour to Kuwait.

Everyone looked at Lucinda in silence. "Oh my God, people," she said, and went back to her plate, stabbing a piece of potato and shoving it straight into her mouth.

Mártir looked around, too. All eyes now turned to her, the

mother. The mother, if she were a good one, would be aware of troubles regarding her daughter. "Yes, Teo and I drove down one night. We were worried—"

"*You* were worried," Teo interrupted. "I almost got arrested."

"You almost got arrested?" his father said.

"You were worried, too," Mártir said to her son. "And it was a night security guard . . . he wasn't arresting you."

"Arrested?" the grandfather said, cupping an ear. He looked at his wife. She shook her head with an expression of equal bewilderment. "What trouble are you in, Teo?" the old man asked.

"I'm not in any trouble," Teo said loudly.

"We didn't bother you, *hija*, because you were studying. Have you heard anything more about Adán hanging around your dorm?" Mártir asked.

"Oh my God," Lucinda said again, this time under her breath. She pushed her plate away. Besides her grandfather, she was the only one who sat at the table.

"Don't be bothering her," Mártir's mother said, and then in Spanish, as if the girl wouldn't comprehend what was being said about her, "You're going to make her not want to eat . . . and she was eating so well."

The reminder caused Mártir to lose her own appetite. In high school, her daughter, who, like Teo, had always been on the chubby side, at some point became a skeleton. Teodoro and Mártir were called to the school for an intervention. They were stunned to realize Lucinda had an eating disorder. Her mother had assumed the weight loss came from excessive dieting. (After all, teen girls were always self-conscious about their appearance.) Trying to force a meal on her daughter, whether something simple like cereal for breakfast or just a piece of fruit, had been met with hostile refusal. When had Mártir become the symbol of sabotage in her daughter's life? It had happened almost overnight.

The matter of the girl's adolescent angst was all way over their heads. The idea that their child would have an aversion to eating, however, doing terrible things to avoid it, as they learned from the doctor later, nearly defeated Teodoro and Mártir. Why had they never been aware of it at home? What kind of parents were they, anyway? Each blamed the other for having failed their family.

But now, Lucinda, from all reports, was adjusting well at the university. The breakup with her longtime boyfriend had been her choice. "A control freak" was how she started referring to the guy she once called her kindred spirit.

Everyone's eyes were still on Lucinda until the girl jumped up with an air of sheer exasperation and dashed out of the kitchen. "Get your daughter," Grandpa Salomón ordered Mártir sharply, giving the floor a pound with his metal cane and in Spanish. "In this house, one eats . . . Mothers who don't know how to take care of their kids . . . it's all that's ever asked of them . . . !" He didn't look directly at his wife, but with the second pounding of the cane, she found a crinkled tissue in her apron pocket and, eyes lowered, wiped her nose. It didn't take much anymore for her to become upset. She had much to be upset about, not all at once or recently but throughout the years.

Her only son lost his life during Desert Storm. She was always so proud to see him in uniform. Such a big, strong man he'd become, she bragged. Her husband did, too. The day the two soldiers appeared at their front door with the news of his death . . . that day was the last for her to have with any peace. It was the same for her husband, except that for some reason, he found satisfaction in putting the blame for their son's demise on an unnamed failing of his wife as a mother. Living with Salomón became, in a word, an *infierno*. Where was she to go? She was no longer close to anyone in Spain. In any case, the woman had become more American than anything.

Mártir reached the bathroom and pushed on the door before her daughter was able to shut it in her mother's face. "Lucinda, come back, please," she begged. "If you don't, they'll all only keep asking." She was relieved when her daughter released her grip on the door and agreed to return to the kitchen.

"Speak up!" Salomón saw no point in letting up on his commands when the women were back. Lucinda took her chair, but this time, Mártir stayed near the entrance. "Is that good-for-nothing bothering you?" he asked.

"Abuelo, no," Lucinda said quietly. In truth, she wasn't intimidated by her grandfather. Just one punch like she'd learned in boxing class would've knocked out the old guy. Besides, when they were alone, he showed himself to be the gentlest man alive.

"Did *you* see Adán down there?" Teodoro asked.

"*I* didn't," Lucinda said, looking up at her father with bulging-eyed resentment. "I told Teo and I told my mom. It was my friend Belkis from Jack in the Box who said she saw him in front of my dorm."

"Belkis? ¿*Quién*?" Doña Cuca whispered to Esteban. Both were leaning against the sink. Holding their dinner plates, they ate standing.

"How did she describe him?" Esteban asked. It was the first time he'd spoken since the family started eating, and everyone turned to him as if they hadn't noticed him before.

Teo pulled off his skullcap. His scruffy hair fell over his eyes, and he swung it back with a quick head jerk. "Maybe your friend Belkis saw *me* that night. You know all us Mexicans look alike!"

Lucinda dropped her jaw to show how offended she was. "What are you talking about, Teo? I can't believe you and Mom actually drove down to my campus to spy on me!"

"We didn't do anything wrong, Lucinda," Mártir spoke up.

"So, what exactly did this Belkis de Jack in the Box say, *mija*?" Teodoro asked. He was now eyeing which pie on the table to cut into first. It was no secret that dessert was his favorite part of any meal. Cherry was the winner. "I mean, does she know Adán?"

Lucinda pushed back her chair. It made a skin-crawling scraping sound. Teo reacted by putting a finger inside his ear; the other hand still held his plate. "Damn, girl."

"Yeah, she met him . . . once, before we broke up, of course. She said the guy was kinda dark. But he had on a hoodie or a cap or something, so she couldn't see his face that well."

"Besides dark and a hoodie or cap, what else?" Esteban said. Mártir looked at her lover, slight build, average height, predominant Mayan features, most likely had gotten his share of being taken for a Mexican, and not in a good way.

"Maybe it was me," Teodoro said.

"Naw," his son said. "You and I went down to fix the tire before all that started."

"Well . . ." Teodoro seemed to want to say something. He stopped himself with a forkful of pie.

Lucinda looked up at her father. She hadn't shared with him the issue with Adán, but she had talked to her grandfather on a visit home. No doubt, in days past, he would've straightened out the kid one way or the other. Now she was certain the old man had told her father.

Teodoro went to serve himself another piece of pie, sweet potato this time. His former mother-in-law made the best pastries, pies especially. He hadn't mentioned anything to anyone, no need. A few weeks before, as soon as his father-in-law had called him disturbed about the kid who used to go with Lucinda, Teodoro had taken off work and driven down on his own to report the matter to the university. They took notes but let him know there wasn't much they could do under sketchy circumstances. Unless they committed some violation, it was hard to go after kids from off campus. Not satisfied with the dismissive tone he received, Lucinda's father hung around the campus the rest of the evening. No Adán showed up.

"Oh my gawd," the girl said. "I wish I'd never mentioned it to anyone." When her grandmother tried to hand her a piece of pie, Lucinda looked like she was about to burst into tears. "If you ask me," she cried, jumping from her seat, "I think it was *him*." She pointed at Esteban. Pulling the cuffs of her sweatshirt over her hands, the girl covered her face.

Everyone turned to Esteban, who looked as surprised as the rest. He was holding the pie plate that he'd just been handed and gruffly dropped it on the table; the fork shook and fell to the floor. Without a word, he was out of the room. Before anyone could react, Lucinda ran out next, also in the direction of the living room. They heard the front door open and shut once, then again.

The others' eyes on her now, Mártir debated what to do. Her mother gave her a slight signal, and the two began to clean up.

Lucinda returned a short while later. She'd run out without a coat and was shaking with teeth chattering from the cold. Sullen and silent, she went to her grandfather, who'd gone to sit in his chair in the living room to watch TV. The old man put his cane aside to wrap an arm around his grandchild. "It's all going to be fine," he said under his breath. Mártir in the threshold between kitchen and living room overheard. What she wouldn't have given to be told those words by the man just once.

In the weeks that followed, whatever was said or not between Mártir and her live-in boyfriend, before he packed his things, managed to move out with help from a friend who had a van, collected some money from her for her half of the car they'd bought jointly and which she wanted to keep, was of little consequence. In passing, Esteban mentioned that he was considering returning to Guatemala. He hadn't decided. Of all things, he left behind his dance shoes. Mártir thought it may have been intentional, a kind of memento of their bittersweet experience.

But one day Esteban showed up. "I forgot my dance shoes," he said, and without waiting for her to fetch them, went straight to the closet where they were left. He came out with a shoe sticking out of each coat pocket. At the front door, they stared awkwardly at each other. "Can I kiss you?" he asked. She may have wanted him to kiss her, but in the following seconds, the feeling passed and she shook her head.

Another chapter closed and with no new life lessons. For all their flash and hoopla, the forties were proving to be recycled tribulations with periodic glimmers of ebullience. A "Row, Row

Your Boat" canon composition. Better luck with the next decade. In many traditional cultures, the fifties were considered the age of sagacity. (That may have been because in former times, people didn't live much past then.) Esteban and she might never have Paris, but they'd always have the milonga on Clark Street. One night they had won a tango contest in the intermediate category and, afterward, had taken the trophy and a bottle of Torrontés to drink, then parked at Montrose Beach. If a twenty-year marriage had been a hard day's work where she could take pride in having accomplished her duties, then the brief affair was the remains of the day, the time in one's life you were meant to take in stride.

One day, after running errands for her parents, Mártir stayed to visit. She and Doña Cuca sat at the kitchen table having espresso and her mother's inimitable flan. "It's a good thing I don't live with you," Mártir said, "or I'd blow up like a balloon in no time."

"You could use a few pounds on you," her mother said. "Now I know where this obsession with being skinny comes from that your daughter has." Doña Cuca held back the urge to really give Mártir a piece of her mind. Why did other people have to worry more about the girl than her own mother, after all?

Last week, although Lucinda was far away at her college, her grandparents dodged a veritable showdown over her. Doña Cuca found her husband cleaning his gun, an Astra modelo 400. It had belonged to his father, used in the war in which he fought hard and proudly as a Republican. Salomón was only seven when his brave father died. The gun was the only thing bequeathed to him.

"What do you think you're doing?" Doña Cuca demanded,

fearful that Salomón with his failing eyesight and unsteady hands would end up shooting himself in the foot right there in the living room.

"I'm going to have a talk with this young man about my grand-daughter," he said. He was already in his coat to show that he meant to go and there'd be no persuading him otherwise.

His wife knew he meant Adán. What a gentleman, he seemed. She'd never have taken him to be malicious, especially to Lucinda. "I won't try to stop you, you stubborn old man," Doña Cuca said. "If anyone tried to hurt so much as a hair on my child's head, I'd shoot him myself."

Salomón grunted and began putting bullets into the chamber from a box so old it was falling apart.

"But no one saw Adán at Lucinda's school," she added. Cuca pulled a dishrag off her shoulder and slapped imaginary dust off the TV screen to give added casual effect to her opinion. "No one we know saw that hardworking boy, who goes out every day in the *maldito* cold with his father to fix people's heaters and who buys his mother flowers for every occasion. A girl we don't know, a so-called Tina de Yakin de Vox . . . *thought* it was Adán? Who is she, anyway? Who is her family?"

Salomón kept at his task, pretending not to pay attention to his wife, but she knew he was listening.

"If you ask me, they're all a bunch of *marijuanos* down there." She didn't look at her husband as she dropped a word he probably didn't know she knew.

He stopped. "What're you saying, Cuquis?" The man never admitted it, but his wife's good sense was most likely the reason he was still alive.

"I'm not saying anything," his wife replied.

Salomón's nostrils flared as he grew impatient. "Speak up, woman!" he demanded, waving the gun as if any second he'd pull the trigger out of sheer exasperation.

Cuca took his bluff and bluster on the chin. It was Lucinda who was important. "If you want to help your *querida* granddaughter," Cuca said, "all I'm saying is talk to *her*. If she doesn't stop all that smoking nonsense, she'll get thrown out of the university. How could her mother not see the reality that her daughter isn't perfect? Mártir herself was blindly in love with a drug dealer." Cuca put her hands on her hips and stared at her husband. She couldn't have been clearer.

"A drug dealer?" Salomón's eyes widened in obvious disbelief. Removing his cap, he scratched his bald head and, after a few seconds, nodded. "I always knew there was something off about that guy. I thought he was just a little . . ." He pointed a knurly finger to his head and gave a low whistle. Letting out a long sigh and having lost resolve regarding the young man in question, Salomón went to his room to put away the antique weapon. In final analysis, it had been intended to represent family honor more than expected to do physical harm.

Doña Cuca decided to call her daughter. Fortunately, Mártir had finally thrown that *tipo* out. Obviously, her daughter must have been lonely since the divorce and her self-esteem left frail; a woman had her needs, but you could still show some pickiness. Cuca felt well enough to do her own shopping nearby, but an excuse to have Mártir pick up pimientos and olives when she went to that fancy specialty grocery store on the North Side would give them a chance to visit.

Not that daughters ever listened to their mothers. Only God knew that if *she* had, Salomón would've been a passing fancy. Then Cuca wouldn't have listened to him later and brought their Spanish-born infant boy to the United States just for him to end up giving his life for the adopted country. The Principle of Cause and Effect, that was Cuca's philosophy summarized.

For instance, the imitation Swiss clock in the living room that cuckooed every hour even at night, which her husband was so fond of and believed his devoted wife had purchased on layaway at Sears to present to him on an anniversary? It was a gift, yes, to *her* from a man on the occasion of the birth of their daughter. Mártir had even met him once, although she'd never remember. "Come here," Cuca had called to the child, who was on a swing that afternoon in the park. Her mother was sitting with a man she didn't know and, curious, Mártir came and leaned timidly against her mother. When the man stretched out a friendly hand to say hello, the little girl, maybe three or four years old at the time, dug her face into her mother's lap and began to whimper.

When the children were small and still dependent on their mother for everything, Saturday was Cuca's favorite day of the week. Her husband always worked on Saturdays to collect extra pay. The young mother played with her children at home, put on records, or tried to help with school projects. Sometimes Cuca read aloud, Mártir always with her head on her mother's shoulder. Cuca blew her nose, thinking about it.

You remembered such moments in later years—carefully preserved in cedar drawers lined with flower petals from last summer's garden, cabinets with glass doors and keys, and wrapped in tissue paper inside fancy boxes placed on top shelves—and pulled them out to hold them again when you were alone and felt wistful.

It was strange what other memories also came to Doña Cuca. She'd have to tell her granddaughter about when she was a child in Spain and went with her mother after women first got the vote. Cuca remembered her mamá dressed in her suit, she had only one, with a tulle gardenia pinned to the collar and how they waited in line for hours.

Later, there was the memory of Cuca herself being arrested for having an abortion. Her family managed to get her released but afterward encouraged her and Salomón to move away. "You made a mistake that not only you'll have to live with," her eldest brother said, "but you have made it so that we all have to live with it, too."

When Mártir's answering machine came on, her mother hung up. She hated talking to those things. Doña Cuca stretched her neck to see if her husband was coming back from the bedroom. It sounded distinctly like he had chosen to take a nap. She reached between the armrest and seat cushion in the sofa and pulled out a pack of cigarettes and matches. Cracking the window to let out smoke but not let in too much cold air, she lit one up and sat down.

Women did all kinds of things that society, religion, or men expected, no matter how they repressed one's innate sense of self. Giving birth to child after child. Wearing a girdle and garter to work and sitting on a hard chair all day while hunched over a sewing machine. You could enjoy baking, sure, but not if it was demanded of you. All this added up to a woman's life.

Even Jackie Kennedy Onassis, chic, wealthy, and waited upon all her life, was admired most for the powerful men she married.

You could become an Emma Goldman. Women anarchists, for all their anarchy, ended up doing things as dictated by men. By the same token, there were women without ideologies and politics, out of the limelight and whose names not even the neighbors knew. These anonymous women went about their daily affairs quietly suffocating under the pressures of society's expectations. On the sly, whether in retaliation against the status quo or out of desperation, they dared break the rules. These insurgents, in Cuca's opinion, were the true heroines of each generation of women.

Mártir's mother patted the back of her head and pushed up stray hairs with a pin. Going to the kitchen, Cuca put out her cigarette under the running faucet and went back to the phone to try her daughter again. Whenever Mártir came over, Cuca would ask her to teach her to drive. Yes, it was time to start taking the car out on her own. Oh, Salomón was really going to "like" hearing that.

The Girl in the Green Dress

THE GIRL IN the green dress—or, rather, her presence—was introduced to Vicenta on her first week at the library. The unsettling story—or, as Mrs. Kantor referred to it, "hearsay"— was recounted to the new librarian not by a co-worker or a regular patron but by a woman checking out a book on Edgar Cayce, a woman Vicenta had never seen before and was not to see again.

"Have you heard about the girl in the green dress . . . here?" the woman whispered, leaning on the counter. She was white, in a cotton blouse and pressed shorts, a bike helmet's strap hung over an arm.

Whenever Vicenta had interactions with white people, she tended to stiffen. English was her first language, but not being looked upon as white, therefore not presumed "American," and especially as a librarian, she felt pressured to use her best English.

Now she surveyed her memory bank for any woman in a green dress she was "supposed" to know about. Hesitantly, she shook her head.

"People have seen her here," said the woman, maybe in her late thirties, early forties, tops. She looked around as if paranoid that the girl in reference would suddenly pop out of nowhere.

"I don't know her," Vicenta said, taking the card from the envelope stuck inside the front cover and watching the woman sign it, then asked, "Is she a friend of yours?"

The woman, in need of some sun after the long winter, went completely pale. "She's decapitated," she said in a secretive voice. Then, taking a step back, "They didn't tell you about her, huh?" She shook her head, a wispy ponytail on top swaying like a crow's tail in the breeze.

Vicenta stamped the card, handed the book to the woman, and gave a furtive glance to Mrs. Kantor sitting at her desk. The head librarian looked up, pushed bifocals up her nose, and with a distinct look of annoyance, went back to paperwork. Showing disapproval was her boss's second nature.

The woman dropped the volume in her cloth tote and rested an elbow on the desk. "Well, *I* hope to see her one day. Although they say she's headless, she's probably got a lot to say, and that's why she keeps showing up around here."

"'Say' . . . how . . . ?" Vicenta asked in a tone she thought would be too low for Mrs. Kantor's deerlike hearing to pick up. Immediately, a bloody image of a murder victim came to mind. She felt chills. *Ay, Dios.* The library was *haunted*?

Vicenta had only heard of ghost sightings. Her father, as a boy in rural Mexico, was coming back one night from the outhouse and met La Llorona, the weeping woman who instantly ran off screaming toward the river. Legend said she'd drowned her children. It frightened her father, around eight at the time, so badly that he was taken to a healer to retrieve the soul believed to have escaped his body by the experience.

Spirituality was complicated, thought Vicenta, but spirits even more so. After she made her confirmation, she asked her parents about Mary Magdalene's encounter with Jesus at the tomb of His burial. Was it a ghost? "Don't be blasphemous," her mother reprimanded. "Our Lord resurrected. He was there in person."

The biblical narrative remained confusing on the subject. Did everyone have the ability to die and appear back on earth or just saints and condemned souls? A woman with no head roaming throughout the neighborhood library sounded like she might belong to the latter group. Then again, there were the martyred Christians. They suffered every form of torture. But it was Chicago 1986, not medieval Europe. Vicenta resisted making a sign of the cross. She glanced at Mrs. Kantor, now on the phone, chastising someone who had numerous books overdue, with the intimidating attitude of a bill collector.

Putting on the bike helmet, the woman ran her tongue around her inner cheek and nodded. She tapped the desk and, pointing to Mrs. Kantor, said, "*She* knows." Seconds later, the woman and her lightweight helmet were out the door.

Because Vicenta's hire required a ninety-day probation, she most certainly didn't ask Mrs. Kantor about a headless girl who visited their building. Instead, she tried to push the grim picture out of her mind, but it was impossible. Whether it was due to the stories told around the dinner table when she was a child or catechism indoctrination, she was convinced that such a hideous apparition would one day materialize, and Vicenta would surely lose her mind. (People said "soul," but in a psychology class she had learned they were the same thing.)

Whenever the young woman went to the staff restroom, not wanting to be alone in the back, she waited until someone was in the adjacent coffee room. She didn't even like to be in the coffee room alone. There was nothing menacing back there, but it was windowless and made her feel claustrophobic, as if she were asphyxiating.

Most days she felt fine at work, but others, an underlying apprehension followed her around, an undefined anticipation of something unspeakable. On the nights they closed at eight, Vicenta practically ran out the door when the lights went off. She came to dread the idea of having to stack books in a dimly lit aisle where a morbid figure might suddenly stick out a skeletal hand.

While no one again brought up the girl in the green dress, another undesirable presence began to haunt the place, a very live one. Deidre, as was her name, or "Bag Lady," as less kind people called her, became almost a fixture. Shortly after Vicenta started at her new job, the homeless woman began parking her shopping cart loaded with junk near a parking meter outside the library. She waddled in, shuffling in oversize boots and, even in summer, layers of cast-off, filthy clothing. Before you saw or heard her, a smell that made your nostrils flare announced her arrival. She'd go over to a shelf, pick out a book, and find a seat. Sometimes she actually read, lips moving. If the gluttonous lady started making loud remarks, a sharp "Shhh" from Mrs. Kantor usually sufficed, and she went back to her book until nodding out.

It was Vicenta's first full-time employment as a librarian. She'd finished college downstate two years before, but planning a wedding and settling into a new life had kept her from pursuing a professional full-time position until then. When she heard there was a post open at the local library, it seemed like the perfect fit. Apparently, the director, Mrs. Kantor, thought so, too. After a brief interview, Vicenta was hired. The library was fairly new and, overall, offered a congenial atmosphere. There was the children's section, and an area had been set aside with computers. Most people weren't familiar with how to use them yet, and Mrs. Kantor aimed to arrange an evening class. "Everything depends on whether or not we get funding," she told Vicenta by way of explaining why her plans for programs were being held up. "And these local politicians would rather line their pockets than give the schools and libraries what we need."

There was another staff member who came in three or sometimes four days a week. "Sharon picks up the slack around here," the head librarian told Vicenta on her first day. The young woman nodded with her brow furrowed as if taking in a serious piece of information when, in fact, she didn't understand what slack in a neighborhood library might mean. Vicenta's husband worked loading docks. Now, *they* had slack when a man didn't pull his weight. It was all about team effort if they were going to keep their jobs.

Sharon held a degree in library science, but mostly what she did was stack books back on shelves. Perhaps it was what Mrs. Kantor meant by "picking up the slack." Restacking books was a job for an intern or college student, Vicenta figured. Why hadn't Mrs. Kantor given the librarian already on staff the full-time position?

Sharon didn't seem to mind. She made little conversation and focused on duties. Pushing back a head full of dreads in a brightly patterned scarf, one of many fabrics she'd purchased on a honeymoon trip to Kenya, with a new device they called a Walkman hooked to a loop on her jeans and headphones on, Sharon went methodically up and down aisles. Mrs. Kantor disapproved of wearing jeans on the job almost as much as listening to music while working, but there were no policies against either, and the most she could do was mutter displeasures under her breath. The part-time employee was expecting, and as her belly grew, it seemed, so did Sharon's impatience. It was possible her boss knew better than to start a feud when she was already short-handed.

During the summer, Vicenta's four-block walk home after the library closed was pleasant, like a scene out of the Wilder play *Our Town*. People went about as bright streetlights blinked on. Parents played at the park with their children on the swings and slides, older kids enjoyed a game of softball or riding bikes. Teens on the basketball court. Young families cooling off under the park sprinklers. The full maple trees were bustling with birds settling just as the sun set, horizon strewn with purple and orange hues. At home, Simón had already made dinner, and as a man in love and desirous of creating a harmonious life, he waited to sit down and eat with his wife.

On those late Thursdays, Vicenta and Sharon occasionally dashed over to Mr. Pagonis's diner on the corner for a quick burger and fries. On one such occasion and away from Mrs. Kantor's acute hearing, Vicenta ventured to query as to why Sharon hadn't tried for the full-time position. Obviously, she was qualified and could use the money. "You know the job offers only a few weeks' maternity leave, right?" Sharon asked. "I'm not coming back after I have my baby. I'd have to hand most of my check to a babysitter. When I'm ready to go back to work, I'll find something else." She shook her head. "I won't miss Mrs. Kantor," she said. "I swear, all she worries about is getting her full benefits when she retires next year. Can't say I blame her after spending half her life inside a library."

Vicenta didn't think it would be a bad life; she liked the atmosphere of her workplace.

"That's why Kantor's so uptight, always worried she might mess up, and then what? No hard-earned retirement check. I swear, she treats that bag lady nicer than she does me." Sharon gave a low chuckle, but it was clear she didn't find anything humorous about what she'd said.

"Deidre, you mean?" Vicenta clarified. She hadn't realized Sharon's resentment before. That made two of them.

"Yes, I mean Deidre," Sharon said, rolling her eyes. "I do feel sorry for her, don't get me wrong. But she completely stinks up the place, or have you not noticed?" Sharon balled up the waxed paper wrapping from her burger and dropped it in the red plastic basket it was served in. "Just thinking about it has almost ruined my lunch," she said, sticking a finger inside her mouth as if about to gag.

Of course Vicenta was aware of the foul odor left in the woman's trail. It was why the young librarian had made it a point to ask the janitors who came early mornings to take extra care in sanitizing the area where Deidre usually sat. Dealing with the homeless had become as unsavory as Vicenta's growing obsession with a possible phantom in the library.

Unsurprisingly, it was Halloween time when the headless girl in the green dress became a topic for discussion. Mrs. Kantor dropped a stack of black and orange construction paper and a box of supplies in front of Sharon and Vicenta. They had a huge bulletin board that was decorated every month according to what national holidays or figures were being celebrated. The two women found a reading table to spread out the stencils, glue, scissors, and other materials. It was a duty Vicenta enjoyed and she started on it immediately. Sharon commenced cutting paper to make black and orange links to string along the bulletin board. It was the extent of her creative talents, she said. One of the patrons who'd been reading at the table offered to help. "I love Halloween," the woman said. "I rent slasher movies and watch them alone just to scare myself."

Sharon held back a snicker. "But have you ever noticed how it's always the 'bad girl,' you know, the sexually promiscuous one, who gets slashed first?" she asked. The volunteer shrugged. Vicenta glanced over at Mrs. Kantor, who was busy with a few people checking out books. Leaning in, Vicenta said, "Speaking of scary, has anyone ever heard of a girl with no head around here . . . in a green dress?"

The volunteer and Sharon both reacted with mildly amused expressions, as if she were joking. Two women at a nearby table, working on a grant for the city to use a vacant lot for a community garden, were eavesdropping. They shook their heads.

"Well, this is a new building," Sharon said. "And I don't think anyone ever died here. Isn't that why they say ghosts appear? They died abruptly, and then their spirits are trapped in that place."

"Maybe it wasn't in this building but whatever was here before," said the lady helping out. "You know, like they always talk about

Indian burial grounds being desecrated by people building over them?"

Vicenta didn't think the girl in the green dress had anything to do with indigenous burials. A man sitting on a comfortable chair a few feet away put down his book. He came by once or twice a week. Retired and with long days on his hands, he was slowly reading his way through the Western fiction section. "When I was a kid, this whole block was lined with Edwardian houses. Impeccable gardens. Bankers lived here. Lawyers. The crème de la crème. The houses were all eventually knocked down, one after the next, due to deterioration and the mayor's plan to make a modern Chicago."

For some reason, everyone nodded. One of the women working on the grant, forms strewn in front of her, put down her pencil. "What kind of green dress?" she asked. It seemed like a peculiar question, especially from someone whose appearance might have been described kindly as casual, if not scruffy, but it set Vicenta's imagination aflight. She envisioned angora, like the winter white beret she was wearing, and the color of the scarf smartly tied around her neck, forest green. It was from Poland or Russia. At least that was what Simón had told her. It was a gift from his last trip to the flea market, where he went to browse for used tools. The scarf was now her favorite accessory.

"An overprotected debutante, no doubt, from back in those Edwardian days," the woman at the table began to speculate, pulling off reading glasses. "Her father forbade her to marry the Italian guy who delivered coal. The girl went up to the attic and hanged herself. Simple as that."

"Why Italian?" someone asked.

The woman shrugged, then said, "When my grandfather came from Italy, that was the first job he had. My mother said there was a lot of discrimination against Italians back then."

"She doesn't have a head. How could she hang herself?" Sharon said. She put a hand on her sore back; it was a hard pregnancy. Picking up the stapler, she took her paper chain to the board.

"So, the dad took an ax out of the woodshed and chopped off his daughter's head," one of the grant-writing women said, as if making an investigative report. Her side of the table was neat, sharpened pencils lined up alongside a portable calculator and what appeared to be an asthma inhaler. "And not because she wanted to run off with some schmuck but because she didn't want to get married at all." As if the mystery were solved, Grant-Writing Women One and Two resumed their undertaking.

"A cemetery's not too far," said Western-book Man. "But it wouldn't necessarily explain why anybody would see a ghost *here*."

"Cemetery?" Mrs. Kantor said loudly. "Headless ghosts?" Everyone turned. "What are you driving at, Vicenta?" she asked. Everyone turned to Vicenta and then back to Mrs. Kantor. The director grabbed her purse and a thick cardigan she kept hanging over her swivel chair. "Take over the desk," she called to Sharon. In a huff, she went outside to smoke a cigarette. Silence resumed.

Vicenta was about to pick up a marker when a small voice whispered, "I saw her." She looked up. A woman of slight build holding her child's hand and an LP of *The Sound of Music* under the other arm was standing next to her. Her abrupt proximity startled Vicenta until she realized they had emerged from the nearby soundproof booth.

"Last time I came, I was in there." The woman gestured with her chin in the direction of the booth; it had dark glass panes, so you couldn't see inside. "I felt something touch my hair. At first I thought it was her"—she used her head again, this time to indicate her child—"but then I saw it behind me in the reflection of the glass."

"It?" the volunteer at the table said.

"Something," the woman said, "with no head." No one spoke, and then she said, "I grabbed my daughter and ran out and told her about it right away." She turned and, with her chin, indicated that she meant Mrs. Kantor, who was still outside. "But she only looked at me like I was crazy."

The lady at the table shook her head and resumed her stencil tracing. Vicenta was speechless, heart thumping hard.

"At home, they told me I was crazy," the woman said, trying to smile. "Maybe I am." She looked down. "After all, I went back in there . . ." Pulling her child along, the young mother returned the album to the front desk and left.

After a few minutes when no one seemed to have anything to remark, Grant-Writing Woman Two cleared her throat. "My cousin killed his wife because he said she was crazy," she shared. "But we knew it was because he was always berating her for not making rice like his mother's."

"What?" the volunteer said. "If my husband said I couldn't cook like his mother, I'd kill *him*." She snorted.

"He only got three years," the woman continued, "and with 'good behavior,' he did less than that."

"You're kidding me, right?" her grant-writing partner said. She slammed her pencil on the table and sat back. "Three years for killing a woman because she couldn't make rice? Was that in *this* country?"

Her friend nodded. "Yes, right here in Chicago. He didn't use that as his defense, of course. His defense was that she came at him with a kitchen knife and he had to shoot her."

The man reading the Louis L'Amour novel (or, as he had referred to it with Sharon, "the president's favorite book writer") stood up. He stuck the novel back on the shelf and gave the ladies a polite nod as he left. Most likely there'd been too much chattering for him. With Mrs. Kantor on break, the women felt at ease to pursue the gruesome discussion.

Vicenta's scalp itched and she pulled off the beret. The woman at the table, now cutting out hunched-cat silhouettes, smirked. "Your hairs are all standing up," she said, pointing at Vicenta. "It's the electricity."

The young librarian self-consciously patted down her hair, put the beret back on, and adjusted her neck scarf. She was going for a Kiki of Montparnasse look. No one around Vicenta had known who the notorious Parisian muse and artist of the 1920s was when she explained her new hairstyle, a bob with bangs. The rare visit to a salon was supposed to cheer her. Making herself over like a woman who knew her own mind was inspiring.

Just before she started working there, Simón and she had gone to the emergency room one night when Vicenta woke hemorrhaging. Since the miscarriage, he'd been doting on his young wife and surprising her with small gifts like the scarf. She hadn't even suspected she was pregnant. Although they were assured she'd be able to get pregnant again, it seemed that afterward, Simón, who rarely showed emotions, had become withdrawn. Slowly, he'd regained his easy-going manner (at least on most days), but it was clear how important having a family was to him.

The unfortunate event had a different effect on Vicenta. Everyone endured unexpected pain and sometimes humiliation. Women spread their legs in love and also because of their reproductive functions. After her womb was scraped, she began to rethink motherhood. She wasn't turned off by the physical discomforts of pregnancy but wondered if her true calling in fact lay elsewhere.

Also, the incident had reminded each of an occurrence earlier in their relationship. Naturally, in the beginning, they were unsure what, if any, commitment they might make. She was in school downstate. He lived in Chicago and worked long hours. Soon after they broke it off, Vicenta realized she was pregnant. She had a long night, several, discussing it with her dorm mates. She called her mother and sister. Finally, the girl decided terminating the pregnancy was the best solution. After they got back together, Vicenta never discussed the anguishing episode with Simón; a year later, when they became engaged, she did so in the interest of being open with her future husband. To the young woman's consternation, instead of displaying compassion or regret for not being present to offer support during a critical period, Simón reacted as if he'd been wronged.

"But we weren't even together," Vicenta said. "I left messages on your answering machine. I was in the middle of studying for exams . . . I didn't know what to do."

"So, you killed our baby?" he asked.

———

As the days grew short, autumn rolled back, signaling winter's approach. Walking the four blocks home when it was dark and with temperatures increasingly dropping was soon out of the question. Besides that, Simón felt uneasy with his young wife on the street, where hardly anyone was out. He bought her a small canister of Mace on a key chain. Vicenta was a city girl. She was smart and alert. It wasn't about that, he said. "You just never know," he told her, "someone could jump out at you from a shadowy doorway . . . or pull you into an alley." It wasn't as if such things never happened. Soon Vicenta welcomed the nightly car ride home from her husband. It was reassuring to see their car double-parked, engine on, warm inside, and Simón, who hadn't seen her all day, anticipating her emergence from the glass doors.

When the cold came to a city known for its brutal winters, it wasn't easy sending Deidre out to the street at closing time. Mrs. Kantor made some inquiries and found out she slept at a church shelter that served evening meals and provided cots. But she couldn't go there until six p.m., when the doors opened. One day, while picking up lunch at the diner, Mrs. Kantor mentioned to Mr. Pagonis the responsibility she felt for the transient woman who'd taken up residence in her library. It occurred to her to ask her old friend, whose diner had been in the neighborhood longer than the library, to allow Deidre to sit in the back of his establishment and have a coffee on the house until the shelter opened up. "Except for Thursdays when the library stays open late," she said, "we close at five. It would only be for an hour or so."

His thick eyebrows went up like a pair of animated brushes. "What do I look like I got here—a charity?" he asked. Mrs. Kantor saw spittle spray from his mouth. "I pay my taxes," he went on. "I give to my church. I voted for the president. What else does anyone expect from me?" Perhaps he was right, she thought, and was about to leave with her carry-out gyro order when he gave in with a reluctant nod and a dismissive wave indicating that he'd either given in, given up, or didn't care. "This is a rich country," he said. "There's no reason why the government lets these people live on the street. You know what should be done? They should round them up, send them away."

"Where do you suggest?" asked his hostess, who was listening in. "Put 'em on a bus to Fort Lauderdale?"

"Florida? Florida!" He turned and looked like he was about to bite off the poor woman's head. "I should be so lucky to retire there someday," he said, practically stomping off, waving as if he wanted to pull out the hair he didn't have. "I don't care where they all go. Just outta my sight and outta my city."

At closing time in the library, it took a few tries to get the cantankerous woman to go to the diner, but eventually, she went on her own.

It was early December, snow shoveled to the curbs and ice on the ground one early evening, when Mrs. Kantor announced the library was closing and, as always, made it a point to call Deidre. Clearing off tables, Sharon yelled, "She's not here."

Eager to hurry out where, as always, Simón would be waiting in the double-parked car, slowing down traffic, Vicenta had already put on her boots and layered up in sweater and coat. She was slipping on fleece-lined gloves when Mrs. Kantor looked her way and ordered, "Go check the ladies' room, Vicenta. Maybe Deidre's in there." Meanwhile, Sharon went to stick her head in the men's room to check, and Mrs. Kantor stepped outside with no coat on to peer up and down the street.

Not because her boss had any right to yell orders at anyone, but Vicenta went to survey the ladies' room. As had become her habit, she drew a hand up to the side of her face to obstruct a view as she passed the soundproof booth. If she ever so much as glimpsed the reflection of a headless figure, she was sure she'd drop dead of a heart attack.

The young librarian made her way to the facilities, which reeked of something putrid. Seeing the familiar raggedy shoes under the stall, she called out, "Deidre, are you okay?" Warily, she stepped toward the stall. The door was unlocked. "Miss Deidre?" Vicenta whispered. Pinching her nose, she cautiously pushed the door open. The old woman grunted but made no move to rise from the toilet seat.

"Can I help you?" Vicenta asked. The door drew closed again, and Vicenta gave it a gentle push open. When Deidre didn't respond, she decided to take action. Holding the swinging door back, she reached out a hand. Deidre looked up with her usual confused gaze and didn't move. After a pause, Vicenta grabbed the woman's hand. "Come on," she coaxed, "let's get you out of here. Everybody's got to go home now." Deidre brusquely pulled away. Exasperated, Vicenta leaned over to get hold of her by the shoulders, hoping, though the woman was at least twice her weight, to lift her. "Leave me alone!" The other woman shrugged off Vicenta's strenuous attempts. Each time, Deidre's delusional responses grew more aggressive. "Who are you?" she yelled. "Where are you taking me? Get out! GET OUT!"

More than anything, Vicenta wanted to do exactly that, leave.

She fought an urge to throw up from the foul smell and, unable to dislodge the hefty body planted on the toilet, also felt helpless. Vicenta's feet slid as if in mud, and she suspected she was stepping in diarrhea. She wanted to call out for the other two librarians to come help, but out of dread that shouting would only cause Deidre further alarm, she tried to stay calm. "Come on, please," she pleaded. "It's all right."

A short time later, when Simón tapped on the locked glass door looking for his wife, leaving his car double-parked with the emergency lights blinking, it was a panicked—or at least breathless—Mrs. Kantor who unlocked the door. She'd met him on a couple of occasions. Putting in extra hours in anticipation of Christmas expenses, Simón was in his gritty insulated coveralls, and it seemed to him the older woman was giving him a once-over or perhaps having trouble recognizing him. For a second they stared at each other, and then he asked, "Is something wrong?" He tried to peek inside, but Mrs. Kantor blocked his view.

When a frazzled-looking Vicenta finally came out, she felt immediate alarm upon finding the two glaring at each other as if in a standoff. They turned to her. "What?" Mrs. Kantor said to Vicenta, who, at a loss for words at the peculiar scene, said nothing.

"Let's go, okay?" Vicenta at last said to her husband, taking hold of his arm.

And the ghastly night was not to be over. In the car on the way home, she struggled to explain why she'd been so detained and what she should tell or best leave out regarding Deidre, the deranged, repugnant old woman nobody wanted around.

"Disgusting," Simón said. "How much is everyone gonna do for that homeless lady, anyway? Shouldn't you call some agency?

Maybe she should be in a mental hospital." His hands gripped the wheel.

Vicenta had never heard that talk from her husband. In a way, she couldn't blame him for being upset. They were both tired from a long day and hungry.

When they arrived at their building, she asked Simón about the way her boss and he had been looking at each other when she came upon them. "Did she say anything to you?" Vicenta asked.

He ran a hand through his thick black hair as if he hadn't figured it out. "Do I look like a gangbanger, babe?" he asked. "Why do some people think that all men who look a certain way"—he pointed to his face—"are open to criminality?" Vicenta didn't answer, and they went upstairs inside the building in silence. "If anyone looks like a potential hit man, it's that old Kantor," he said, yanking off his wet boots to leave outside the apartment door.

Vicenta took a seat in the living room. She felt like a blow-up float, Snoopy, for example, in the downtown Christmas parade, that was losing all its helium.

Arguments between couples sometimes erupted from a flammable pile of emotional debris, requiring only a match to burst. In their case, the pile never went away. Each time it became more volatile. He was always sorry afterward. "Since losing the baby," his apologies would begin by way of explanation. Now, as she started to see their fights, that seemed like an excuse. They'd end with small offerings, like the Eastern European scarf or a bouquet from the supermarket.

They didn't peel off layers of clothes, as they usually did when they arrived in their warm apartment. No one went to prepare dinner. Each sat, one in the living room, the other on the bed in the bedroom, waiting for the bell to ring to announce the start of the fight. The fire of an imminent argument had been ignited by her delay at work. "If we're going to start a family soon," Simón said from the doorway, "I don't think I can let you stay working."

Vicenta couldn't believe her ears. Simón had always been encouraging of her career goals. When she was in school and working part-time at the college library, it was he—a hardworking guy with a full-time job on the docks—who paid for her textbooks.

"Who'd take care of our baby?" Simón asked. "Assuming we ever have one."

With or without her husband's support of her working outside the home, she was going to keep striving. Then again, she remembered Sharon's point about the lousy employee benefits for women regarding children. Would it even be worth it to work outside the home?

Simón went back to the couch, an ankle resting on the other knee, his grimy stockinged foot shaking with agitation. "If you think I'm gonna wait until I'm a middle-aged guy to have kids," he said, "too old to enjoy them, *estás loca*." As if immediately regretting his phrasing, he added, "I hope you understand, Vicenta."

Understand what? she asked herself, but was exhausted from a long day and didn't want to argue. It was late and she'd lost her appetite. "I'm going to take a shower and go to bed," she said, hoping the retreat would serve as a kind of white flag to their conflict.

"Yeah, good idea," Simón said. "Make sure you throw those clothes in the hamper, too, or maybe in the garbage can. You smell like shit."

Despite the fact that there may have been some truth to his complaint, Vicenta felt the blow of her husband's rejection.

"Don't be so sensitive," Simón had started saying whenever he'd level a criticism at her and she responded only by looking hurt. As the object of his scowls, she had started acting like a trembling rabbit. In the bathroom, removing items of clothing, she sniffed, and indeed traces of Deidre's funk were there. Still, who wouldn't feel offended to be told they stank? Simón's world of rough-and-tough guys on the dock was different from hers; maybe he just forgot that sometimes.

After washing up, Vicenta went to the hall closet and pulled out a sleeping bag. If she was so repulsive, Simón could sleep on the floor that night, for all she cared. She flung the heavy roll in his direction; it landed at his feet, where he was still sitting on the couch. "See what I mean?" he said, face red. "You're crazy." Almost by reflex, he reached for the beer bottle on the end table and, with the quarterback's aim that he had in high school, hurled it directly at his wife. She reacted quickly, scarcely dodging the flying object, feeling a splash of beer as the missile hit the floor with a crash, glass and liquid all over. Anger brimming, Vicenta looked around for something she might sling back. Simón looked ready, sitting up straight with both feet on the floor. She remembered the cut on her leg from the Sunday before. They'd argued, and a cozy afternoon watching a rental video had become a war zone. When she got up, heading to the kitchen, something had struck her on the back of the leg. It was the framed wedding picture that sat on the shelf in the living room. The metal corner cut her skin just before the object hit the floor. A startled Vicenta stared at the broken object on the floor. Simón hadn't even bothered to see where it landed, having already retreated to the bedroom and slammed the door.

Now, another argument only a few days later. If she continued the fight, she suspected matters would escalate quickly. What would be next? The young wife preferred not to find out and went to the bedroom, closing (not slamming) the door behind her. When Vicenta peeked out later, wondering why the apartment was so quiet, Simón was gone. Whenever her husband felt the need to cool off, think something over, or just be alone, he often drove around. Near midnight, she was still unable to sleep and returned to the living room. Simón wasn't back. Vicenta went to the window, peering through the venetian blinds; the street, without sound or movement beyond snow flurries wafting in the wind, under other circumstances would feel peaceful but instead felt foreboding. In addition to worrying about her husband and hoping he'd be home soon, she was anxious about the Deidre incident. Vicenta felt guilty having left Kantor and Sharon with the horrible mess—horrible and unmentionable. But what else could she do when Simón came looking for her? If she'd insisted on staying or dared to explain, in his eyes she'd go from the girl who once could do no wrong to the woman he married who did only wrong.

The next morning, the walk to the library was practically in arctic conditions. Sidewalks were so treacherously icy at the early hour when residents hadn't yet thrown out rock salt that Vicenta slipped a few times but luckily avoided a fall. Simón and she weren't speaking, but she assumed he'd come by for her that night as usual. Despite the painful exchange the evening before, she trusted they'd work out their differences.

Mrs. Kantor always opened the library, and Vicenta was immediately troubled when she arrived first. Her boss had not been late before. After switching on lights, getting off wraps, and removing snow boots to slip on street shoes, she went to check the thermostat. It was nippy, and she deliberated whether there was a problem with the heat. She hoped not. The library would get intolerably cold if the furnace went out. Denial was never a wise option, but for the present, the library's second-in-command raised the thermostat, certain the heat would soon kick in.

Instead of going to her desk, Vicenta moved briskly around to stay warm while anticipating the janitorial service to show. Her stomach was rumbling loudly. Not a breakfast person—as usual, she'd had only coffee at home that morning—she was suddenly starved. After the argument, she hadn't had any dinner the night before—she thought. That morning, the pan with leftover lasagna that the couple had pulled out of the refrigerator to reheat still sat on the stove, covered with a sheet of aluminum foil. But *had* she had any? Why was she having so much difficulty remembering the previous evening? As if from a hangover, her head throbbed.

Vicenta was trying to decide what Mrs. Kantor would want her to take care of in her absence when she noticed the odd presence of an old thick volume lying plainly on one of the reading tables. At the end of each day, they all made sure to tidy up. On the other hand, the evening before had been an exception—nicely put, but more accurately, a tragedy in two or three parts. Vicenta picked up the book, tattered at the spine and with yellowed pages, just as two people from maintenance turned up, rapping hard on the windowpane. She set the rogue book on the returned-books pile, hurrying to unlock the door.

The men were busy scrubbing the ladies' restroom when Sharon turned up. She drove to work, but since the library didn't have a parking lot, the walk from where she found street parking to the building left her quivering. She was disquieted, too, at the director's absence. "Maybe we should call her house," she suggested, glancing at the head librarian's vacant desk. Vicenta thought it best to give Mrs. Kantor some time. With the inclement weather predicted later and temperatures dropping, traffic on the highway was most likely at a crawl. "Maybe she's just late," she said.

When the cleanup duo was done and about to leave, they stopped at the desk. "Who made the mess in there?" one of the guys asked. He was short, stout, and with a beard that nearly disguised his whole face. The other man nodded, wiping sweat off his brow. They seemed revolted.

"A homeless woman," Sharon replied with what Vicenta interpreted as glibness. The men may have taken it the same way. They looked uneasy. The other guy, buttoning his pea coat, asked, "Did she make it to the hospital or what?"

"Hospital?" Vicenta asked. "Why do you say that?"

"What do you mean?" It was the bearded guy asking. "With all that blood we had to clean up? It looked like a . . . like a . . ."

"Like a fucking massacre took place in there," the second guy said when his partner held back. "Excuse my French, ladies."

Vicenta and Sharon looked at each other and then back at the men. "It wasn't blood, fellas," Sharon said.

"Hell if it wasn't," the second guy said, signaling with a jabbing elbow to his partner to take off. "You ladies, take care. Stay outta trouble, all right?"

After the men left, Sharon said, "Who mistakes shit for blood, anyway?"

It gave Vicenta her first smile in the last twenty-four hours. "Right," she said. "They'll probably put it in a report, and we'll have the cops here in no time to arrest us."

"Over that gross old bag lady," Sharon said. "After I left here yesterday, I was sick all night." She gave Vicenta a peculiar once-over, which made Vicenta self-conscious, provoking a questioning nod from her.

"Oh, nothing, I just thought it was funny how you're so fixated on a ghost chick hanging around here, and right now you look like one yourself."

Vicenta's jaw dropped.

Her co-worker continued, "You're all pale and bony, nonstop shaking—and in a *green* dress."

No one had ever referred to her as bony. As for pale—she was dark-skinned even in midwinter. Her outfit, a merino sweater and matching skirt, were teal. "We need to warm up," Vicenta said, and headed to the coffee room. Sharon wobbled behind, hands on her swollen belly. "Get it together, girl," she said, although it was obvious Vicenta was ignoring her sharp comments.

There was an electric coffeemaker in back, but when they tried, it didn't work. With overhead lights flickering, the two concluded that, along with the heat in the library, the electrical was acting up. "It has to be this damn cold," Sharon said. "They said it's gonna drop way below zero—maybe eighty below with the wind chill factor." Unable to have her usual hot tea, she announced she was running down to the diner to pick one up.

Meanwhile, though the library was officially open, nobody had come in yet. Who could blame people for not stepping outside in such hostile weather? Vicenta herself would've preferred staying under the warm covers that morning. She went to her desk to turn on the reading lamp and found it wasn't working, either. When she reported the electrical problem, she hoped they wouldn't send the same two guys who'd cleaned up. Instead of assuming it was just a tripped fuse, they'd probably come up with another sinister scenario, like claiming someone had cut the wires.

Just then a patron blew in along with a blast of fierce wind. She recognized the man, who went straight to the rack where she'd just laid out the daily papers. He picked up a few but held out the *Chicago Tribune.* "Frigid Temps," read the headlines. "People were freezing to death out there last night," he said aloud as he went to find a seat. When Vicenta looked up again, she thought she saw a dark figure lumbering toward the front doors—maybe it was Deidre. It quickly turned into nothing. She didn't know what to think.

Sharon was back. Unable to bundle up because of her huge stomach, she was shaking from the walk.

"Where's your tea?" Vicenta asked.

"Oh, I was so cold, I just drank it there," she said, teeth chattering. "Guess what? The hostess asked about the bag lady, since she didn't turn up last night." Sharon groaned. "Lord, Lord."

"Well?" Vicenta said.

"I said we didn't know anything after we got rid of her last night."

"Did you say it that way? 'Got rid of her'?" Vicenta said.

"Didn't we?" Sharon asked with a kind of trembling sigh. "Mr. Pagonis just stood there by the cash register, all quiet."

"What should he have said? Would he know anything?" Vicenta asked, knowing he didn't, but starting to feel irritated with Sharon's cockiness. The visceral unease throughout her body wasn't just because the library was fast becoming an icebox.

Sharon's dark side lay just beneath the Rasta peace-and-love posturing. As much as Vicenta had initially thought they'd be friends, she didn't trust her co-worker. Then again, everyone had a dark side that surfaced under particular circumstances, didn't they? With some, it came from sheer self-defense, and when it erupted, it surprised everyone. Others released it from deep-seated rage. Violence caught others off guard, no matter what the reason.

Vicenta started sorting the returned books and, upon picking up the one she'd found that morning, realized there was no shelf mark on the spine. It also wasn't wrapped in a protective plastic cover, as were all hard copies.

Sharon remained with coat and gloves on, standing in the same spot, and Vicenta went over to hand her the book. Her colleague gave it a once-over and then said, "This isn't ours." Her expression was off.

"Are you all right?" Vicenta said.

"I'm not sure," the other woman responded softly. "I think my water just broke." They both looked down on the tiled floor and saw she was standing in a widening puddle.

"Don't worry," Vicenta said, scrambling to her desk to call an ambulance. With a hospital nearby, it arrived fairly quickly. After seeing the mother-to-be off safely, now the only employee on hand, Vicenta ran back inside the building to answer the telephone, which had been ringing incessantly. It was Sharon's husband. A resident at Mount Sinai Hospital, he hadn't been home all night.

"She's gone off in an ambulance to have her baby," a breathless

Vicenta informed him. She cradled the phone receiver between ear and shoulder while rubbing her coat sleeves. The thermostat was either broken or crashed. Outside was fatal.

"What are you—a doctor?" he asked. "Sharon's not due for another month."

He knew full well she was a librarian, like his wife, and if lack of sleep had provoked such condescension, Vicenta didn't care. Obviously, sarcasm ran in that family. As soon as she had a chance, she'd check her horoscope in the *Sun-Times*. Surely it would read something like "Today would be a good day to stay home."

It was time to track down her boss. Vicenta was flipping through the cards on her Rolodex where she had one with the director's home number, when the phone rang. It was Mrs. Kantor. Before Vicenta had a chance to start telling her about the catastrophic morning she was having, the other woman said, "I'm at the hospital."

Vicenta gasped.

"No, it's not like that," the woman said. "After my son picked me up last night, we got in an accident. With all that ice, he lost control of the car . . ."

The young woman gasped again, louder.

"No, it's all right. I mean, he's gonna be okay. But I've been here with him all night. As soon as someone from the family can come stay, I'll go home."

Vicenta wished her boss well, assuring her that everything at work was under control. It didn't seem right to burden Mrs. Kantor with such things as faulty lights, heat gone out during the coldest day of the year, and left alone in the library. Not far from Vicenta's thoughts was an upcoming evaluation. Being able to handle challenges would surely be noted in her file.

"Hey, listen," Mrs. Kantor said, "have you heard anything? You know . . . about Deidre?"

Vicenta said she hadn't. There was a moment's pause on the other end and then what sounded like a sigh. "I haven't, either," the director said. "Not on the news, anyway. Well, I'm taking up this pay phone, and there's a line behind me."

They hung up just as an overhead light flickered out. It was overcast outside, so now the place was nearly dark. Vicenta looked over where the man had been reading the papers, but he was gone. She sat for a couple of minutes and then went back to Mrs. Kantor's desk to call maintenance. Trying to make the reports during raw weather only added to the ongoing turmoil. Heating and electrical were separate departments, lines jammed. It took determination or, by then, desperation creeping up to finally get through to the correct person after dialing a few extensions and each time getting placed on hold. When the right dispatcher answered and assured her that an order was in to send someone, Vicenta felt proud of herself and relieved. "You'll have to be there to let them in," said the lady at the other end. "Otherwise they might not be able to get back there this week, with as many emergency calls as we're getting. So hang in there, okay?" Vicenta confirmed that she'd wait. The library closed at five. She only had to hold on until then.

Remaining seated in her coat and gloves at the desk, she noticed the antique volume she'd found that morning. She couldn't recall having left it on Mrs. Kantor's desk, but that was just as well. Maybe its owner would return to claim it. As if about to unlock a treasure box but prolonging the expectation, she ran a hand over the front cover. Indeed, there were fewer riches more exciting to a bibliophile than discovering a rare book. The lone librarian lifted it to her face and inhaled. It smelled of the inside of her great-grandmother's steam trunk, the one she'd brought with her from Mexico during La Revolución with all the family's belongings. The woman was long dead, as were the uncles who rode with Pancho Villa, but the trunk survived.

Dim natural light made Vicenta squint while trying to read the first page. The publishing house was established in Chicago in 1909. The publication itself was in 1913. That was an exciting time in the vibrant city of more than two million. The Chicago and Northwestern Railway Terminal had recently opened. Kroch's bookstore was established. Later it would become Kroch's & Brentano's, still going strong. In those years, the city was a main hub for publishing. The printing company, also in Chicago, had printed one thousand copies, which must've been a major run back then. Then came the title page, like the crown on any story. What she saw caused her to rub her eyes before reading it again: *The Headless Girl in the Green Dress*. A black-and-white engraving of a castrated figure walking along a path was opposite the title page. No author.

Vicenta put the volume down. So that was it—the story was a novel, pure fiction. It had to be what that woman on the bike was referring to back when Vicenta was new there: a famous bit of the city's history, or at least its legends.

Vicenta's teeth were chattering, and she got up to go to the back room for her wool hat, the scarf her mother had knitted, to wrap up. It probably would be prudent to leave. To hell with it all. Who'd blame her if she closed a neighborhood library without waiting for official approval? Would Vicenta be fired? She sat in the coffee room trying to decide whether to stay or go. She'd have called her mother for advice, always so practical and sound, but her parents had left for Mexico. They were constructing a house for their retirement and both had taken a leave of absence from their jobs to supervise the house project. While hesitant, Vicenta could page Simón. After their awful fight, however, most likely he'd wait until his lunch break to call back, if even then. Was waiting for maintenance part of her job description? Stalwart Mrs. Kantor never would have abandoned her post.

There was a battery-run clock on the wall—you could practically hear it clicking each second—but Vicenta's brain was going numb, and pulling back the thick coat sleeve at her wrist and two sweaters, and pushing down the thermo-glove, she checked her watch. It was almost noon.

A draft whirled in, slamming the coffee room door and causing Vicenta to jump up. Someone at the front entrance? "I'm back here!" she called out. An infusion of cold rushed in, and the overhead light in the coffee room went out, whoosh, like a candle. The windowless room was black, and Vicenta stretched out her hands, hoping to find the door.

There were footsteps out there. It could be the city-employed maintenance engineer come to see about the lights or heat. Maybe it was the mailman. Someone might be needing help finding a book or information and there was no one at the front desk. Or perhaps, as on normal days, it was a stranger looking for directions on foot or by car. Whoever it was, they were being silent. "I'm back h-here!" she stammered, realizing how meek her voice sounded. Who would hear? Then Vicenta noticed something else coming from outside the room. Not a stench like excrement or urine and whiskey, so familiar now with the homeless people who came in to get out of the cold. It wasn't rank at all . . .

Vicenta sensed an energy, perhaps in the form of an angel, just outside the coffee room.

No, that was stupid. Poetic but illogical.

She couldn't find the door, much less the handle, which would take only a twist and push out. Vicenta felt for her pager in a pocket and got it out to contact Simón but, unable to see anything, put it away. Maybe Simón, thinking about her, feeling remorseful in any way, to any extent, would try calling her. The thought brought a fleeting sense of calm.

"*Hello?*" Vicenta called out, then louder, trying not to sound foolish or too vulnerable, being shut in the coffee room. It was just the kind of situation Simón warned her about. Where was the Mace? In her purse—inside her desk—out there. Shaking, Vicenta crossed her arms tight. *Find the door*, she told herself. *Run out, grab your purse from the drawer in your desk. Don't look around. Where are the keys to lock up . . . ?* She couldn't recall.

It was one thing to explain why you'd left a nonfunctioning facility under dire circumstances, another to leave it open and risk vandalism. It'd been a chaotic morning. She was so cold now she could hardly remember her full name. Wait until she told Simón all about it later, when they were having dinner at their little kitchen table in their warm flat. He wouldn't believe it. What a laugh they'd have. She herself could hardly believe what was happening. In the future, perhaps, she might even try writing a story, "The Girl in the Green Dress." Something to be considered for the Nelson Algren Award. It wouldn't be about a headless woman but, instead, a woman who refused to have children. The professional lady would hold office in city hall, where she'd make sure people got what they needed, especially during catastrophic conditions.

The steps stopped right outside the door. Vicenta cocked her head. "Hello?" Silence. She inched sideways and found the counter with the coffeemaker and assorted items. Hand moving around, there was the sink. Over the sink, she knew, hung a small mirror, perhaps the industrial developers, thinking that instead of a window with a view—which was impossible, given the location of the building—people would like to look at themselves. Was she looking into it?

A careful step back—she bumped into a chair, pulled it out, and sat down.

"'Take me out to the ball game,'" Vicenta began to hum and then sing in a low voice. A long time ago she'd learned the tune in day camp. If the bicyclist woman had never mentioned a headless girl the first week Vicenta was there, why would she ever fear something ungodly was nearby? If it had breath, she'd have smelled it, surely rancid, foul. Was something reaching behind her now? She shrank back.

It was no more than the power of suggestion or the result of a whimsical mind, like the faint music she was distinctly hearing from outside the door, the same imagination Simón, her parents and siblings, and even friends thought she'd been born with, if not gathered from her fondness for books.

But what about the young mother who listened to musicals in the booth, who felt her hair stroked? She *saw* it in the glass. No one had told her anything before about a headless girl there, had they?

Maybe she *was* crazy. Or maybe she'd overheard the conversation and made up the account. People did things like that to get attention. Vicenta reminded herself that she shouldn't be so quick to call another woman crazy. Too many women throughout history, even in her own century, had ended up in sanitariums, with lobotomies, drugged or alone and homeless. Brilliant women like Camille Claudel, who apprenticed under Rodin and was rumored to be the true artist behind his masterpiece *The Thinker*, ended up abandoned and destitute and then judged harmless as a solitary house mouse. Oh, but if that house mouse had comparable friends—that would be an invasion. You couldn't tolerate such an assault on the order of things. Zap. Zap. ZAP. *Away and be done with you, bold little mice. Die, die, die.*

Vicenta never told anyone, not even her mother, in whom she confided everything, of the time recently when Simón had put his large hands around her neck. She didn't want her family to think badly of him. They'd reject him, and there'd be no bringing him back to the fold. He'd caught himself quickly and apologized. It hadn't happened again. That night, marks visible, Vicenta had thought many things. It occurred to her to sneak the thirty-five-millimeter camera out of the closet and take pictures of the marks. Documentation. Just in case. But if she called the police, what would they do, anyway? They'd chalk it up to a domestic quarrel.

Feeling nearly paralyzed now in the blacked-out coffee room, Vicenta was certain she heard the melody playing in the next room. *Take me out to the ball game*, it repeated over and over. It sounded like an organ playing ever so faintly. With each note, she felt lulled. Or was it hypothermia? *Ay, no.* Impossible. She was inside. *Get up,* her brain instructed. *Go out there. Walk around. Find your keys.*

Go home. In the background, the ballpark melody continued. Was it in her mind or out there? Her eyes closed, and for a fraction of a second she saw her parents in their new home in Mexico. They were working on a luscious floral garden.

Where had she read that when people passed away, they'd already said all their goodbyes?

Vicenta crossed her arms to rest her head on the table and felt a book there. She was about to push it aside. Sharon often grabbed one off the rack to skim through when on break, sipping herbal tea. But had there been anything on the round white table before light evaporated? Vicenta tried to recall. (It was important to stop letting her mind play tricks on her.) There couldn't have been anything. She would have noticed any book left there. But there it was, in her grip. If she brought the volume to her nose, what would she smell? Dandelions in spring, human feces, or perhaps blood?

Vicenta shook her head, trying to clear her mind, and readied to stand up. She'd dash forward, and there'd be the door magically in front of her. She'd run out of the library and wouldn't stop until she got home.

The keys were probably on top of her desk. What made her so reluctant to pick them up, lock up the facility, and head home, treading cautiously all the way over glassy pavement? How glad she'd be, back in the warm apartment. Tomorrow would be another day, a better day. Sharon would have had her baby. Mrs. Kantor, recovered from the horrific evening before, would be back at work. That night, Simón would hold her close, breathe in *her* smell of citrus oil, orange blossoms, and lemon (and most definitely not of shit). They'd love each other forever.

Take me out to the ball game, she heard the tune repeat, now less like an organ and more like a child at a toy piano, tapping one key at a time. Why were Chicago winters so excruciating that you might fall asleep remembering the green grass of ballparks, people's exuberant laughter and shouts, the anticipation of a game, which on summer days was like none other? *Take me out to the ball game*, it repeated.

Vicenta closed her eyes. Her dad was a handyman. Even if he'd been around, she wouldn't have called him because the city had strict rules about the union. But she could have called to ask his opinion about the electrical. "Don't worry, *mija*," he'd have said, "it'll get fixed."

Take

me out

to the ball game . . .

Don't worry, mija,
It's gonna be all right.

Vicenta heard a voice so sweet, like agave syrup, her arms yearned to reach out and touch it, but her limbs were tingly and stiff. Anyway, could you caress sound? *Yes, of course,* came the answer from an indistinct source. *You can smell us now, can't you?* it said. *We smell of caramel corn and steamy hot dogs. We are Abuelita's hot chocolate on Noche Buena.* This Christmas, Vicenta and Simón had invited their siblings over. They'd planned on making tamales and hot chocolate, the foamy Mexican kind, rich with whole milk, that they all had grown up having on special occasions.

A minuscule faint blue light appeared at the center of Vicenta's mind. It didn't grow. It didn't fade. It was like the Star of David flashing brightly in the night sky.

Cross yourself in the name of the Baby Jesus, she heard her mother's younger voice instructing the children just before lights went out.

The phones were ringing. *I have to answer,* Vicenta thought, but was surprised when she couldn't get up. The ringing stopped, then started again. Was it Mrs. Kantor? Fleetingly, she felt glad she couldn't get to the phone and admit to her boss just how bad things were, but not answering would make her director furious. *If I'm being such a fuckup, I should be dismissed,* she reprimanded herself.

But maybe it's Simón. She felt overcome with sadness not to be able to speak with him. He was her husband, after all, her partner in crime, as they enjoyed teasing each other. There was no judgment between them, nothing they'd keep from each other. It was what they'd always said.

What are you thinking?

You're not going anywhere, Vicenta. Vicenta. Vicenta.

The Night at Nonna's

HAVING BEEN SEATED next to each other in homeroom, Lulu and Marie became best friends their first day in high school. The teens were ecstatic when they realized their families lived only a few blocks from each other. Marie had attended Catholic elementary, while Lulu and her siblings went to public school, so until then neither girl had ever seen the other around. On that first day, the new best friends passed their phone numbers to each other. "Don't call after nine," Marie said, "my parents don't let me get calls late." Lulu nodded. "Mine don't, either." It was true. Her father worked the graveyard shift, and it was his call at two in the morning, which her mother always got up to answer, that was the only one allowed after bedtime.

Marie's Italian mother insisted she go to Catholic school. However, by the time she was ready for high school, the girl's Protestant father had outvoted her mother, and Marie got her wish to go to the local coed public high school. Besides homeroom, she and Lulu had other classes together. Instead of catching the bus after school, they started taking their time by walking the two and a half miles it took to get to their neighborhood. If it rained, one pulled out an umbrella and they hooked arms, jumping off curbs over water rushing into sewage drains. All the way, they never stopped chatting and laughing at whatever the other said or did. Marie, who'd never worn a hand-me-down in her life, was stylish, unlike Lulu, who had one pair of "school shoes" and one new purse to use all freshman year. Soon her best friend was loaning her items, a mohair sweater brought to school in a paper bag or a pair of capris. In turn, Lulu fixed Marie's hair every morning. Both tried out for cheerleading and neither made it. They decided to join the French Club. At lunch in fourth period, they sat together, and other kids quickly learned the pair wasn't interested in anyone else's company.

They were inseparable. If what they felt in common wasn't enough, as with all alliances during war and peacetime, what sealed the bond between them was a secret that, if found out, could ruin either or both.

It was October in Chicago, and autumn had already made its majestic entrance. Buckthorn leaves turned fiery red and golden. Deep orange maple leaves drifted in a dance through the air, landing gently on damp sidewalks. In the sky, formations of birds were heading south. Everywhere were signs of winter approaching. Most of all, the air was different. "I woke up this morning and I did like this," Marie said, moving her nose like a bunny sniffing or maybe the actress on the TV show *Bewitched*. Neither could twitch her nose without using two fingers to do it. As the girls giggled, one snorted, causing them to break into near hysterics. When a passerby gave the pair, who were bent over, each holding her stomach, a curious second glance, it ignited a new round of laughter.

Now summer was officially gone, and it was time to bring out jackets and wool socks. "The air *smells* different," Marie said as they strolled home. They walked so slowly, sometimes they didn't get home until dinnertime.

Lulu nodded. It was her opinion that one day Marie was going to make a very good schoolteacher, which was her goal, to follow in her mother's footsteps. Marie's grandmother, her nonna, hadn't been a teacher but helped teach catechism at church, so she was like a teacher, too.

"I felt it last night sitting on the porch. It *felt* crisp and I knew it was October," Marie said. "The air *smells* crisp."

"Yeah, crisp like a potato chip," Lulu said. "A Lay's potato chip!" She gave her friend a side glance to see if the girl picked up on her attempt at a double-entendre.

"Lay's?" Marie muttered.

"Yeah, LAYS. Man, don't you get it? October got laid."

"I swear you're so silly sometimes . . . and with a mind in the gutter," Marie said, still scratching her head. The two stared at each other and then fell into laughter again.

Each looked up at a cloudy sky and nodded as if they'd landed on a new planet and decided that it was habitable.

Lately, Lulu would have agreed that something did feel different. If you gave autumn a color, it would be purple. Purple was the color of the robe the bloodied statue of Jesus was covered with during Holy Week. At the wake her mother made her go to one time for the husband of a lady who also worked at the factory, the man in the casket had on a purple tie. Lulu didn't quite understand why a dead man was to be buried, left in a box six feet under the ground, dressed up in a suit. She shuddered. "That thing you sense in the air, Marie," she said, "is the announcement of death."

"I swear," her friend said, "sometimes you say the weirdest things."

"I know," the other said, "that's because I *am* weird."

"Yeah, you weirdo."

The girls walked for a while, then Marie said, "I'm not going home right now. I have to go sit with my nonna. She just got out of the hospital, and my mother said we all have to take turns watching her."

Lulu knew about her best friend's maternal grandmother because she was Marie's favorite person in the world. The first Saturday the girl came to Lulu's home, she brought a paper sack of homegrown tomatoes. "I'm so embarrassed," she whispered to her friend after she handed it to Lulu's mother. "But my nonna made me. She said you never go to someone's house empty-handed."

Lulu's mother was delighted with the gesture and the wonderful tomatoes. After that, anytime Lulu brought up Marie's name, her mother would say something like "What a nice girl. How's her grandmother?"

The week before, Nonna had been taken to the hospital with stomach pain and had been admitted. "They removed her lady parts inside," Marie wrote in a note she passed to her best friend. It was a funny way to refer to a hysterectomy. The girls had learned about human anatomy in health class. Now Nonna was home, and the previously independent fifty-year-old widow who took care of everybody now needed looking after, at least until she was back on her feet.

"Do you think you can come over with me? I'm gonna get bored sitting there by myself. My nonna will be in bed, I think," Marie said. "My mother is leaving some mostaccioli and we can eat dinner, you and me, without grown-ups or anyone around. Come on! I can help you with our essay that's due in English class . . . I know you probably haven't even started it." The petite girl made a "pretty please" expression with hands together which busted up her friend.

"I have to ask my mother," Lulu said. "Maybe tomorrow." It would take some finessing. Lulu would use the tactic of doing the school assignment with her straight-A friend. Lulu hated writing compositions, and the book the teacher had assigned recently, *Lord of the Flies*, put her to sleep after the first three pages. It was almost as bad as *The Scarlet Letter*. The class had one copy and passed it from student to student, reading the whole thing out loud.

It wasn't unusual for Lulu to go in her mother's room at bed-time to talk. She'd crawl into bed and sometimes fall asleep, her mother softly scratching her scalp. They didn't talk about every-thing, but they did share a lot. Lulu already knew she was going to go to beauty school. Her mother thought it was a worthwhile plan and offered to pay the tuition. "Just don't tell the rest," she whispered. "Your siblings will want me to help them with what-ever they come up with, too. And your father will say you should go to work to pay for it. It's better to keep it between us."

That evening when Lulu went into the small bedroom where her parents' full-size bed was up against two walls, she used the school angle to convince her mother to let her go with Marie. "What would your father say?" her mother whispered. "You know he doesn't like you kids out during weeknights. Well, okay. Just make sure those people bring you home. It's too late for you to be on the street alone." The fact of the matter was that the city of Chicago had a ten thirty weekday curfew for minors.

"Marie's uncle Luca is going to drive us home," she said, "but not until after eleven."

"Eleven?" her mother asked. "Oh, *hija*, your father will kill us both if he finds out."

Lulu saw her mother was trying to play hardball, so she said, "Marie says maybe her uncle will hire us to work there next summer, making pizza."

Her mother shook her head. "No, *mijita*. You and I have already decided. You're going to sign up for cosmetology—that's if you don't fail a class and end up having to go to summer school. Who knows? Maybe one day you'll have your own shop, and I can quit the factory and work there." In the end, as was usually the case, Lulu got her way and was given permission to hang out with Marie at her nonna's.

All the next day, the girls were almost giddy with anticipation of an unsupervised evening together. Now that Lulu was in high school, she was growing up, and quickly. She could take the bus every day by herself. Although she had to be careful no one at home found out, she wore makeup at school. The knee-length skirts her parents approved of were rolled up at the waist to make them into minis. And then there was the matter of boys. One in particular.

That afternoon in the hallway, Lulu passed a note to the guy who had most recently asked her out, a senior. Asking a girl out meant to be his girlfriend. Alfie wasn't that cute, but he was tall and had an after-school job. He even had a car. He seemed to really like her. He always smiled and found something to say to her when they'd pass each other in the hall. "Hey, foxy lady," he might utter. Then one day he stopped at her locker and asked her out. Lulu nodded. Immediately, her musings took flight. It would be so cool if one day he could pick her up in his car and take her to a movie.

That afternoon when she caught sight of him, she gave Alfie the grandmother's phone number and address. "Pick me up at nine thirty," she wrote in the note. She'd have over an hour to ride around with the kid before he'd drop her off. They'd probably just park and make out. Thinking Marie's uncle was taking her home, Lulu's mother would be none the wiser.

After last period, the girls met at their neighboring lockers, as always, and hurried off to Grandma's house like a couple of Red Riding Hoods. Nonna and her family lived in an old two-flat graystone on a short residential block off Blue Island Avenue. It was yet another advantage for Lulu. At least ten blocks from her house, she'd be out of sight of anyone in her own family.

That afternoon, instead of taking their sweet time walking, they caught the bus, so anxious they were to get to the grandmother's. When they jumped off at their stop, gripping hands and skipping, they began to sing. "'Over the river and through the woods,'" they sang, laughing, "'to Grandmother's house we go!'" Of course, they didn't expect any wolf to be waiting under the bedcovers, and if there was: "I'll smack him with my satchel!" Marie said, swinging her book bag. "Yeah," Lulu said, "and then we run!"

The girls stepped into the front hall; wooden stairs led up to the second-floor flat, flanked by a polished walnut-stained banister. The door immediately upon entry to the building was Nonna's. Lulu rubbed the newel cap like a crystal ball as Marie searched for the spare key, which must've fallen to the bottom of her book bag. When her mother abruptly pulled open the door, both girls were startled. "Mommy," Marie said, "you scared me."

"What took you so long, Marie Ann?" the woman scolded, going off to pick up her coat and purse, laid carefully on the sofa. "Didn't you take the bus here today, like I told you? Now I'm late at the rectory." Marie's mother had taken over Nonna's duties at the church. Dabbing herself from a small bottle of Tabu from her purse, she rattled off instructions. "Your nonna's asleep. Keep the TV low. And lock the door behind me. Don't open it for anyone." She left.

The girls both sighed with relief. "Want some cookies?" Marie asked, flinging off her jacket onto the sofa. "We can watch *Soul Train* . . ."

With days growing short, it was completely dark by five o'clock. It felt odd to Lulu not to be at home after the sun went down. Except for school, the girl was never away from her family. She watched as her friend obediently turned the bolt to lock them inside.

"Are you okay?" asked Marie, who was sensitive to her friend's feelings. "You're shivering."

Lulu kept her coat on when her friend invited her to take a seat. The abrupt sensation of being cold was reminiscent of the year before, when her grandfather from New Mexico came to visit. He stayed at her aunt's house. Lulu and her family went over there on Sunday. The old man never stopped regaling them with stories about growing up on the *rancho*. Lulu thought it was in Mexico, but her grandfather corrected her. "New Mexico's been a state of the union since 1912," he said gruffly. "We're Americans, but we are also Spanish."

Lulu always thought they were Mexican. Her mother was from Mexico City. "Is Mexico City in Mexico?" she asked.

"Of course," her kid brother answered. "Stupid."

"Don't use that word in this house," the aunt reprimanded the boy.

The whole afternoon and into the evening, the abuelo went on as if he'd been gagged all his life. After dinner, everyone crowded in the cramped living room as he started a story about when he was a kid and told to guard the sheep all night. Something was getting in the pens.

"Like what? Bears?" Lulu's little brother asked. "A wildcat!" said the other brother.

"Coyotes, most likely!" guessed her aunt. Lulu's older sister, always with a nose in a book, looked up and offered, "Wolves . . . of course."

The man nodded each time but never said. Maybe he never knew. He just went on with his story. "There I was, all alone," he said, smoothing out his bushy mustache. "A little kid, just a *mocoso*, with this big shotgun. I knew how to use it, too. The bear, coyotes, or mountain lions, whatever—wouldn't have gotten me alive!" He laughed and everyone else laughed, too. Lulu tried to smile but kept wondering what horrid creature was harming the ranch animals every night.

"At one point," he added, "maybe I'd fallen asleep or maybe it was a dream but I heard a woman . . ." For whatever reason, he pinned his gaze on each of the women around the room. "She whispered, 'Come with me . . .'" The abuelo's voice changed, high-pitched and eerie.

Lulu, sitting on the floor with the kids, shrank back. She saw her brothers shrink away, too. "Come with me," the abuelo repeated, each time creepier. Then, with a sudden leap, he grabbed Lulu's stockinged foot. She tried to pull it back, but he held on firmly until the sock was off. "Let me go!" she shrieked. While the grown-ups tried to laugh it off, everyone was left uneasy. The grandpa guffawed and stood up. "Ah, those were the days," he said. "Everybody had to help out back then. If you didn't, you wouldn't eat." He seemed angry more than nostalgic, thinking of those times.

Later, as the family readied to head home, the grandfather frightened Lulu again. His gnarly hand came up from behind to tickle her neck but instead felt scratchy, like a bird's claw. "Come with me . . . !" he said in that raspy smoker's voice.

After Lulu heard her grandfather had returned to New Mexico, she spoke to her mother. "I didn't like him picking on me," she said.

"Your abuelo was just playing around, Lulu," her mother said, offering a faint smile for reassurance.

Despite her mother's words, later, Lulu overheard through the wall that separated their bedrooms her parents discussing it. "That's just how my father is," Lulu's father said. "He raised all us kids like that, teasing, poking . . . He thought it would toughen us up."

"I'll show him tough if he doesn't leave my daughter alone next time," her mother said.

Now Marie turned on a living room lamp sitting on an end table and then another at the other of the couch and called out to her grandmother. While she went to check in with the woman, who was in her bedroom, Lulu glanced around. The heavy drapes in the small living room were drawn. *How strange*, she thought. The drapes were deep purple, the exact shade she'd had in her mind earlier. Maybe she was clairvoyant, like Marie said. "I knew you were going to wear that today," Lulu would say when they'd show up wearing similar colors or outfits. "That's why I put this on, so we could match."

At the funeral home where the girl with potential powers had gone with her mother, curtains reminiscent of Nonna's hung behind the casket. The whole time Lulu sat on the hard chair next to her mother in silence, she kept wondering what was behind the curtains. She asked.

"Nothing. It's just a wall," Lulu's mother replied, putting a finger to her lips.

You couldn't see in through the grandmother's drapes from the street, but you also couldn't see out onto the street, where Lulu knew rush-hour traffic had picked up and streetlights had switched on.

She'd been so excited to have a chance to escape from home for the evening and the watchful eyes of her family, she'd hardly slept the night before. Now she felt utterly alone, like they had abandoned her. It was dumb, because naturally, it wasn't true. When Marie returned, she brought over a knitted afghan from an easy chair and wrapped it around her friend's shoulders. "Man, Lulu. What's wrong?" she said. "Are you coming down with something?" She touched her friend's forehead with the back of her hand the way her mother always did when Marie felt ill.

Something *was* off, Lulu thought. From the second she'd walked into the flat, no, even in the hall, she'd begun to feel indefinably odd, like she was there but not there. If she did make an excuse that she felt sick so as to leave and run home, she wouldn't get to meet with Alfie later. When would she have the chance to sneak out again? Her parents were so strict she almost never got permission to be out. She took a deep breath and threw off the afghan and then her coat. "I'm okay," she told Marie, managing a smile. "We can start on our homework." She looked over her shoulder toward the dark threshold of the grandmother's bedroom. The nonna had always been such a strong-looking woman, it was hard to imagine her bedridden.

While Marie went to check in with her grandmother, Lulu took in the surroundings. Damask wallpaper was all across the flat, which was crowded with bulky furniture and walls lined with family photographs and prints of Jesus, the Madonna, the Last Supper, and one of President Kennedy. Lulu was too little to remember when he was assassinated, but everyone around her honored him, the school, her parents—there was even a picture of him at the church hall, like he was a saint. Lulu could see the dining room with its hefty oak table and six high-back chairs. There was a china cabinet with glass doors that contained the family's best dishes and crystal glasses. On the far wall of that room was a huge photograph of a bride and groom, parents on each side. By the styles, she presumed it was Marie's parents and two sets of grandparents. Everyone looked so young and pleased. The bride was in a lace cupcake gown. When Lulu married, she'd have a big wedding, too, with lots of bridesmaids. There'd be all kinds of presents, and although she'd heard of people going to Niagara Falls for their honeymoon, she'd fly to Paris on Pan Am above the clouds.

Nearby, on the television console, were two large framed pictures neatly arranged on a crocheted runner. Marie was learning from her grandmother how to crochet, but she wanted to make things like the caps Ali MacGraw wore in *Love Story*, which were popular among a lot of girls. Maybe she'd even start a small enterprise, she said. One picture was in sepia tone, and it was obviously Marie's grandparents' wedding picture. The nonna was a slight girl then; her chiffon chemise went to midcalf, but her veil dragged on the floor. Seated next to her was a portly man projecting authority. His pocket watch chain hung over a fat belly. Marie's grandfather had died before she was born. The other picture was the same couple, apparently taken shortly before the nonno's passing. Both at the center, they were surrounded by grown children and grandchildren.

In order to not make her protective father angry, Lulu knew she had to marry as a way of getting out of the house, but she had no interest in having kids, at least not right away. With her husband, she hoped to have adventures—not only to see the Eiffel Tower but perhaps to ride in a gondola in Venice or spend a New Year's Eve in Times Square . . . Maybe she'd get into Studio 54 and run into Cher or dance with O. J. Simpson. Lulu began to relax, thinking of the what-ifs of the future, like what if she got to meet Diana Ross and was asked to be her hairstylist. People didn't know Lulu had dreams, and those dreams didn't include staying in Chicago. She could be a beautician anywhere.

The teen leaned back on the couch, and a white doily placed there stuck to her puffed-up hair. Taking it off, she felt like a little girl about to make her First Holy Communion. From the bedroom, she overheard the brief exchange. "You remember Lulu, Nonna," Marie said softly.

"Yeah, yeah. She's a good girl," the grandmother said. "You girls have some tiramisu. Your aunt brought it this afternoon . . . I'm not gonna eat anything, just sleep."

When Marie returned to the living room, she said in a near whisper, "Let's go to the kitchen. We can work on the table there." Lulu got her book bag and followed her friend. Marie put WVON on the radio atop the fridge but kept it on so low they could hardly hear it. "Do you think you can get permission to go see *Lady Sings the Blues* with me and my mother on Sunday?" Marie asked. Lulu shrugged. It was doubtful. On Sundays after mass, Lulu's parent insisted everyone stay home. It was the only day of the week the whole family was together at once.

After the girls had tiramisu and milk, they started working on their papers. Neither got past writing in the heading and the title before the chatter started up again.

Lulu hadn't entirely gotten rid of the ominous feeling she first had when coming inside Nonna's flat. Everything seemed so out-dated, like she was in another era. She wouldn't be surprised if the place was haunted. "Did I ever tell you about my grandfather from New Mexico?" she asked Marie. Her friend nodded. She remem-bered how excited Lulu had been to meet her father's dad for the first time last Christmas.

"He told us about this strange experience he had out there, where he grew up raising sheep," Lulu said. Marie loved ghost stories. She'd make sure to put her friend in a good mood before saying anything about meeting Alfie later. "My grandfather was a kid, maybe around our age, when it happened. Anyway, one time when he was out there all by himself, guarding the sheep—"

"Like the little shepherd boy who watched over Jesus?" Marie asked.

"No, *pendeja*," Lulu said. Leave it to her goody-goody friend to think of God at that moment, when she was trying to evoke ghoulish images.

"Don't call me that," Marie said. She didn't know Spanish but figured it was a cuss word. "Puck-face."

Lulu gave Marie a gentle shove on the shoulder. "Anyway, *Marie Ann*," she got back to her story, "he was watching out one night because something was attacking all the sheep, you know . . . eating out all their guts."

"What was it?" Marie's big eyes grew wider.

"Whatever it was mutilated one of the sheep every night." Embellishment came easy to the girl. Marie put a hand over her mouth. "Poor little lambs."

"My grandfather said late at night, out there all alone, he felt something nearby . . ." Lulu leaned in. One hand started taking finger steps across the table toward her friend. "'Come to me,' he heard a voice, like an old witch whispering in his ear, 'Come to me, my pretty . . .'" Marie pulled away and leaned back on the kitchen chair so swiftly she fell, hitting the floor. Her head missed the refrigerator door. While both were first stunned, after seeing her friend was all right, Lulu started to laugh. Instead of laughing along, Marie was upset as she got up. Straightening herself and the chair out, the girl sat down and returned to her work. A little while later, her anger seemed to pass and she said, "My uncle Luca can bring us a pizza when he comes tonight. I can call him at the restaurant. Do you like anchovies or sausage?"

Lulu wasn't interested in Marie's uncle's pizza, her aunt's tiramisu, or her mother's pasta in a big pot on the stove. She was beginning to think food was all her friend thought about. Marie had never had a boyfriend; she'd never even had a kiss. She was pretty, but she was so shy around guys, they just left her alone.

"I'm gonna have to cut out at nine thirty," Lulu finally announced, almost holding her breath. There was a good chance Marie wouldn't cover for her.

The other girl seemed surprised to hear her friend's news. Then she nodded. "Oh, I get it," she said. "Alfie?" All the way to the nonna's house, Lulu hadn't stopped talking about her new boyfriend. She'd drawn a big heart on her notebook with their initials. By next week, Marie figured, they'd be over. Meanwhile, who'd be there to pick up the pieces again? Her, the loyal best friend.

Lulu nodded. "He's gonna pick me up here. Don't worry, Marie, he'll drop me by my house by ten thirty, so you won't get in any trouble."

Marie didn't like it. She didn't approve of being used as a way to sneak around with a guy. If Lulu got caught, Marie would get in trouble, too. She knew that Lulu's father left for work around that time. What if he spotted her friend in the guy's car? She wasn't allowed to have a boyfriend, and neither was the other girl. They weren't supposed to get in any boy's car or be alone with a guy anywhere, for that matter. That hadn't stopped her best friend, who seemed to be getting bolder by the day.

Angry at the thought that Lulu had come over only to use her as an alibi, Marie slammed the book shut and got up. "I'm gonna peek in on my nonna," she said as an excuse to get away and calm down.

Lulu heard the two in the tiny bedroom speaking in Italian. She dug in her bag. Without an allowance like Marie got, Lulu had to skip lunches to save up to shop at Woolworth's. At the very bottom, she hid a small pouch with makeup. She pulled it out and went to the bathroom to fix herself up for her date. It wasn't really a date. Alfie was her third boyfriend, but she'd never been on a real date. She blamed her parents for that, since she wasn't allowed out on weekends.

Her first boyfriend had dropped out of school and enlisted in the army. She got a letter from him and found out he was headed for Vietnam. "Wait for me," he wrote. Later, she heard he'd written the same thing to a couple of other girls. The second boyfriend didn't even count. He asked her "out," which meant they were going together, and then he showed up in front of her school, holding hands with a girl who looked older, like she wasn't even in high school. Marie was the first to see them, giving Lulu an elbow. Initially, Lulu was mortified and couldn't even speak. Some kids were standing around watching. One girl called out, "Aren't you going to say anything to your boyfriend?" Humiliation took hold of her whole being, and Lulu turned off, dragging one foot in front of the other like she'd been blasted with atomic smoke. Luck, so far, wasn't on her side when it came to guys.

With makeup on and long hair teased and sprayed, Lulu felt disappointed when her best friend came back and made no comment. The two always complimented each other. Lulu pretended to focus on her schoolwork. Marie did the same, except she was probably getting something done, when both girls suddenly heard a woman's voice cry out. At first neither put her pen down, each most likely thinking it was her imagination, but when they heard it again, they looked at each other. "Go away!" It was the nonna. "Oh, Madonna *mia*," they heard the woman moan.

"She's probably having a nightmare," Lulu whispered. Marie nodded. They had returned to their books when Marie said, "I'm going to confession this Saturday. Do you want to come with me?"

Lulu didn't know what to say. Saturdays were mandated by her mother. The boys cleaned up their room and took care of the front yard. Meanwhile, her mother and older sister washed, ironed, swept, mopped, and everything else. Except for maybe changing her bed linen, Lulu was given no chores. She wasn't the baby, but she was the youngest girl, and both parents tended to favor her.

Her mother's LPs played low so that the music didn't disturb the father's sleep, he worked late. Sometimes their mother played José José or Raphael, but usually, it was the Animals. She had three albums and usually went back, steadily setting the needle to play one favorite song over and over.

One time as Eric, her bulky older brother, went by, he shoved Katia, who was vacuuming, "by accident," into the record player on a stand. It would have crashed to the floor were it not for the two kids catching everything in time. The incident ruined the album. And Lulu's siblings were duly reprimanded, albeit in a whisper so as not to wake the dad, but at least they didn't have to hear about the house in New Orleans again.

In the afternoon, before the boys got permission to go out and play basketball in good weather or street hockey in winter, her mother sent the kids to confession. It was a long shot, but if Lulu asked permission to go with Marie to her parish, she might be able to meet Alfie somewhere instead.

The girls finally settled into writing. Both were singing along softly under their breath to "I'm Stone in Love with You" by the

Stylistics when the radio went crackly. Each looked up. "What's happened?" Lulu asked, as if Marie could know. The other girl got up to readjust the dial.

"Did you hear that?" Lulu asked.

"What?" Marie said, as she went to try to get their favorite station back. It all sounded garbled. Although nothing had been announced, maybe there was going to be a thunderstorm.

There it was again, the faintest voice coming from the radio, like a faraway signal. Lulu felt her arms covered with goose bumps. *Come with me.* When Marie didn't seem to hear it, but kept moving the dial around, Lulu figured she was only imagining it. "It's okay," she said to her best friend. "Let's just get back to our essays."

Marie was about to click the round dial off when Lulu heard it again, this time less audible. Someone seemed to be calling from inside the radio. "Did you hear *that?*" Lulu asked, putting down her pen and starting to stand up.

Marie shook her head. In the back alley, tires went fast over tar, and a cat let out a loud screech. Both girls jumped.

"I'm gonna see if my nonna's all right," Marie said.

"What if she's dead?" Lulu whispered.

It caused Marie to stop, but instead of finding the suggestion offensive, she said, "Don't make me laugh." Her best friend's warped sense of humor wasn't for everyone, but she had one, too.

"Wait," Lulu said, and picked up the cake knife they'd used to cut the tiramisu. "Take this . . . just in case there's someone else there . . ."

"What good is that gonna do?" Marie said. Spinning around, she reached behind the stove where a few cooking utensils hung and took hold of a small cleaver. "This will do, madame!" she said with an exaggerated grin and left. Just a few minutes later, she was back; her nonna appeared to be asleep.

After sitting at the table, presumably to get back to their school-work, Marie remembered she was upset with her friend. After a few minutes, without looking up, she said, "He's got a girlfriend, you know."

Just another ploy to stop her, Lulu figured. "You lie like a rug," she said.

"I know her," Marie said. "We went to grammar school together, and she's going to Saint Michael's High now. She's a sophomore."

Lulu waited.

"They've been going out for over a year," Marie added. "Every-body knows. I heard he brought her to his junior prom last year."

Lulu thought about the news. She didn't have Alfie's home phone number to call and ask him. Now she figured it was because he didn't want another girl calling his house. Marie had never lied to her before. Maybe she was making up a story about a girlfriend because she didn't want Lulu to leave her alone there. Or maybe she was just jealous. Marie was always saying, "All these guys chasing you all the time."

The tension between the girls grew heavy when Marie said, "I'll tell her, Lulu."

"You wouldn't dare," her friend said. Somewhere inside, she knew her friend always meant what she said.

Then Marie got that self-satisfied look she sometimes had in science class when she was first to finish an experiment, like any-one cared about the power of friction or what caused density to increase. "No," she said, with the smug face that made you feel like smacking her on the forehead like Moe always did to Curly, "I won't tell her about Alfie. That would only hurt *her*. I'll tell her our secret."

Lulu didn't know if her eyes ever got as wide as her friend's, but she felt bug-eyed. "Marie," she said, "you promised . . ."

"I'll tell her," Marie said firmly, avoiding the other girl's gaze. "I swear I will."

"You said you got rid of it," Lulu said.

"Well, I didn't," the other girl said. Her tone indicated she knew she was gaining the upper hand. "It's here." She pointed down to the basement.

Lulu looked behind at the paint-chipped door right off the kitchen. A lot of basements were dark and dank. She imagined that one was no exception. There was probably a washing machine down there and maybe a clothesline. Exposed pipes overhead. She remembered Marie talking about the homemade wine in jugs her grandfather left behind after his death, her nonna's mason jars of tomato sauce which she'd helped can, and how the family used the basement to store all their junk.

"I brought it here because I didn't want any temptation to look inside," Marie said.

Lulu leaned back. What proof would her friend have, anyway? It would be her word against Marie's. "If you tell on me," she said, "you'll be telling on yourself, too."

"I don't care," Marie said. "Hardly anybody likes me, anyway."

Lulu shrugged. She picked up her pen, but her glazed vision made it impossible to make out the page. She was so upset with her friend she couldn't even speak. Alfie hadn't called yet, but she had to figure he'd be out there on time. As soon as Lulu ran out, she could be sure Marie would be on the phone with his girlfriend. "I don't believe you," she challenged Marie.

"I told you," her friend said, "it's downstairs." She set her pen down. "You want to go see for yourself?"

The truth was Lulu didn't. She feared basements more than she did sleeping without a night-light. It was one of the reasons she'd sneak into her mother's bed—nothing unsettled her more than the dark. She shook her head, hoping to pull off indifference.

When Lulu was studying for the Sacrament of Confirmation, the nun said, "Jesus teaches us every day." What Jesus taught her the afternoon when her second boyfriend showed up with an older girl at *her* school to embarrass her—just because she was only a freshman, a virgin (who knew why guys did what they did?)—was to "toughen up." Her abuelo might have toughened up his kids by poking at them, but Jesus had taught Lulu that just being out in the world on her own was going to do it.

Marie got up and went to a drawer next to the sink. Getting out a flashlight, she said, "Come on, scaredy-cat. I'll show it to you. Go out with Alfie if you want. But by tomorrow, he'll know. Everyone will."

"They'll know about you, too," Lulu said, although it was clear her friend wasn't concerned about being found out.

Marie opened the basement door and started down. Momentarily, a dim light came on. Lulu had no choice but to follow. If she refused, Marie could talk about that, too, how terrified she was of going into her grandmother's basement. Kids at school laughed at everyone. Everything got around so fast in high school. That time of cheerleading tryouts, the day wasn't even over before kids were snickering behind her back about how she'd failed at doing the splits. Obviously, it wasn't everyone. Most people at school didn't even know she existed.

Lulu reluctantly followed her friend down. Even if the box that the girls had packed together one afternoon in a kind of ritual was down there, which she desperately hoped was not the case, could Marie prove Lulu had anything to do with it?

A bare lightbulb hung from a wire above the stairs. Lulu stretched out her arms to each side of the wall to steady herself as she went down. It was just like she'd imagined it. The jars of tomatoes and the jugs of wine on rustic shelves. There was a washing machine, and Lulu had to duck beneath the clothesline strung across beams. A big pair of pants, which she assumed were the uncle's, hung from the clothesline. Everywhere, piles of boxes, bikes, tools, and junk.

Marie went straight to it. It was a Pampers box, and when Lulu recognized it, she held her breath. Her mind was racing. In grade school, she'd had best friends. Now she knew why no one lasted. One day a kid was offering you her custard pudding at lunch, and the next, with the other kids, she was mocking how you ate.

But this was different. "You two look like a couple of love-birds," Marie's mother had said sweetly when she found the two girls sitting on the carpet, facing each other and talking quietly. Not everyone felt that way about the pair. "Yous two are thick as thieves," said nonna one time, "I dunno if I like it."

Marie aimed the flashlight at the box as if it were a murder victim.

Lulu swallowed loudly. "That doesn't even look like the same box," she said meekly. It was only a couple of weeks before, but already it felt like a lifetime ago.

"You don't think it's all in there?" Marie said in a tone Lulu hadn't heard before. "We packed it up together. We lit candles—the ones my mother saves in the pantry to light at mass—and said a prayer together. Remember, Lulu? 'Our Father who art in Heaven . . .' In heaven, not like us who are going to hell." She gave out a laugh as if to show she was joking, but she wasn't convincing.

The other girl was trying to get her bearings. The basement reeked and made her stomach turn. "We did it for your sake, Marie. Why didn't you leave the box out on the curb for when the scavenger truck came by, like we agreed?"

The scavenger truck went through all the neighborhoods, picking up stuff people wanted to throw out, a card table, a couch, a baby carriage, old clothes, broken appliances, and boxes. "I changed my mind," Marie said. "Maybe in the future, I want to remember when we were such good friends."

The repellent atmosphere and, most of all, Marie's peculiar demeanor made Lulu dizzy, like when you stepped off a roller coaster ride. She sat on a couple of stacked boxes. "But we are," Lulu said, no longer believing it. "You're my best friend, Marie."

The other girl dismissed the proclamation and brought down the Pampers box that had been stacked on other boxes and set it on the floor before Lulu. "Open it," she said. "If you don't think it's the one we packed, you and me together, see for yourself."

"Forget you, Marie," the other girl said, and started to head back.

"Oh, I think you should check," Marie said. "Because if you think I don't have evidence, Lulu, I do. I'll call Pamela Esposito, and she'll tell Alfie. It'll make him feel like a fool going out with you. Tomorrow you'll wish you were dead."

Lulu couldn't think straight. When had Marie started resenting her so much? Then it occurred to her that maybe she was bluffing.

"I don't believe you, Marie," she defied the other girl, now growing angry. "You goody-two-shoes. That's why you don't have any other friends."

"Oh yeah?" Marie said. "Well, at least I'm not a whore." She pushed the other girl, who lost her balance but managed not to fall. As soon as Lulu was back on her feet, she gave Marie a harder shove. Marie fell back on some boxes. Before she was able to get up, Lulu began opening up the box. It hadn't been sealed with tape but simply closed with a cross weave of the four flaps.

She was still hoping it wasn't the same one they'd so ceremoniously packed, their shame synchronized. They'd never speak of it again, they vowed. Marie would put it outside before going to school the next day, and the scavenger truck would haul it off, no questions asked.

Instead, there it was. The basement was dimly lit, but Lulu could see the carnage inside. A head of luxurious hair, a naked torso, a limb. Then another body part and another head and remnants of yet more.

The new best friends had discussed it just before Marie's fourteenth birthday. It was time. Lulu hadn't a choice to stop playing with her toys, the tea set, her favorite stuffed animal, and even her kid roller skates—her mother had gotten rid of it all without asking. But Marie had a whole playroom to herself. She was in high school and still wearing a training bra and playing with dolls.

Sometimes after school, Lulu went to Marie's to play with her games and toys. Most of all, the girls adored the Barbies. There were thirteen plus four Ken dolls. There was also the sports car and Dreamhouse. The girls dressed and undressed the dolls, from bikinis to sequined evening gowns. Barbies played tennis and studied nursing. They spun around Malibu in the convertible and went to their secretarial jobs. They were tanned and blond or pale with black hair, brunette or redheaded with freckles. Lulu had Barbie and Ken make out. "No," Marie said. "They'll end up with a baby." She reached over and picked up a life-size baby doll that looked like Godzilla next to the Barbie and Ken. Lulu and Marie laughed so hard, rolling on the carpet, that each nearly peed in her pants.

"Can you imagine," Lulu said, propping herself up on an elbow, "how painful it would be to get that baby out?" Her hand landed on Marie's lower abdomen.

The girls were staring at each other. "You know you can't get pregnant when you have your 'friend,'" Marie said, gently pulling the other girl until Lulu was on top of her. "Show me," she said, surprised at her gruff voice.

"What?" Lulu said.

"You know," Marie said. "Show me what they do to you. I have to know . . . in case . . ."

The likelihood of her best friend ever being alone with a boy seemed slim. Lulu thought there was a better prospect of an earthquake. She'd started to laugh at the idea of Marie alone with a boy when the girl beneath her pulled up her sweater. Underneath her pristine training bra were nipples protruding like small buttons. Lulu was already in a 34B bra. She wanted to pull away, but she also didn't want to hurt her friend's feelings. Marie was self-conscious about being so flat on top while her thighs grew thicker every day. Lulu put a hand to Marie's bottom. "I got touched there," she said.

"Someone felt up your ass?" Marie said. "You don't even have one."

Lulu tried to smile at the biting remark, but the truth of it made her blush. She moved her hand from Marie's butt cheek to between her legs. "And here," she said. At first she did it to embarrass Marie, but when the girl slightly opened her legs, Lulu kept her hand there.

"Show me," Marie said again.

Lulu recalled the feelings a guy could bring out in her and instead rolled off and lay on her back. "I don't know anything," she said.

"I bet."

"Marie, you're almost fourteen," she started. "What about if we do something like a ceremony or something? Let's get rid of these Barbies and Kens. It's time to stop playing with dolls."

"You play with them, too," Marie said. "And you're already fourteen."

Lulu's face on the floor was a few inches away. She studied Marie's long eyelashes. *She wouldn't even have to wear mascara,* Lulu thought, *to have movie-star eyes.* But just then she didn't like what she was seeing, a friend who was quick to point out her flat ass and how she, too, still played with Barbies. She sat up.

A doll in a miniskirt and halter top was nearby. Lulu pulled off the tiny clothes. Next she started wrenching off its head. "What're you doing?" Marie asked, reaching unsuccessfully to grab the doll. Lulu scrambled up and continued to tug the toy apart, limb by limb. Afterward she threw it down and picked up another.

First Marie let out a soft gasp, then a whimper. Tears filled her eyes. As if forcing herself not to let Lulu get the better of her, she plucked a Barbie out of a toy pile and began to annihilate it, too. She picked up a pair of scissors, the little kid's kind with round edges, and started cutting off the hair. The girls continued their spontaneous rite of passage until they'd ripped apart all the dolls. When they were done, they looked around as if gawping at a massacre, aghast but oddly satisfied. There was no turning back. The days in the playroom were over.

Before Lulu left, she helped Marie clean up. Marie came back from the kitchen holding two lit candles, solemn as an acolyte. "Let's say a prayer for their souls," she said. Afterward, she got one of the empty boxes her parents kept on the back porch to use for storage or trash, and they threw in the plastic pieces. "I'll leave it out on the curb for the scavenger truck," she said. "It comes by tomorrow."

Marie was pointing the flashlight at her face. Lulu looked up. "Stop that," she said, squinting and putting her hands up.

"Marie Ann?" It was the nonna. "What're you girls doing down there?"

"Yeah, Nonna?" Marie responded.

"The phone's been ringing . . . you expecting a call?" the nonna asked. "Get back up here."

"Yes, Nonna," Marie responded.

Just then the bare bulb above the stairs went out. In all likelihood, the grandmother had yanked the string to the light without thinking. Except for the flashlight, there was no light. Marie closed the box and kicked it next to some others. She pulled up her knee socks and pointed the flashlight ahead; a broad beam like a halo, formed by progressively smaller halos within, led the way.

"Wait up," Lulu said. She could hardly see in front of her. Marie knew how afraid she was of the dark.

Then Marie switched off the flashlight and everything went black.

"Cut it out," Lulu said. She felt the other girl's hand reaching for hers.

"Come with me, my pretty," Marie said, feigning a sinister voice. Each step creaked as the girls took uncertain steps up. At the top landing, there was the nonna's shadow, cast by the light upstairs filtering through the half-closed door. When the girls reached the kitchen, they were confronted by Marie's grandmother in housecoat and hair disheveled. She had a hand on one hip and held a wooden spoon in the other. Lulu thought the spoon was for the pasta now simmering on the stove, but with the face the woman had, it was possible she planned on giving someone a whack.

"What were you girls doing down there, anyway?" she asked, looking at one then the other. Each shook her head. Lulu wanted to grab her coat and make an exit but couldn't find an excuse. "I've got a good mind to call your mother," the nonna said to her.

"Me?" Lulu questioned, pointing to herself.

"Yeah," the nonna said. "Who said you could give my phone number out to any boys?"

Lulu's aim for the night with Alfie hit the floor. So much for her clairvoyance; she never saw her plans being foiled. On the other hand, the inevitability of her mother grounding her if Marie's grandmother ratted on her was probably the foreboding she felt earlier. Then to Marie, Nonna said, "What do you have to say about that box down there?"

Marie and Lulu looked at each other.

"Is that how you treat your toys? You destroy them?" The grandmother's voice grew louder as she spoke. She was pointing with the wooden spoon. "If you don't want your dolls anymore,

Marie Ann, give them to your cousins or to the church. I swear you act more spoiled every day."

They should have guessed Nonna would come upon the unfamiliar box in her basement. It seemed unlikely to Lulu that the woman would understand how much the girls were ready to grow up, graduate, move out—escape. It was the Age of Aquarius, for Christ's sake. It was possible the old lady didn't remember what it felt like to be treated like a kid by everyone.

Marie had once told Lulu how her grandmother was married off at fourteen in Italy to a much older man, her nonno.

"Wow," Lulu said, uncertain whether she was impressed that a fourteen-year-old could run a household or sorry that she was made to do so.

Now the grandmother was treating the girls, of the same age she'd been as a bride, like they were babies. "Come 'ere, *bambina mia*," the nonna called Marie over to put her arms around the girl. "Don't worry," she said to Lulu, "I'm not telephoning your mother. But don't think I'm letting you go anywhere until Luca gets here to take you girls home."

When Marie had first told Lulu all about her favorite person in the world, her grandmother, it felt to the new best friends like they could have talked throughout the night if they were allowed. "My grandfather wanted to come to Chicago to start a restaurant with his brothers," Marie said. "When they left Italy, my grandmother was pregnant with my mom. A year later, my uncle Luca was born. Then came my uncle Vince. My nonna always says for the first ten years of marriage, all she knew was washing diapers."

Lulu pinched her nose. Marie nodded in agreement. Yeah, life could be a stinky business if they didn't watch out.

Doña Cleanwell Leaves Home

THE DAY AFTER Katia's high school graduation, her father woke her with a round-trip airline ticket to Mexico City. "Bring back your mother," he said. Then he pulled out another ticket, one-way. "Tell her, her children need her." As if to give his eldest the chance to ask something, he hesitated. She didn't. Instead, holding both tickets, she sat up on the couch, arm frozen in midair.

The class of '74 held its commencement on a Thursday night because the rented auditorium wasn't available on a Friday in June, the month when there were graduations being held throughout Chicago. The class of about two hundred sang "The Way We Were," which didn't resonate with many of the teenagers. Most of the seniors had voted to sing "You Ain't Seen Nothing Yet." Then Mr. Foster, the principal, who always had the last word, said he wouldn't allow rock music at the commencement of his school. The students were given no choice but to sing nostalgic lyrics about a past youth while they were all looking toward the future. Nevertheless, when Katia noticed a few girls getting teary-eyed while singing, she felt a lump in her throat.

No one in the family came to Katia's graduation. Her father worked nights. Her kid sister, Lulu, was a sophomore at the same school, and they hardly spoke to each other. The only thing the girl liked to read were magazines like *Glamour*. As for interests and hobbies, it was "I'll take guys in all categories, please." Lulu had practically unraveled the telephone cord from stretching it until the handset was inside their parents' bedroom and she could shut the door to talk privately. With the father gone all night at his work, the mother now absent, she acted like it was her personal hangout.

The two brothers wouldn't go on their own. The boys would have had to take two buses to an unfamiliar part of the city. Once arriving at the auditorium, like most kids, they'd feel awkward among the crowd of strangers. Katia attended alone and, afterward, dropped off the cap and gown backstage and caught public transportation home. After midnight, her dad called on his break to ask how it went. "So, you got your diploma?" he asked.

"Yes," Katia said. No one before in her family had finished high school.

"*Qué bueno*," he said. "That means you can find a good job now, eh?"

"Yes, Dad," she said. Javier, her father, knew she planned to spend the summer working at the gas station.

"You can take your time," he said. "Cashiering is good training. You can use that skill at another job."

She could, she thought, if all she wanted to do was cashier. Her father's break was soon up, and they said good night. After hanging up, she lingered, seated at the telephone gossip bench idly staring at her feet. Katia noticed a tiny hole on the toe of her right sneaker. With the next paycheck, she'd get a new pair. She liked Keds white sneakers. You could do anything in them—walk for miles, dance, dash if you had to catch a bus or, if necessary, run for your life. Not the heel type, she'd wanted to wear the scuffed shoes for commencement, but the teacher in charge announced that without proper attire, no diploma. Katia sneaked a pair of L'eggs pantyhose from her mother's drawer and also borrowed a pair of black pumps. The shoes were tight on her, and although she carried them to and from the graduation ceremony in a bag, wearing sneakers en route, the girl already had a blister when she went onstage, trying not to limp.

In anticipation of the occasion, some of her classmates had gone with their mothers or friends for manicures. Most who polished their nails did it themselves, so going to a salon for an occasion felt akin to ceremonial. Katia didn't wear nail polish, seeing all beauty products as part of the conspiracy of the patriarchy to make women sex objects. She stopped shaving because it was one more form of women's oppression. She once found a paperback in the bathroom at the gas station, and even though it talked to and about white women, Katia, being in the US, nevertheless related to an extent. It was called *The Feminine Mystique*. She read all the time, if not books, magazines—*Ms.* was one—and newspapers, the *Sun-Times* or *Tribune* from cover to cover.

Clothes weren't that important. She wore her favorite bell-bottom jeans every day. Katia decided she wasn't going to be trapped in a job where looks were a consideration for a woman's employment. It was bad enough to know she was seen as a second-class citizen because of her Mexican background. Her complexion wasn't that dark, not like Lulu's or her little brother's, who resembled their dad most. It was Tina, her Spanish-dominant-speaking mother who always told her children, "You speak English. That's all you need here to get ahead." Still, people could tell Katia wasn't white, and whether her mother realized it or not, there were all levels of guardrails keeping people in their place.

One Saturday her father and Katia's brother Eric went out to the supermarket and bought *barbacoa*—steamed lamb—warm tortillas, and all the fixings for tacos. They happily gathered around the table. At one point when she reached over in her sleeveless blouse, Katia's father reprimanded her, "Don't come to the table like that." Her brothers and Lulu broke out laughing, covering their mouths, acting like they weren't making fun of her, although they were. When her mother was around, her father passed on such disapproval to his wife so that she'd speak to the girls privately. Now he just said things outright to his kids without much regard. Whether it was due to respect for his authority or the way her brothers started imitating a monkey scratching his armpits, the embarrassment sent Katia back to shaving.

Soon, however, she'd get to do whatever she truly believed was right. Her aim wouldn't be to "look beautiful" (which seemed to be Lulu's ambition) but to make the *world* better. College students and young people everywhere were marching against the Vietnam War, civil rights, dictatorships in South America, and for women's lib. Katia went to one anti-war demonstration held downtown. It was the only time in her senior year that she missed school.

It was her friend's idea, Jay from English class. He was a slightly built Black kid from way on the South Side who donned a huge Afro like a crown. Principal Foster tried to make him cut it with threats of expulsion. Jay's parents came to school with their lawyer, and that was that. Katia's friend kept his 'fro and became somewhat of a hero around school. A small group from the senior class, led by

Jay, went to the demonstration. Moreover, they informed the principal that was why they weren't in class that day. "We have power in numbers," Jay said when the students were relieved to see the principal didn't suspend anyone.

A long-haired white guy passing out pamphlets about Marxism handed Katia a sign, and she held it high throughout the march. "POWER TO ALL THE PEOPLE," it said. "Gay, Women's Rights, Black Power, American Indian, Students United," various signs read. Katia brought the sign home and taped it to the bedroom wall. Surprisingly, Lulu, who preferred her posters of José José and El Puma, didn't complain.

Katia got ready for sleep on the couch with a new issue of *Time*. There was a short article in the back about the United Farm Workers and César Chávez. Mexicans in California weren't taking exploitation by "The Man" anymore. Perhaps after graduation, she'd get the courage to go there and join them. *La Causa*, they called it.

The morning he gave her the airline tickets, her dad, forty on his last birthday but already with a small-plate-size bald spot in back that gave him the look of a tonsured monk, said over his shoulder while heading to his room for some daytime shut-eye, "The suitcase is in the hall closet."

It was the same blue suitcase they had taken turns lifting and going outside with for a bitter minute on New Year's Eve. It was a silly practice to indicate your wish to take a trip in the coming year. When Katia's mother abruptly left, however, she didn't take the blue bag. She didn't take anything, just herself.

"Don't pack too much in case your mother needs room for her things. I'll drive you to the airport in the morning," Katia's dad instructed. It was how he always addressed his eldest, like she was a subordinate on his drifting crew. Pulling all-nighters at the plant as a machine operator, without regular sleep, and over the last months not having much of an appetite, Katia's dad had come to look like a faded palm frond that might blow away with the slightest wind.

Striations of sunlight came through the venetian blinds, hitting the opposite wall, cluttered with family photographs. As the kids grew up, Katia's mother dragged the family to Sears for formal family portraits, usually after mass on Easter or around Christmas, when everyone dressed up. Every holiday and milestone of the children's lives had been marked with dime-store greeting cards, school citations, and ribbons. Then, last year after Thanksgiving, their mother left without notice, and all such markings of time stopped.

That unforgettable day, Katia's mother didn't come home from the factory where her father worked the graveyard shift. Monday through Friday, he'd get up in the afternoon, wash, and get ready to pick her up at the same plant where a few hours later he'd return to work. On the way back, the pair stopped to do an errand or two, then came home, where the mother prepared dinner. Katia had a part-time job. Lulu, almost sixteen, was in beauty school. After regular school, she commuted to the Loop and took evening classes to get licensed as a cosmetician. Her mother had been enthusiastic about Lulu's goal and apparently had paid for it in advance. The boys, fourteen and twelve, had after-school activities. Consequently, no one ate at the same time. Food was left on the stove, and as they came home, they each made a plate. Their mother often sat at the table to keep them company.

By six o'clock that frosty evening in Chicago, when their father returned without his wife, it was pitch-black out. The day after Thanksgiving was a holiday for public schools, but their parents had to work. Katia was just getting in from her job where she'd put in a full day. She was about to take off her snow-covered boots to set on the pile of other shoes they kept by the door on newspapers when she sensed something was off. Dark kitchen? Odd. Light from the TV on but no volume. Equally odd.

"Where's my ma?" she queried aloud but heard her voice sound more like an utterance. In the living room, the father sat as if strapped to his chair, and Lulu was on the couch. The boys, who spent the day at the local recreation center, weren't home yet.

"Ma took off," Lulu said with the blasé attitude she'd acquired lately. Being in beauty school seemed to have gone to her head. "You act too big for your britches" was what Katia often said to her. Her trend-seeking sister had lightened her long hair again, from an orange shade (meant to be auburn but left a brassy yellow) to a shade going for dark blond. The first time Katia's younger sister dyed her hair, their dad, seething, threatened to make her quit cosmetology. "I don't care what it cost," Katia overheard him say to her mother. As usual, Tina sided with Lulu and reminded him that she'd been the one who paid for the course. Before marriage and children, when such aspirations were possible, Tina said she, too, wanted to work in a hair salon. It was glamorous work, not drudgery like the factory. In an act of defiance against Javier's old-fashioned ways, Tina let her daughter cut her own long hair and dye it. She became a redhead, much to his displeasure, although after that he went silent on the entire subject of beauty school and his baby Lulu who was growing up too fast.

Katia didn't see it that way. It was the era of women's liberation. Her sister wasn't a child but a young woman. Ladies, who before couldn't hold a credit card in their own name, were doing as they pleased, whether it was wild hair changes or *Alice Doesn't Live Here Anymore* or an extreme move like her mother had suddenly made. Katia was left to wonder what revolutionary act she might end up doing to combat the establishment.

The Friday after Thanksgiving, her parents used to work and Katia had to be home watching her younger siblings all day, instead of as a family going downtown to watch the Christmas parade on State Street. Now everyone went their separate ways.

Katia stood in the living room in argyle stocking feet, waiting for one of the two to tell her what "took off" meant. If they had an explanation, neither Lulu nor their father offered it, sitting so quietly and one might even say calmly. Katia suspected they had some idea. Katia's kid sister had an alliance with their mother, and they were confidantes. Just as their mother always covered for her, Lulu wasn't about to tell on her mother. As for the dad . . . the couple were always tight-lipped about their relationship. She never saw them argue, but she also never saw them lovey-dovey.

Perhaps it was just how older people behaved, holding everything in, or maybe it was cultural. Her father, Javier, was raised on a *rancho*, where he worked hard outside and, growing up, learned not to waste time chitchatting, as he called what most thought of as conversation. Now, during his spare time, Katia's father preferred to work on his truck. Sometimes he just sat in the garage, listening to a game on the radio. He watched TV in silence. Except for the usual questions about chores and school, he said little to the kids. Katia suspected her father had grown up believing it was best, at least for men, to keep emotions to themselves, lest they come off as weak.

Now he pulled the lever on the side of the easy chair and leaned back, feet up. The TV was directly in front of him, but Katia could follow his field of vision and see that he stared into space.

She made an about-face to the hall to remove the layers of winter wear, knitted scarf and wool hat and gloves that were shoved into coat pockets and the thick sweater she always wore as an extra layer and left inside the coat. Just as the boys arrived, Katia shuffled back to the living room. As with Katia, the boys, immediately sensing something awry in the home, hurried in and received the news from their father: Mother was missing in action. For some reason, no suspicion of foul play.

Junior became weepy. The older son, without a remark, went in a huff to the room the boys shared, slamming the door behind him. His little brother followed, doing likewise.

Where oh where could their mother have gone? Tina never went anywhere on her own. Her social life consisted of occasional church functions, the rare family treat to Connie's for pizza or Chinatown for egg foo young or chow mein, and visits with extended family. Relatives—Javier's—resided in the nearby town of Aurora, and visiting was done as a group. In any case, she wasn't close to them, and a call verified they knew nothing about her absence. The fact that there was no mention of calling the police made Katia certain that although she didn't know why or where, nor exactly when or how, the leaving was her mother's choice.

The following evening, once they were all home, the father told his children what he'd found out. After making several calls, he was led to reach out to his wife's mother in Mexico City.

Tina was there.

"I'll tell her to call home," the older woman said.

Since then, Katia's mother had telephoned seven times and spoken to each one at home. She kept it all so brief you'd have thought she was being held hostage. She always called collect, but whenever one or another asked why she left, what she was doing in Mexico, or if she was coming back, the woman remarked that the bill was running up and cut it short. "Make sure you keep your grades up," she told the boys. "Try to find work at a beauty shop!" she said to Lulu for when the girl finished beauty school. And to Katia: "Take care of things at home," as if by default, such duties had fallen on the eldest.

Not just Tina but Javier expected her to take on the household. She tried to recruit her siblings to help, but they only blew her off. Their mother had been strict about each having chores. Now, without parents after them, they just didn't do it. The big sister had no authority. When she tried to keep them in line or to express interest in her brothers' homework or to worry over Lulu about everything, "You're not my mom to tell me what to do" became an anthem. Her father never backed her up. She was the oldest, but the boys were going to be men one day, and that trumped her seniority. As for Lulu, no one told her what to do.

Months before, Katia had caught her sister slipping out of their bedroom window. No parents were around at night, but the brothers tended to act like they had sovereignty over the girls, and Lulu feared waking them up. Katia tried to pull her sister back with no luck. Near dawn, when the girl was climbing in through the window before their father got home from work at six a.m., Katia was waiting up for her. A whispered argument ensued until the girls began to wrestle on the bottom bunkbed. Lulu's head hit the wall hard. After that, they stopped speaking to each other. Katia, to avoid further confrontation, started sleeping on the couch and stayed out of her sister's business. It wouldn't surprise her if Lulu sneaked in a boy to stay over.

Now, graduation behind her and life ahead, on that morning when everything still felt in between, her dad pulled down the blinds in his room and, shutting tight the door so as not to be disturbed, he went to bed. Katia bathed and got ready for work. It was three long blocks away on busy Cermak Road. That Friday was to be a full day, from noon until eight. Now, done with school, she planned on working full-time. Cashiering at a gas station might have limited prospects, but she needed the money. Graduating fourth out of over two hundred in her class, Katia was aware she could set her goals higher, but college was out of the question.

Her parents had made it clear there was no point in more schooling. Maybe the boys could apprentice as electricians, the mother suggested once. Mexican kids, Black kids weren't allowed in the union, her father said, so what was the point? Her mother encouraged Katia to take typing and stenography in school. She did, hated them, and her skills were abysmal. She excelled in sports, math, and science, but unlike a few of her classmates, who were like rockets ready to launch into wondrous and exciting times, she couldn't see past the summer except for knowing she had to find an occupation.

On Career Day, numerous people came to the school to talk about their professions. It was set up like a fair in the gymnasium.

When Katia recognized the pretty local news anchor, she went over. The young woman, tall, white, and thinner than she looked on TV, was surrounded by a group of white students. Katia waited until they moved on to get closer. "What do you have to do to get a job like you have?" she got the nerve up to ask.

To Katia's surprise, the anchor didn't reply but turned around and sat at the folding table next to the cameraman from the station. Noticing Katia still waiting for an answer, the young man looked at the anchor and then at Katia. As if her patience were being tried, the young woman put her hands up in the air and, looking at the brown-skinned girl in front of her as if she were delusional, finally said, "You'd have to cut your hair, and anyway, you're not tall enough. Besides that, you have to speak English."

"I speak English," said Katia, who had asked her question in that language.

Again, when the haughty anchor said nothing, the young man looked at one then the other and spoke up as if volunteering to translate. "Oh, I think Sherri means you have to speak it correctly. And you can't have an accent."

Katia turned away, wondering if she had an accent and, if so, what was it? She understood Spanish well enough, but it wasn't her first language. Glancing back, she saw the pair at the table looking at her like a stray dog that needed shooing.

Katia arrived at the gas station with ten minutes to spare before punching the time clock to relieve the cashier who did the earlier shift. Mr. Vinny came in from pumping a customer's gas and was headed toward his messy desk when Katia went up to him. He looked at the girl as if her very presence flustered him. They rarely exchanged words.

"I can't come in tomorrow," she said. Knowing the ill-tempered manager would be put out to have to find a last-minute replacement made her anxious. The macramé strap of her suede bag was across her chest; Katia pulled open the flap and reached for the airline tickets. "My father . . . I . . . I mean . . ." She became tongue-tied, having never told anyone about her mother leaving home.

Mr. Vinny interpreted her travel to be a pleasure trip. "You don't have vacation time here," he said. "You're supposed to be my full-time cashier now."

"I'll only be away for a few days," she said. The return was on Tuesday. Her father had obviously not meant the trip to be any kind of vacation, either. "I can come in and do the evening shift on Tuesday—"

"Who's gonna replace you tomorrow?" her boss demanded. Before she could give an answer, he scoffed, "Never mind. Go." He waved. "Pick up your check next week or whenever you get back. I'll find someone else."

She wasn't being allowed to put in her shift, a day's pay Katia had been counting on. Being fired left her with nothing to say, and she started to leave.

"Wait," he said. "You're a good worker. If you need a job later on . . . My brother just bought a motel near the airport. I'm gonna be leaving to be night manager there. I'll get you in to clean rooms if you want."

She didn't "want" but nodded so as not to antagonize him any further and give El Vinny, as her father liked to refer to him, a reason not to release her final check. "Thank you," she said, and made her way back out to the street. The glass door shut slowly behind her, and an attached string of bells gave soft chimes as she heard Mr. Vinny yell, "Mexicans! Always going back to Mexico!"

What did that *mean?* Katia asked herself. She was born in Chicago. She'd never been to Mexico City, where her mother was from. Her dad was from New Mexico. When he came up from Albuquerque, he and Tina met filling out applications at the factory, where they'd worked ever since.

For some reason, Mr. Vinny's bogus behavior made Katia want to sit on a curb and give up. She pulled out her aviator sunglasses and slipped them on. It was the boys' last day of school, so they'd be let out at lunchtime. They might come home, raid the refrigerator, and watch the White Sox opening game on TV. Feet up on the coffee table and snack crumbs left on the couch, they never heeded her complaints. Or they might both take off to the ballpark without their father's permission. Javier was rarely aware of what went on at home most of the day while he slept.

Katia decided to take a detour on a tree-lined street where people prided themselves on their groomed front yards. It was where their one relative in Chicago lived, her paternal grandaunt. Tía Jimena was busy pruning rosebushes as Katia approached. She didn't push the chain-link gate open to go in but gave a faint wave at the older woman, who was surprised to see her. "Are you off to work now?" Jimena called out. Katia shook her head.

Her dad's aunt was about sixty years of age, wiry but not frail. With shears still in hand, Jimena came up to the fence. Before their mother left, Katia and her kid brother Junior used to like dropping in on the older woman, who lived alone. Jimena served as a grandma figure in lieu of their father's mother, who passed long before they were born. She put them to work making savory sopapillas while telling stories about growing up on a sheep farm in New Mexico. When the pastries cooled a bit, the kids poured honey inside them and ate with eyes closed as if in prayer. Since their dad didn't talk much, Jimena's reminiscences filled in some of the blanks about how his life was growing up in the Southwest. Family in Aurora said Jimena was widowed young when her husband was killed in the war. She had no children.

Katia began to explain to Jimena what was going on, how she was going to Mexico to fetch her mom. She felt nervous and took a deep breath. The urge to cry returned. It was PMS, she told herself, and did her best to stay composed. Acting natural with her father's family was important, or it might give them more reason to talk. It was hurtful how they went on about how her mother had abandoned her family.

"Well, why doesn't your father go to Mexico himself?" Jimena asked. "After all, it's his wife!" She shook her head of short graying hair and wiped her brow. The June day was humid.

Katia shrugged. Jimena had a point. Knowing her father, who never missed work, fear of losing his job was probably enough reason. It also occurred to her that he was worried his wife would reject him.

She showed her grandaunt the airline tickets. Jimena refused to handle them, as if they were official documents. She'd never seen airline tickets before; no one in their family had ever taken a plane. "I'm sure it'll be fine," she said. She didn't sound sure. "Did your father give you any money?"

He hadn't. He might before she left, Katia hoped. But if he didn't, she had some.

Jimena pulled out a change purse from her apron pocket and clicked it open. Taking out a five-dollar bill and then a crumpled ten-dollar bill, she started to hand them to her grandniece. She reached inside the front of her blouse and pulled out a neatly folded twenty and gave her that, too. Katia, thinking about Jimena's rent, refused.

"Don't get yourself lost trying to catch a bus there," Jimena said, insisting. "Take a taxi. Just go do what you have to do and come right home." She made a hasty sign of the cross in Katia's direction as if believing a blessing, too, was an obligation to a girl whose mother hadn't cared enough to finish raising her children.

"You had a good graduation?" Jimena asked about the night before. Except to visit family and walk to the grocery store, Katia's grandaunt didn't like to go anywhere. Jimena had relocated to Chicago to be nearer to her relatives who'd moved up north for work but hadn't much use for city life. She went back to her gardening.

Katia nodded and stuck the bills in her wallet. She composed herself and headed toward the main street. There was a pay phone outside a convenience store. She took out a dime and, after inserting the coin in the slot and getting the dial tone, dialed one of the few numbers she knew by heart.

Santiago was definitely not her boyfriend. She had taken a survey in one of Lulu's *Cosmopolitan* issues: "How to Know If the Right Man Is Wrong for You." Santiago fell somewhere in the middle, rating neither wrong nor exactly right for her. Just as she'd thought. The young man, out of high school two years and always worried about the draft, worked at his uncle's auto repair shop.

You could say he was her best friend. But marriage material? And who was thinking of ever getting married, anyway?

Although she had to let the phone ring incessantly, someone eventually picked up, and it was Santiago.

"My father's making me go to Mexico," she said. She had much to explain to her friend, since she'd never discussed what was going on at home, but summarized it by simply saying, "My mother's in Mexico." The truth was, at the moment, what troubled her most was traveling by herself, flying for the first time, making her way around a strange city in a foreign country, and then, the worst part, facing her mother. How she would convince Tina to come home was beyond her.

"What?" Santiago asked, understandably disturbed by the news. "You're going back to Mexico?"

"I'm not from Mexico," she said, already frustrated by his tendency to jump to conclusions, always trying to be helpful. Over a year before, it was Santiago who'd told her about the cashier job at the gas station when she'd said she needed to earn her own money. (Her parents didn't believe in allowance.) Her mother had gotten upset when Katia brought up various fees for senior activities at school and when she started pleading about the new coat she wanted for the forthcoming winter. "If yours doesn't fit anymore, wear my old one," said Tina, who was slightly larger than her daughter. She'd never have said that to Lulu. The moment Katia's sister mentioned wanting anything, their mother would say, "Wait until Friday, when I get paid."

Santiago fell silent when he heard for the first time that Katia's mother was gone. He didn't know anyone who got divorced, much less deserted their family. "Man, Katia..." was all he said. Early in their friendship, she'd had the erroneous idea that Santiago had the ability to fix anything, just like he did with cars. Soon she realized his efforts to make things okay were a kid aiming to please a girl he liked. No one could make everything better, especially not her life.

In the background, repair-shop racket drowned out their conversation, and then his boss-uncle shouted, "Get off that phone!" The young man, whose hands were always black in the creases from engine oil, promised to call her when he got off work, and Katia started making her way again without any hurry.

Her father would probably freak out on her for getting fired. He'd accuse his daughter of not having put it to El Vinny how it was a family emergency. In a way, her dad treated her with the same impatience she'd always thought he had with his wife. He didn't criticize Tina for anything she did at her job, since they weren't in the same department; they didn't even work the same shift. He rarely interfered with how she took care of the children. It was little stuff. He complained about how much salt his wife put in the food or if she didn't leave the tub scrubbed to his liking. His criticisms that he saw as his right to give were like the sound of the constant faucet drip from the kitchen sink that kept Katia up at night.

Now his wife had left him. Katia didn't do anything she thought would bum out her father. She felt sorry for him that he'd been left by his wife to take care of the home and family alone, and she didn't want to add to his ire. Nevertheless, he occasionally found things to nag his daughter about, too. Had she forgotten she was supposed to take Junior to his dentist appointment? Was it too much to ask her to iron his shirt collars properly? She had begun to contemplate moving out. It would get heavy with her father, but he couldn't stop her.

How could she go anywhere now without a job?

When Katia reached their rented bungalow, the place was quiet with no one around, except for her father snoring loudly in his room. After making a pitcher of grape Kool-Aid—the boys' favorite—and putting it in the fridge for whenever they got home, she went to the hall closet to get down the blue vinyl suitcase stored on the top shelf. It was weighty, and Katia was surprised to find her mother had carefully stored inside it the nativity scene and manger she usually set out under the tree.

Last Christmas, her father hadn't brought out any of the decorations. It was as if, with Tina gone, the family was in mourning. Every house on the block had lights outside except theirs. On Christmas Day, along with Tía Jimena, they went to his sister's home in Aurora. Katia's aunt had just left their centuries-long faith to become Pentecostal. No celebrations for the Baby Jesus there.

Katia put away the manger and nativity figurines and took the bag to the bedroom. As her father had recommended and because it would be a short trip, she packed only the most pertinent items, Noxzema, toothbrush, underwear, a pair of jeans, and a few other items. She'd wear sneakers for the journey.

The next morning after Javier had his coffee, he drove her to Midway. It was a small airport, but he asked if she wanted him to wait with her. He was half asleep and seemed relieved when she declined. Katia was looking for her gate when a white woman came out of nowhere and whispered, "You'd better find the ladies' room, honey. It looks like you've had an accident." She pronounced it "aksy-dent." A combination of the stranger's powdered face so near her own and the realization that her period was gushing down left Katia so mortified she only stared back. "You speak English, hon?" the woman said, and then practically shouted, "I THINK YOU'RE BLEEDING," as if the assumption that the girl didn't understand English also equated deafness.

Without answering or looking around to see who'd heard to add to her shame, Katia dashed to find the restroom. Once there, she turned her khaki skirt around and saw a splotch of fresh blood, brown against the fabric. Had Katia left blood on the passenger seat of her father's car? If so, he'd be mad as hell. She prayed he wouldn't bring it up and embarrass her.

She was trying to scrub out the stain with soap by the wash-basin when the cleaning lady, taking a cigarette break, her huge cart left in the corridor, said, "There's a Kotex machine." Rolling her eyes as if the girl were the worst mess she'd seen all morning, the woman pulled a quarter from her uniform pocket and handed it to the girl.

As she made her way to the gate, miniskirt on backward, holding the macramé strap so her bag would cover the damp spot, Katia felt the gut-wrenching start of menstrual cramps. Around stewardesses, nothing short of classy in starched uniforms with perfect makeup and sparkly jewelry assisting mostly white passengers dressed like they were going to church or a business meeting, Katia took her seat by a window, wishing she were invisible. Sick, terrified about flying, and sensing she looked like a wrung-out mop, she put her head back and closed her eyes.

Being above the clouds was surrealistic, a Dalí painting, everything below instantly becoming tiny. Right after takeoff, Katia felt her extremities grow cold. The stewardesses moved up and down the aisle serving drinks and fresh coffee and then lunch, which consisted of miniature chicken enchiladas and clumpy orange rice, a festive meal in honor of their destination. No sooner was the tray picked up than Katia felt like heaving and grabbed the vomit bag from the seat back pocket in front of her, holding it over her mouth just in time. The white man next to her in a sport coat shifted away to lean toward the aisle. Katia's cramps were bad enough, but the airsickness in front of the other passengers was mortifying. The way the stewardess took the vomit bag, barely hiding her disgust, didn't help.

Katia wasn't the wailing baby across the aisle, bounced by a young red-haired mother, the stewardesses saying, "Aww," every time they passed, but she felt as miserable as the baby. Maybe eighteen-year-olds on a mission to retrieve delinquent mothers deserved no pity. But it also seemed that girls who looked like newly arrived immigrants from developing countries, surviving by the skin of their teeth in the great land of opportunity, didn't merit compassion.

Despite getting sick midflight, Katia decided flying was pretty cool. There were no words to describe seeing cars below like lines of ants, tops of high-rises, and then going through the clouds. She couldn't wait to tell them back home, especially Eric, who'd gotten mad because their father hadn't sent him, too. "Man, I never get to do nothing," he complained. She'd rub it in his face. Lulu also asked, and their father said, "You? Knowing you, young lady, you probably would stay in Mexico with your mamá!" No one said anything, because that sounded about right. As for Junior, Katia would have enjoyed her kid brother tagging along. When they were away from the others, they had fun. The previous summer, they spent nearly every day riding all over the city on their bikes.

The hippest part of the whole trip was when the plane landed in the sprawling capital, el *monstruoso* Distrito Federal. Back on earth, she instinctively made a sign of the cross and followed everybody off, then to retrieve the suitcase and go through the customs process. When she asked for directions, someone pointed to money exchange, another to pay phones and how much a call cost, twenty. "Twenty pesos?" she asked. "No," the man said like she was dimwitted, "twenty centavos."

At the line of pay phones, as soon as someone hung up, the girl snatched the receiver, still warm to the touch, and carefully pulled out the paper with her grandmother's home telephone number. On the way to the airport, her father had handed it to her. "Make sure you let your abuela know as soon as you arrive," he said, and added that he'd already informed his mother-in-law that his eldest daughter was on her way.

"Did you speak with my mother, too?" Katia asked. She wished beyond any actual expectation that her father had somehow eased the task ahead of her. He shook his head.

Her grandmother answered on the third ring. "*¿Bueno?*" she said in the brusque tone Katia identified with her mother's mother. Brusque or impatient, not necessarily unkind, but you wouldn't want to depend your life on her. It was the impression Katia had always gotten from her mother about the abuela whom she hadn't seen since Lulu was born; Katia herself was only around two, so she didn't remember the visit from the grandmother who'd journeyed by bus and train all the way to Chicago to see her newly born granddaughter. The abuela stayed through the holidays, but with the first blasts of cold in El Norte, she headed back to Mexico.

"It's me, Katia," she announced. She was soft-spoken, and with all the hullabaloo at the airport, she had to repeat herself several times during the brief call, and each time her grandmother seemed to grow further irritated. "I can't hear you," the woman kept saying.

Finally, the abuela instructed, "Find a taxi and come here. You have my address, right? If your mother comes around or calls, I'll let her know you're on your way."

Katia felt confused. How was it that Tina wasn't expecting her?

Katia went out where a swarm of people were going every which way, vehicles pulled up at the curb and others double-parked. A long line of cabs caught her eye, drivers hanging around, smoking cigarettes, chatting among themselves, leaning against their cars and reading newspapers. Lugging the suitcase, shoulder bag pulled in front of her to cover the dried stain on her skirt, and breath surely smelling of throw-up, she tentatively approached a reserved man with the bearing of a grandfather. He looked at the address she held up and nodded. "It's not the best *colonia*," he said. "I know the street. I'll take you, señorita, but you have to be very careful there. You're unescorted."

He put his folded newspaper under his arm, grabbed her bag, and threw it in the trunk.

They began the slow bumper-to-bumper trek through relentless traffic, sometimes with go-cart-style maneuvering and at other times speeding. The broken springs in the backseat hurt her behind with each pothole dip and bump, until they reached the area where her grandmother resided and the driver slowed down.

Throughout the ride, the scratchy radio was on full blast, combined with the traffic and street noise, all of which Katia might have endured without being overcome were it not for the man constantly eyeing her through the rearview mirror as if she were in some noir story. She tried to ignore his gaze by looking out the window, and then he began to ask questions. At first they sounded as if they were coming from idle curiosity during the long ride. "Do you know the Basilica of Our Lady of Guadalupe isn't far from where you're staying? Are you a believer? Of course you are, all Mexicans are . . ."

She wanted to say she didn't think she believed in the Virgin Mary (a *virgin* birth?) but thought it prudent not to argue with a stranger and gave a simple "*Sí.*" Maybe her father was right, she read too much for her own good. "One day you're gonna go blind," he often said whenever he caught her with nose dug in a book.

The interrogation continued. Who was she visiting? Was she married? Did she have a boyfriend? And finally, just before dropping her off at her grandmother's, he muttered something over his shoulder about wanting to take her out for coffee. No, no, she declined, heart starting to pound. What if he drove off with her? *What a way for the life of Katia to end*, she thought, *so young to die in a city far away from home at the hands of an old lecher.*

"My grandmother will worry. She's expecting me for lunch." Even to Katia, her excuse of such a proper and attentive abuela sounded improbable, but to her relief, the man stopped eyeing her through the rearview mirror and scarcely mumbled a few words when he dropped her off, collected his fee, and left her bag at the curb.

She saw the number of the house was right, but when she pushed in one of the pair of humongous antiquated doors and stepped over the slat, she was dismayed to find herself in an expansive concrete courtyard with apartments all around and up three floors, doors facing out. People everywhere visiting with each other, hanging clothes on lines strung from one building to another, washing laundry in public sinks, children scurrying and shrieking, aimless dogs, lazy cats, dozens of mucky pigeons, varied music coming from radios all about, and nowhere a sign of her grandmother.

Katia asked a woman giving a toddler a bath in the sink and then the next person who looked her way and finally put the suitcase down and stood there until someone came up to see what she was doing there. The woman pointed up, and after climbing two flights of stairs, Katia found the right door. It was open, and as soon as she peeked into a dark room, she saw the abuela seated by a small rustic table in a room where the only light came from the open door. The old woman held a cup, and with her free hand, she waved Katia inside. "Close the door," she said. "I don't want nosy neighbors sticking their heads in to check out who's come to see me."

The place consisted of two rooms, no closets, pantries, or bathroom. In the room where her grandmother sat, she saw a hot plate and dishes but no sink. "Toilets are downstairs," she was informed, "they're shared by everyone. Make sure you take the roll of paper with you." Katia indeed needed the facilities badly.

She had brought a couple of sanitary napkins in case her period came down that weekend and got one out of the suitcase. She wanted to brush her teeth, too, but her father had warned her not to drink tap water. "It'll make you sick as a dog," he had said. She was thirsty and asked her grandmother if she might purchase water somewhere, as her father had recommended.

"Serve yourself," the abuela said, indicating a large clay jug on the makeshift counter. "A few people around here with children and babies keep water dispensers. I've arranged with them to sell me some in that jug. Don't worry. It's good."

A clay cup covered the jug's spout. Katia got out her toothbrush. She didn't have toothpaste because she'd assumed her mother would have a tube in her bathroom. Katia didn't want to use up too much of her grandmother's good water and poured enough to brush her teeth over a white enamel pan on the counter.

Idly humming to herself, the old woman stared into space as the girl tidied up. Katia still needed the restroom, but her reluctance to see what it was like made her sit down. "Your mother never calls," the abuela said, "she just comes by . . . when she feels like it . . . she's always been like that. I sent word. Let's see if she shows up."

It turned out the phone number Katia had was not her grandmother's line. Anticipating the granddaughter's call earlier, the abuela had been waiting in the neighbor's rooms. The lady who was on the floor below charged people for its use. "Another family with a television set lets children watch a cartoon show for a whole peso each in the afternoons," the grandmother said, as another example of the enterprising practices in the neighborhood.

Where was Katia's mother? For some reason, the girl felt uneasy coming right out and asking. It may have been because, for whatever reason, the abuela also wasn't saying.

"You know she ran off with someone she met at work," Tía Elida had whispered to another relative in the kitchen last Christmas Day when they were all together in the aunt's home in Aurora. Katia knew they were talking about her mother. It was the first hint of the lowdown as to why her mother had left. "My poor brother," Elida said. "He never had any luck with the girls. The idiot still loves Tina." The women in the kitchen started chuckling under their breath. Until then, they'd forgotten that Katia was sitting in a corner reading. When she looked up, they went quiet.

That winter afternoon, when it was already dark out by four, Katia had returned to the small living room where her father, brothers, uncle, and cousins were watching a soccer game from Mexico on the Spanish-language channel. There weren't enough chairs, and the boys sat on the floor. Lulu put her coat on, and when a car honked outside, she announced she was leaving. Elida came from the kitchen to reprimand Katia's father. "Since when does a fifteen-year-old go out without asking permission?" When Javier didn't respond, she added, "That girl's gonna take off on you, too, Javier."

A few minutes later, Javier gathered up the children, hastily getting on coats and hats, packed up any leftovers Elida wrapped up, and they went back home. He didn't speak the whole way, and the kids, feeling they may have done something wrong, were sullen, too. Katia had never been so glad to have the holidays over and be back in school. She looked forward to freedom in a few months.

Now in her grandmother's home in Mexico City, she began to

wonder what freedom would actually mean. What exactly defined freedom for an independent young woman of the seventies or any single woman?

The abuela lived alone. She'd had one child and, as far as Katia knew, had never been married. Did freedom mean you had to be lonely? And if you were lonely, were you "free"? Was it for the sake of freedom that her mother had practically washed her hands of her family in Chicago? At school, when Katia talked with friends in the girls' locker room or at the lunch table in the cafeteria, they all assumed that turning eighteen and finishing high school amounted to an independence that would allow them unprecedented joy and satisfaction. Whether the plan was to marry right away, move out with a roommate, start college, or join the army, they'd have their own money and not be answerable to parents or teachers.

No one cared if the apartment with the roommate might be roach infested. It was their place to decorate with psychedelic posters and drink gallons of wine and smoke pot with boyfriends who could come and stay over whenever they wished. If marriage was in the picture, they'd look forward to babies and, of course, live happily ever after. The army sounded like an adventure with benefits when you got out, and for the lucky few who made it to college, they would get to have lives as nice as whites—in the suburbs. No matter what you did after high school, freedom was so spectacular that you'd be thrilled every minute because you were answerable only to yourself.

But two days after graduation and a month since her eighteenth birthday, Katia already knew something she didn't see before about freedom. Even if it was as splendid as she had dreamed, it was ridden with pitfalls, a yellow brick road where "lions and tigers and bears" to watch out for were real, if metaphorical and not totally imagined like in the *Wizard of Oz* movie they watched on Thanksgivings at home.

One pitfall that came with her abuela's freedom was that, with her decrepit body, she obviously couldn't easily get to the toilets downstairs. It explained the basin Katia spotted on the floor by the bed in the next room. Outhouses were located in the court-yard just across from the public sinks. At last going down her-self, she found the three toilets dark and reeking like backed-up sewers. Katia needed to urinate and she changed the sanitary pad, but after the experience, she vowed she'd not go there again. The wooden floor was rotted and grimy, and when she went to the sinks to rinse off the soles of her shoes, she felt the eyes in the courtyard watching her. Katia waited for a woman to finish scrub-bing clothes before taking her turn to rinse her hands. A couple of kids using the other sink began shrieking at a fish that'd come through the faucet and was splashing around the basin.

Katia hurried back to her abuela's dimly lit rooms and found the old woman sitting in the same spot, smoking a hand-rolled cigarette. Her grandmother was using an empty food can as an ashtray. Katia had never seen a hand-rolled cigarette and at first, mistaking it for a joint, was taken aback. She took the other chair in the room while her abuela finished the smoke. It crossed the girl's mind that maybe her grandmother had trouble walking, since she had yet to stand.

There was no refrigerator, nothing but the hot plate. It was obvious Abuela wasn't going to offer a meal to her newly arrived granddaughter. As if reading her thoughts, the old woman said, "I used to have an icebox, but a few years ago, the iceman stopped coming." Katia nodded politely, although she didn't know what the woman was talking about. A man who delivered *ice*?

"Just like the tortilla man," Abuela continued. "All my life, someone came by every day to deliver fresh tortillas. I was never that good at making my own. Even in this place, with so many people all over, a man came into the courtyard with his cart of warm tortillas. Women ran out to get them for the meal. One day he stopped coming. Times are changing. My neighbor brings me a dozen from the tortilla factory nearby. Sometimes fresh eggs, too. Now and then they pick up sweet bread for my coffee, nice and warm. My favorite are the sweet-potato turnovers."

Katia smiled. She liked the *empanadas de calabaza*, too. Her mother and Lulu preferred *conchas*, and the guys ate any and all sweet bread whenever her parents brought some home from the Mexican bakery.

"When I was a little girl," her abuela said, "we lived on a ranch. We had all kinds of animals—chickens, goats . . . My mother used to have a big garden. She could grow anything. We didn't have shoes, but we had plenty to eat." What Katia's grandmother was describing sounded like an ideal childhood. Katia imagined kids running gleefully through cornfields, sunlight creating shadows along the tall stalks.

"Then one year my father decided we were all going up north to work in the fields. We picked cotton. It was very hard work. You can't imagine it. Gringos must be slave drivers by nature. I was fourteen. It didn't go well for me. I had your mother here in the capital. We lost our ranch, so we had to live here." As chroniclers went, the abuela made no effort to embellish. Nevertheless, her granddaughter took and saved each word, like in a game of marbles, to play at a later tournament, the tournament of being out in the world, and when someone asked, "Who are your people?," she would have something to shoot back. Katia wanted to know so much more now that the abuela had opened up, but the woman pushed the can aside and stood up. Gabbing over. She was surprisingly agile despite looking like a turtle on two hind legs, thick flesh-colored stockings rolled down to grossly swollen ankles, gritty cloth slippers on her wide feet.

A small round clock on a shelf with a loud ticktock showed it was three o'clock. The abuela stared at it and then said without looking at Katia, "I'm going to sit outside to wait for your mother."

There was a crude bench outside the door, not big enough for both. Before arriving at her grandmother's, Katia had wanted to wash out her soiled skirt and bloodstained panties, but now she figured she'd just get out something clean. She asked to use the back room for privacy. The abuela waved a hand as she made her way out the door.

The small bedroom was crammed with a bed and its iron headboard against one wall, an armoire, nightstand, boxes, clothes hanging on a wire that went from one wall to another, and no window. Lit votive candles cast a dim light that barely let her see. There was no space anywhere for a second person to live. Where did her mother sleep? Obviously not there. Katia couldn't fathom it.

After changing, she set the suitcase back in the kitchen. It still wasn't clear whether she'd be staying, since her abuela hadn't offered.

"What's this?" Katia's grandmother said when the girl stepped outside and handed her an elegant red and black box of Maja soaps. She felt her face grow warm. There wasn't even running water in her grandmother's home, and she was gifting her a box of perfumed soaps. "It's for you, Abuela," she said. The night before, just before he left for work, her father came out of the bedroom and gave Katia the box. "Is this for my mother?" she asked. In fact, the soaps were her mother's. One Mother's Day, the kids bought the present at the neighborhood pharmacy. It remained unopened.

"Give it to your grandmother," her father said. Next he pulled out fifty dollars in ten-dollar bills. Katia's eyes widened. Her father had never handed her so much cash. "This is for any expenses that come up for you and your mother. Offer to buy your grandmother some food. Maybe you can go to the market and get a chicken to make while you're there."

Now, finding her grandmother not just living in squalor but hardly able to get around, Katia assumed her father had little idea of what was going on in Mexico City. Even if Katia did offer to go to the market, where would they cook?

Lunch on the plane came on a small tray with silverware and a dainty cup in case she wanted coffee or tea. It felt like a pretend meal served in a futuristic fantasy, "Katia Goes to Mars (Really Mexico City)." Hunger pangs were winning over cramps. Although she had no idea where the nearest place to pick up ready-made food might be, she heard herself offering: "I could get us something to eat." From the taxi, she'd seen open-air places with rotisserie chicken and spit-grilled pork tacos.

"Don't bother," her grandmother said. "They'll be bringing me food later." She didn't clarify whom she meant by "they," but Katia had already concluded that her grandmother wasn't of the mind to give accounts. *That, too, must be a benefit of leading a free existence,*

Katia thought. Even though, at the moment, she felt like the source of her grandmother's irritability, she admired the lady's stalwartness.

As if it just occurred to her that Katia might be hungry after her journey, the abuela said, "There's some fruit on a shelf in there. Help yourself."

Katia nodded but went inside primarily to get away from the endless clamor of the *vecindad*. On the shelf, she found a spotted banana, two bruised red apples, a squashy avocado, and something she wasn't sure about but was probably a shriveled mango. She picked up an apple but, after detecting a suspicious wormhole, put it back.

Retrieving a steno pad and a pen from her bag, she also took out a paperback. Katia always carried a book to read whenever she had time, like between customers at the gas station or on the bus. She'd brought along a new one, *Looking for Mr. Goodbar*, but was so miserable on the flight she didn't even take it out.

Katia dragged a three-legged stool, which her abuela had kept her feet on while at the table, over by the doorway, where she could sit with some light. She was wiping off a smudge on her polished white canvas shoes when she spotted a trap by the baseboard with a dead rodent. Its bulging eyes seemed to stare at her and she just about freaked. Katia jumped up, praying she wouldn't end up having to sleep on the floor. The girl was still trying to make up her mind whether to read or write at the table—there was a bare bulb hanging over it from a wire that she figured worked—when she heard the abuela talking to someone. Immediately recognizing the other woman's voice, Katia stuck her head out.

They locked eyes. *What a trip to see Tina again, like out of nowhere,* the girl thought. Her mother stepped forward to kiss her on the cheek and right away started babbling. "How was your flight? How are your brothers? How's your father? Lulu?" Her mother was acting so light and airy, you'd have thought they were two girl-friends who'd run into each other at the mall. But Katia scarcely had a chance to respond when her mother made a motion to head out. "Okay, so . . . ready?"

Ready for what? Katia thought.

Then Tina, starting to sound like the mother she remembered—in other words, bossy—ordered, "Get your things." Without asking why, the girl did. When she came out, about to say goodbye to her grandmother, who was still sitting but now holding a paper bag with oranges that Tina had brought, Katia remembered the money for the chicken. Reaching into her purse, she took out ten dollars. It would probably buy the old woman a week's groceries.

"What's this?" her grandmother asked, holding the bill between two fingers as if she might blow her nose on it.

"For the love of God, Katia," Tina said, "don't you have pesos?"

Pulling out her wallet, the girl started fussing with the weird Mexican money, and then an impatient Tina stuck a hand in, counted out a few paper bills, and gave them to the abuela. The grandmother nodded and shoved the currency inside her vest pocket.

"It's so they can bring you food later," Katia told her grand-mother. The "they" were obviously whoever came by.

Tina bade a brief goodbye, promising to return soon and insisting on carrying the suitcase, and commenced ordering Katia to keep up. "*Andale, mija,*" she kept repeating as her daughter followed her down the stairs, through the courtyard, and out the immense door of the *vecindad*. There was a ride waiting.

Katia, moving as fast as she could, had already assessed distinct changes in her mother. It seemed Tina had put on weight. Also, she was now wearing makeup. Black roots from the auburn color treatment had left an unkempt appearance, but Katia's mother was also now donning a shag à la Farrah Fawcett. Also—and this, too, was new—she had on a pair of white capris. Katia had never seen her mother in pants, even in winter.

Another variance in her mother was blowing her way. Although Katia suspected it was out of uneasiness, her mother never stopped yakking and grinning like everything was all hunky-dory, like one fine day she hadn't gone to work and never come home. Although Lulu and Tina identified with each other in many ways, the fact was their mother's personality had always been more aligned with Katia's, withdrawn, even sullen. Obviously, grown-ups had no obligation to explain anything to kids, but seeing her mother transformed into another woman caused chills to run over Katia's body. Instead of feeling comfort to be reunited with her mother, she was shocked by the stranger who'd shown up.

The ride waiting was a beat-up Buick double-parked and with a woman behind the wheel pressing down on the horn, cussing back at irate drivers having to go around. After Tina and Katia scrambled in, the latter in the backseat, and quick introductions were made, they sped off. "We only live a short way," Tina said with a carefree air, as if they were in a sports car on a drive to Acapulco. She got a tube of pink lipstick out of her clutch bag and dabbed it on her lips.

The streets exploded with people everywhere; on the block where they parked was no different. The women led the way through a laminated gate, past a side walkway, to an old coach house. "Here we are," said the other woman, whose name was Valentina. "I always went by Tina until I met your mother," she explained at the outset to Katia. "Well, we kept getting everyone confused, back in Chicago at the plant. Someone would say, '*Oye*, Tina,' and both of us would turn around. I finally started telling people to call me Vale. *Vale*. Get it? The Spanish say it all the time to mean 'okay.' But *vale* for us Mexicans still means it's worth something." Then Valentina, who had chosen to let the world know she had value, laughed. Tina laughed, too.

They went inside the small, cramped house, where it was brightly painted but the walls were stained and, near the ceiling, watermarked.

"You're staying on the sofa," Vale announced. Everything she said sounded like a proclamation. Katia almost saluted just to kid but thought better of it. Tina gave her daughter an apologetic look and touched her shoulder. "We only have one bedroom . . ."

Vale put the suitcase down. For the first time, her face became serious. Katia noticed how she looked at Tina as if expecting her to say more, and when she didn't, Vale left the room. She was a compact woman, but her bulk enhanced a bristly disposition. Vale wore men's work boots, and Katia had no doubt that if someone made her mad enough, she might stomp them to a pulp.

The girl stood in the living room, pretending to study an enlarged framed photograph on the wall. It was of the two women seated at a table, her mother in a party dress and Vale in a starched shirt, arm around her mother's shoulder. There was a tablecloth, and Vale had her free hand on a beer. It looked like they were at a wedding reception or some sort of occasion, and they seemed happy. The realization that her mother had run away from home to make her life over with a woman she'd met—and apparently fallen in love with—sank in slowly. When it did, Katia fought an urge to feel rage and indignation on behalf of her siblings and father. But the fact was, instead of feeling betrayed, she felt assailed by a day of too many firsts.

What Katia felt above all else at that moment was a sensation she'd carried about her mother for as long as she remembered. It didn't take Tina leaving home for Katia to feel her mother missing in her life. Even as a child, she'd longed for her mother's embrace, a smile, a word of encouragement or a pat on the hand or shoulder when she needed it.

It would be easy to say since Tina came from an unloved background herself, she didn't know how to express affection. But among her kids she had her favorites.

And now, this. This was what? Tina had found within herself the ability to love Vale or at least to coo with and caress her the way no one had ever seen Tina do with Javier. Surprise at her mother's courageous or crazy ability to commence a new life and toss the previous one like an old *chancla* conflicted with Katia's genuine wish for her mother's personal fulfillment and her sense of abandonment. Staring at the picture, the girl folded her thin arms tight and thought her knees might buckle.

"Are you hungry?" Tina, oblivious to any signals her daughter's body language might reveal, called out. Heading toward what appeared to be a tiny kitchen, she began whistling along with the radio she clicked on. It was Los Ángeles Negros.

Katia was hungry, but also the stomach cramps were worsening, and she let herself flop down on the narrow sofa that felt like a board. She wasn't about to get much sleep there.

Vale was back, saying, "I need to take a siesta. Let's rest awhile." Tina stepped out of the kitchen. "We'll get some tacos later," she said to Katia. "We've got a good place to take you. The best *tacos al pastor*." She bunched up her fingers and kissed them.

Katia felt too miserable to eat. The first day of her menses was the worst. She forced herself up to go to the kitchen, where her mother was putting dishes away, to ask for a sanitary pad. Tina led her to the bathroom and pointed to a box on the floor near the toilet.

When Katia came out, her mother said, "Lie down. We'll go eat as soon as Vale is up."

Back on the sofa, the girl balled up with hands on her stomach. When Tina came over, she said, "I don't know why you get like that. Your sister and I got our periods at the same time every month, exactly twenty-eight days. We have it three days, and then it's over. But you ... you've always had so many problems." It sounded like an accusation.

"I don't know what you're trying to get at, Ma," Katia said, so irritable she wanted to scream. She couldn't sit up; she was in too much anguish. "I don't get cramps because I'm doing anything bad." She kept her eyes shut. It wasn't the first time her mother had insinuated that the cause for such problems was from sleeping around and maybe even having contracted something. If not, something worse, like a secret abortion, which had just become legal in her home state, but it was a subject women and girls only whispered about.

Katia, otherwise healthy, didn't know why her periods were irregular or so difficult. The family doctor had said something about her ovaries or fallopian tubes, which her mother and she didn't understand and he didn't explain. They simply took his word when he said, "It's nothing serious."

"Make her a cup of tea!" Vale shouted from behind the closed door.

"I've got some pills," Tina said. Back home, there was one product meant for women's menstrual discomfort, and it never helped Katia. Perhaps her mother had discovered something else in Mexico.

The bedroom door swung open. Vale was in a man's T-shirt and boxers. "I'm telling you to make her some yerba buena tea. I know what it feels like. Pills won't help."

The tension between the women was palpable. Not wanting to get in the middle and feeling no better to be the cause of it, Katia mumbled, "I'll try anything . . . Thank you." She leaned over, laying her head on a hard cushion, and did her best to get into a fetal position and pretend to sleep.

Katia couldn't recall the last time her mother had hugged her—not the kind of phony hug in front of the abuela earlier, but a loving one. A few years ago, the father off at work, the girls would get into bed with their mother. Their father kept the graveyard shift because it paid more money. Lulu did it first, crept into her parents' room to sleep with their mom. Occasionally, Katia, not liking the feeling of being left out, joined them. Sometimes the mother sent them back, complaining that she needed her sleep for work the next day. The parents had a portable TV in their room, and one Friday night after *Johnny Carson*, the three lay awake in the dark. Their mother, in the middle, put an arm around each girl.

"What was your dad like, Mami?" Lulu asked. Whenever she talked to her parents, she'd do it in a baby voice. Katia was curious about their grandfather, too. She always assumed her grandmother was widowed.

"I never knew my father," Tina said after a pause, as if considering how to answer her daughter. "All my mother ever said was she was working up north, and the foreman took advantage of her."

A man raping a girl, Katia thought, was not a grandfather.

The next morning, Tina, Vale, and Katia were all in a better mood. The evening before, the girl still unwell and tired, they'd enjoyed an order of assorted tacos and bottled Coca-Colas that Vale had gone out and brought back. They watched a bit of TV, a silly variety program replete with merengue pies in the face and off-color jokes that made Vale slap her thigh like it was a hoot and a half.

Katia had yet to bring up the purpose of her trip. Her father might have told the abuela, who most likely would have informed Tina, or she herself might have figured it out. What else would Katia be doing in Mexico?

However, she'd discovered her mother had fallen in love. In fairy tales this meant your life was magically transformed. In the "Story of Celestina," at thirty-eight years old, once a wife and mother of four in Chicago, dedicated to her assembly-line job and devoted to her household, she was now another lady. In her daughter's eyes, the new Tina lived in La Capital—a metropolis teeming with Mexicans day and night. She lived with a girlfriend, drank beer, wore pants, and didn't stifle a laugh by covering her mouth. The Mexico City Tina, like the Chicago mother, however, still worked hard to make a living. Now it was by selling wholesale merchandise.

Cardboard boxes labeled "Donna Clean Well Supplies" were piled up to the low ceiling, against a wall in the living room. "It's our own business," Vale announced almost as soon as they walked in the house. "The company is from England. They make excellent products."

On the products, there was an illustration of an Anglo-looking "housewife" with a pencil-point nose, blond hair, tiny waist in frilly apron and heels. She held a sponge emitting soap bubbles. Vale ran her finger over the lettering. "Doña Cleanwell," she said, like a teacher pointing at a blackboard, unaware that she mispronounced the product name or had inadvertently translated. "You wouldn't know this company in the United States. They don't import to Gringolandia."

The way Vale said "the United States," Katia couldn't tell if she meant that it was because the US would consider the products inferior or if the company considered the US unworthy.

Tina nodded. "We sell very well. We work on commission. There's a demonstration party tomorrow in the home of a neighbor—well, not far."

The hostess of such a get-together, Tina explained, would invite her friends and family. She'd serve refreshments while Tina demonstrated the efficacy and efficiency of the products. They'd play a few games with samples as prizes to get people motivated, and then take orders. "My job is mostly carrying boxes in and out of the car," Vale said to Katia. She went to the small refrigerator and got herself a beer. "Tomorrow you can give me a hand, *muchacha*."

The next morning, Tina fixed fried eggs on an iron skillet, fresh hot green sauce, and beans with tortillas. Katia had missed her mother's *salsa de tomatillo*, but all she said was "It's good, Ma." Vale was always nearby, and Katia found no opportunity to have a private talk with her mother. There was a lot she wanted to ask, although she probably wouldn't have anyway. But there was also the matter of her purpose there and how to best approach it. She wondered if she should suggest they call her father and let him ask her to return. None of the possible scenarios, however, seemed viable to Katia with Tina's paramour hovering over them. Vale's eyes rarely moved away from her girlfriend's every move.

Late afternoon rolled around, and Tina told Katia to help Vale load boxes into the large trunk of the Buick while she got herself ready.

They rode from their busy block, Katia in the backseat feeling every speed bump and pothole with shocks shot, to yet another jammed street. Nowhere had the girl seen the city not bustling and at all hours. When she mentioned it, Vale said, "Do you know that by the twenty-first century, we'll have more than twenty million inhabitants here in the capital?"

"Wow," Katia said under her breath.

"Well, I won't be around by then, anyway," Tina said with a little chuckle.

"What do you mean, we won't be around by the twenty-first century?" Vale asked.

"You'll only be in your sixties," Katia said, doing the quick math in her head.

"Oh, no," Tina said. "My mamá is in her fifties, and look at her. I'd rather be dead than get old."

Vale stopped and double-parked. A woman in a mandarin-colored pants outfit waiting outside signaled they could leave the car in her driveway. "I'm so excited!" Margarita, the hostess, kept repeating. *"¡Qué emoción!"* All four, carrying supplies, made their way into the lady's house. Tina took charge setting up and giving instructions as to how to arrange things.

Margarita was a large-breasted woman with a heavily made-up face and a prominent beauty mark painted right below the corner of her bottom lip. With her short blond curly wig, it appeared obvious she was going for a Marilyn Monroe look. It took a second, third, and fourth look, but mostly it was her voice—and Adam's apple—that convinced Katia the lady was a man.

Except for parodies of women on TV portrayed by comedians like Milton Berle or, lately, Flip Wilson, Katia had never seen a man dressed like a woman. Although she thought of such acts as just silly, it seemed that they implied there wasn't supposed to be anything more ridiculous than a man dressed as a woman, cheap wig, girdle, painted face, pumps, and all. A high-pitched voice projected a manipulative personality spewing mostly nonsense.

On the other hand, when a woman dressed in men's attire (like Vale preferred), it didn't seem funny at all. Instead, people seemed to perceive the intention was to impose (or assume) authority. Katia had noticed public glares at her mother's companion with disdain for her boldness, the audacity to try to be a man. One or two even whispered insults her way, which Vale and Tina both ignored.

Now, upon arriving at the location of the demonstration party, the girl was seeing a man actually living as a woman. This was big news to the self-styled feminist, especially because Mexicans took gender roles so seriously. The hostess's live-in companion was a man in men's attire. It was all blowing her mind. As far as Katia could tell, she was deep in the underground of a subversive culture. Katia suspected she'd best not remark on it to Tina or anyone else around. If the girl was to phrase her curiosity wrong, she might come off as offensive. The last thing she should do was anger her mother when they had yet to discuss the point of her visit, which was sure to send Tina into a spin.

Soon guests—or, as Vale and Tina saw them, prospective customers—started showing up; most, she assumed from their behavior, were couples—brown, working-class, gloriously and ardently themselves. Katia kept up with the women's movement. They went braless and even topless at music festivals, joined communes, and traveled the world hitchhiking. She'd descended upon a new world, an aspect of her Mexican culture that she'd never imagined.

Even if Katia was a "gringa," like Vale kept saying—she seemed surprised that the girl had grown up on rice, beans, and tortillas and not just burgers and hot dogs—Katia had always felt herself to be Mexican, Mexican-American, or even "Hispana," like her father liked to say they were, being New Mexican, seven generations back to the Conquistadors. Their Catholic beliefs forbade both men and women, boys and girls, from even thinking about sex. (It was anti-evolution, of course, because everyone thought about sex.) Perhaps what she had come upon was the sexual revolution she only read about.

Throughout the evening, Katia said little and did her best to project the image of the ideal daughter. She'd been raised to display only the best manners in public, which included speaking when spoken to and doing as she was told. It had taken no more than a stern look from either parent for any of the children to shut up and sit still whenever they were out. Following her mother's and Vale's instructions, Katia distributed samples, made out orders, handled cash, and gave out receipts.

Everyone was in gleeful spirits. They chugged beer from small brown bottles or guzzled homemade lemonade and nibbled dainty cookies from a bakery. They teased one another and guffawed at their own jokes. At one point someone went to the record player and put on a 45 of "Me Gusta Estar Contigo" by Angelica Maria. All at once, the party was swooning and singing along, forgetting all about the demonstration underway until Vale shouted, "Cut that out!" Someone snapped a switch on the record player, but instead of shutting off, the next 45 dropped and a hit by Diana Ross began. It was a huge smash in the States, but apparently, people knew it in Mexico, too. Everyone jumped up and started swaying and singing along: "Tush mi in de mornin' . . ." The hostess grabbed Tina's hand, and they started twirling each other around.

Katia, who at the moment was sitting next to Vale, couldn't believe what she was seeing. Her mother dancing was always a novelty, like when Tina and Javier slow danced at a family party. But the Hustle? Katia felt her face grow warm with embarrassment at her mother's girlish behavior. Vale noticed and elbowed her, as if to say, "Come on, it's all right." Everyone was singing along to the English lyrics. Vale, too, almost howled, "There's no tomorrow!" Then leaning over, she whispered, "What does the song mean?" She knew few English words. When Katia interpreted, Vale's face turned into a ripe tomato and then, gaining composure, she nodded and gave the girl a soft pat on the shoulder, as if to thank her, but with such a direct woman-to-woman look that Katia felt it wasn't only about the song. When the record ended, everyone, out of breath and sweaty, took their seats, backs straight and hands on their laps as if they were back in a classroom.

Tina started a game of musical chairs. A cheerful participant won a sample bottle of rug cleaner, and everyone clapped. She seemed thrilled even as she blurted, "I don't have any rugs . . ." Vale snatched the rug cleaner out of the woman's grip and placed a sample of a drape spot cleaner in her hand. "I'm sure you have curtains!" she said.

Next Tina held a raffle, with Katia walking around passing out scraps of paper and a pencil, and used someone's sweaty cap to drop in names. Her mother instructed her to pick one out, and just as she was about to say the winner, a protest was armed. "It's rigged!" "Unfair!" "Do it again!" "Get someone else. It's Tina's daughter!" To avoid further ruckus, Margarita took over. Everyone soon calmed down, and the winner was elated with the prize—a sample of powdered laundry detergent. Then someone said, "Don't you say you don't have drawers to wash?" Everyone cracked up.

It was around then that a pint-size box-shaped woman appeared, wearing an oversize short-sleeve man's shirt and huaraches with soles made from tires. Her long hair was slicked back in a tight braid. She didn't seem interested in Doña Cleanwell but moved around as if she were an inspector. First, picking up this or that sample from the table where Tina had laid out all her products, the newcomer sniffed or pretended to read the English labels. A tense silence covered the room, eyes on the stranger. Maybe ten minutes later, two other women turned up, giving hairy eyeballs to anyone who glanced their way. It had been a very warm day, and a soft rain outside made the house humid, but one in an oversize thick motorcycle jacket left it on.

At one point, Katia saw the first woman elbow the hostess, "Who's the gringa?" She asked loud enough for everyone to hear.

"She's my daughter." It was Tina who responded, not looking at the woman but maintaining the merchant's smile she'd worn since arriving.

"Why did she call me gringa?" Katia whispered to Vale, who was nearby. She didn't think she looked white. The thought suddenly occurred to her that perhaps only in Chicago was she considered Mexican. Ironically, in Mexico, she was a *pocha*. Over the last few days, everyone had treated her like a foreigner, she figured, because of her accent. Wasn't she Mexican? "Where are you from?" they asked with a sneer. Chicago born but if she were a *white* gringa, would they instead have praised her ability to communicate in Spanish at all?

Katia learned her second language from both parents, who, being from different places, spoke Spanish differently. She recalled one Sunday recently, Javier's day off, when he began telling them about the history of New Mexico. It had become a state some sixty years earlier. "Basically, New Mexico was part of Spain. We were settled by the Spanish. We're Spanish," he said with hands motioning around the table. No one dared or bothered to raise questions. Their mother came from Mexico City. The kids were all born in Chicago. Was your ethnicity about cultural affinities or ancestry and not where you were born? If so, she *felt* Mexican. Was that enough to claim it? If white people lived in Mexico or grew up in a barrio in the States and felt Mexican, could they claim that, too? For Christ's sake. What made you Mexican?

Talking about cultural nuances, what made you a women's libber? If her mother—who read nothing, discussed nothing—was starting her own insurgency against the patriarchy, wasn't she at the forefront?

Katia was doing all she could to keep it together at the Doña Cleanwell party.

"It's your denim pants," Vale said, referring to the flared jeans Katia had on that were so popular with guys and girls back home. She was still in grammar school during Woodstock, but the festival defined for every young person what was hip. Back then Katia stitched patches on her bell-bottoms with frayed hems, a peace sign, "Make Love, Not War," and although she had tried it at a party only because it was antiestablishment, she added one of a cannabis plant.

"No one wears those except hippies." Vale spoke out of the corner of her mouth as if they were in a movie theater but loud enough so that a couple of guests turned around.

Meanwhile, the "inspector," whom Katia overheard called Lucas, was causing a distraction by acting all freaky-deaky. Lucas picked up a bottle of stain cleaner, took off the cap, sniffed it, and was going around with it as if she might pour it on someone's head. "Go home, Lucas," the hostess said, yanking the bottle from the woman's grip. Rings of sweat showed on her shirt's underarms as

Lucas made a show of acting like she was being run out. The rest weren't laughing but starting to get uptight.

It was time to wrap up the demonstration party. Tina handed her daughter the vinyl pouch with the book of orders and cash. "Put this in that box over there," she said, "and make sure you close up the lid. Don't put it in the trunk; keep it in the backseat. I don't want to lose track of it."

Katia did as she was told and with Vale started taking boxes to load up in the trunk of the car. Then, without having been asked, Lucas picked one up, too.

Outside, night had come, but the street continued to burst with activity. Katia was about to get in the backseat of the Buick when Lucas came forward and said, "Allow me," trying to take hold of what Katia had in her hand.

"What're you doing?" Vale said.

There was a momentary standoff and then Lucas let go. The busybody stuck her chin out as Vale came up. Katia took her opportunity to lug the box into the backseat of the car.

The people pouring out of the party onto the street, seeing a potential rumble brewing, stopped their jovial goodbyes to watch. Margarita, her wig now somewhat off center from so much hugging and kissing, stepped forward but said nothing.

Katia, in the backseat, started when she heard the front passenger door open. Tina stuck in her head. "Do you have the bag with the money?" her mother asked in English. In Chicago, Katia's mother always spoke in Spanish in public when she didn't want people around to understand. Now she was doing the opposite, speaking English as a private language.

Frightened by the brawl about to erupt, her pale daughter

pointed to the box. Instead of getting in, Tina slammed the door and went around to where the pair who'd come with Lucas were snooping inside the trunk. Katia twisted around to see what was going on in the back, and saw her mother slam down the trunk lid, making the two step back. Right off the curb, Vale and Lucas were cussing at each other, voices growing louder when Vale lifted a thick fist and punched Lucas right on the jaw. Pop! One of her gang jumped in. Katia scrambled out of the vehicle, frantic to fetch her mother, but Tina was nowhere in sight.

Instantly, a pile of women, one on top of another, formed on the street, and cars and passersby stopped to gawk. Someone yelled the police were on their way. Margarita, now sans wig and sleeves pushed up, was making circles around the stack of human bodies, all pulling hair, ripping off clothes, scratching flesh, or having someone in a choke hold. "Stop it, you *locas*! The cops will take you all to jail!" The hostess's companion pulled her away. "Come on, let's go in before the authorities put all the fault on us."

At last, Katia spotted the white pants her mother had worn again that day. Tina was crushed beneath the heap of women. "Ma!" she called, grabbing her mother's foot, her silver ankle bracelet glimmering beneath the streetlamp.

As soon as the sirens grew close, everyone started dispersing on their own. Lucas, a stream of blood running down her nose, braid undone, and shirt torn, gave Vale one last scowl, nostrils flaring. She allowed herself to be led away by her pals but not before she called, "I'll find you," flitting something gleaming beneath the streetlights. Vale returned the defiant look as if a knife threat meant nothing. Katia helped up her disheveled mother, who'd lost an earring and was looking around for it until Vale pulled her by the elbow. "Let's go," she said to both mother and daughter. "Hurry, before we end up arrested because of these idiots."

"*Ay, Dios mío,*" Tina said in the car as the other woman drove like a fiend but in silence. Tina seemed to want to take the other woman's hand, but she kept pulling away. Until they got in the house, Katia wasn't sure what her mother had been fussing about in the front seat. It turned out Vale's arm was slashed, and Katia's mother had managed to wrap it with her sweater.

At home, Tina tended her lover's wound. Fortunately, it appeared to be a superficial cut and wouldn't need stitches, or at least, Vale insisted she not go to a hospital, where she'd be forced to file a report. Understandably beyond upset, Vale finished washing up in the kitchen and went to bed. Tina came to sit with Katia on the sofa. Tina made a futile gesture at dusting herself off. The white capris were ruined, one earring, Fawcett-do amok, she lit a cigarette. Katia watched her mother blow a smoke ring. There was no end to the new Tina.

The airline reservations were for the next morning. Katia decided it was now or never with regard to telling her mother why she'd come. She suspected Tina had an idea, although she hadn't once asked. When the girl pulled out both return tickets, her mother immediately seemed overcome with a new level of angst. After a hard night, she now had another matter to face. Tina snatched the tickets and studied them. If she were to return to Chicago, it would be first thing the following day. Ticket in hand, the obviously overwhelmed woman got up and headed to the bedroom, closing the door quietly behind her.

Katia nearly tiptoed to the kitchen to check the time on the wall clock. She switched the light on long enough to see the time;

it was almost midnight. She went back to sit on the sofa, knees up. Light from the street came through the flimsy curtain and hit square on her face. She was already contemplating the consequence of her failed assignment and how her father would express his disappointment at the airport. He'd probably stop speaking to his eldest, who always, in his eyes, managed to screw up.

A plan started forming. She needed a job. Maybe with Mr. Vinny at the motel. Once she saved enough, she'd move out and find her own apartment. The mere thought was daunting. Then she recalled her mother. If Tina had the courage to leave home, why shouldn't she? Before long, Katia became aware of intense whispering in the bedroom.

"They're my children," she heard her mother say in a tone of restraint. More whispers and then it was Vale: "And what about me? Don't I mean anything to you? What about all the sacrifices I made . . . for you . . . for us?" Katia couldn't hear the rest of the reproach. She sat up and tiptoed to the door.

It wasn't long, however, before the discussion escalated into a loud argument. It no longer mattered who heard, and Katia returned to the sofa, actually resisting the urge to put her hands over her ears. At one point, it was her mother: "I'll come back, I'm telling you. I just want to see my children."

Then Vale: "I already know you'll stay in Chicago. You still love him, that's what it is, isn't it?" Their exchange grew to all-out shouting. Katia had never heard her mother raise her voice like that, not even at her younger siblings, who could test anyone's nerves.

Katia's hand landed on the Marlboros her mother had left behind with a compact box of matches. Smoking, another aspect of Tina's new life. Katia didn't even like the smell but pulled one out and, with the matches, tiptoed to the front door with the thought of going outside to have it while the women decided their fate. In the dark, she struggled with the row of locks on the door and gave up.

For the next hour or so, the heated discussion continued, as did crying, followed by pleas, and at one point Katia thought she heard a shattering on the floor. She started to get up, but all in the bedroom went quiet, and then the couple resumed their whispering.

A constant tap-tap came from the flat roof, and Katia realized it was raining hard. Between the pitter-patter above and the whispers of passionate lovers on the other side of the wall, at last Katia was lulled to sleep.

Early the next morning, Katia woke to the sounds of her mother packing clothes into the vinyl bag in the living room, throwing in heels, a purse in which she'd thrown all her costume jewelry, and several Avon products. There was talc and honeysuckle body lotion, but when Tina tossed in a men's cologne in a rare-car decanter, Katia couldn't help but reach in and study it. "When I first got here," her mother explained, "I tried selling Avon. I'm taking that for Eric. He's at that age where he wants to attract the girls."

The three women had coffee, and when Katia asked if they should call a taxi, Vale insisted on driving them to the airport. There was a traffic jam, and the long ride seemed never-ending. Katia couldn't decide from the couple's expressions whether they had come to any mutual agreement or if they were over. She also didn't know by her mother's reticence if Tina was angry at her for somehow being the cause of the disruption of her new life.

Vale towed the suitcase, bulging with Tina's belongings. Before leaving the house, there had been a conversation as to whether

Tina should take any Doña Cleanwell back to Chicago. Vale was certain the merchandise would be a hit, especially with the women at the factory, assuming Tina got her old job back. Tina was dubious about the products, since people weren't familiar with Doña Cleanwell in the US. "Oh, but you know how people are, Tina, they always crave what's new." The two went back and forth until, finally, Tina accepted a box of samples. It wasn't clear how she'd get the orders filled. Vale convinced her they had ample stock and that she would ship to Chicago until she herself could get there; then she'd make sure the entire inventory was sent ahead of her.

At the busy international airport, Katia carried the Doña Cleanwell box, walking behind the two women as they all went to check in at the counter. When her mother noticed Katia's long hair caught by the heavy box she was carrying, she grabbed hold of the long tresses to tie them in a rubber band she found in her purse. "For God's sake, Katia," she said, a little too loudly for the girl's comfort when others turned around. "You're always so disorganized."

Checking in, the flaps of the Doña Cleanwell box were folded into each other, and it took extra time for the reservationist to secure it with packaging tape. "Ay," the reservationist sighed after tossing the box on the conveyor belt behind her and wiping her brow in a silent complaint about the package's weight and perhaps the advantage passengers took in the things they carried.

Vale and Tina walked arm in arm, making their way up to the customs checkpoint and Katia lagging to give them privacy. "Call me!" she heard Vale shout. Turning around, they could hardly see her, left behind with the crowd waving departing loved ones goodbye.

Bringing her mother home was turning out to be the most significant accomplishment in Katia's young life, already trumping high school graduation. No tears, apologies, or even signs from heaven would completely eradicate the fracture in their family caused by Tina's deliberate absence in the last months. But it was a fracture, not a permanent break—or so Katia hoped as she helped her mother snap on the seat belt and get ready for takeoff.

Now she knew that her father and Lulu had been regularly in touch with Tina. Maybe Eric, too. As for herself, she was of age now, a grown-up able to make her own decisions. It was Junior, her baby brother, who had been left in the cracks of the family. "Did you bring Junior an Avon gift?" she blurted.

Her mother's expression seemed surprised. "Of course," she said.

Katia started to say how cool she thought flying was (despite throwing up on her first flight, but then, if she did mention it, her mother would probably repeat, "Oh Katia, you're always so disorganized.") when the pilot gave his remarks over a speaker as he turned on the engines, and the two automatically grabbed each other's hand. They were equally anxious about flying; putting aside their usual inhibitions about being demonstrative, they held each other. Only when lunch was served did the two let themselves exhale. It was American food, something neither had heard of before—Salisbury steak, with mashed potatoes and green beans and the smallest square of vanilla cake with chocolate frosting for dessert. Not only was the experience of flying alien, but being surrounded by white monolingual stewardesses and passengers also made Katia and her mother feel out of place.

After trays were gathered up, Katia's mother began to ask about the children again. "What do you think of Lulu's not being in school anymore?" Katia asked.

"Oh, your sister and I have had a few conversations on the phone. She's a beautician now. She'll find work," her mother said almost offhandedly. "Your father, too, has filled me in on you kids." She had the window seat and turned to look at the clouds. She and Katia both had a fear of heights but agreed that being so high in the sky was nothing short of a miracle.

"When did you speak with my father?" Katia asked. The only occasions Katia had been aware that her mother called were the rare Sundays when each member took a turn saying hello to Tina.

"Oh," her mother said, "he calls me collect from work in the middle of the night sometimes." It was the usual call on break. Obviously, Tina's departure hadn't ended the habit. The mother turned back to the window, indicating she had no interest in elaborating. It was obvious now to Katia that her father knew she didn't stay with her mother in the *vecindad*. Had he also known she was living with Vale?

"He missed you, Ma," Katia said quietly.

"Your brothers are just boys," Tina said, detouring any conversation about her marriage. "They still need their mother." She reached into her purse and pulled out a daily prayer pamphlet and began reading to herself. Katia closed her eyes and pretended to rest, while her brain was going faster than the plane.

She turned and watched her mother's profile, almost a silhouette against the sunlight. She had a pleasant face, but when Tina laughed, revealing a gold-capped tooth, it looked to Katia like a gaudy attempt at showing off. On the other hand, her mother was repulsed by her eldest daughter's armpit hair. "I'm not shaving just to impress men, Ma," she'd said. Now, she began to consider that maybe it was more than a difference in style or popular opinions.

Her mother was as far from being a feminist as Katia was from buying the bride magazines that Lulu pored over.

Katia wondered if older people like her parents still had sex. Being a virgin, she had every question in the book about sex. "Ma," she ventured, "what does it feel like to love a woman?"

Tina put down the pamphlet and stared at her daughter. After a few seconds, she let out a heavy sigh as if every memory of her life had just gone through her body. She picked up the pamphlet to resume reading. Katia decided her mother wasn't about to indulge such a bold question when instead, Tina answered, "It feels like you've found your soulmate."

Coming from her mother, devoted to her faith, the concept sounded peculiar. Katia didn't have a clue what having a twin soul meant. Her guess was that it was related to the zodiac. Everyone was always going around asking someone new, "What's your sign?" Depending on what you said, people decided whether you'd get along. Katia must've looked as confused as she felt because her mother added, "I never encountered anyone who understood me so well."

They were silent and then Tina said, "I'm going to see if I can find some work like I was doing in Mexico, selling products on my own, giving demonstration parties. It was enjoyable and I earned good commissions. I don't want to go back to the factory."

Katia nodded. She had some decisions to make, too. It reminded her of what Vale had advised without being asked: "Do what you want to do with your future. Who the hell cares? It's your own *pinche vida* to live, after all." Later, Katia pulled out the pocket English/Spanish dictionary she'd brought along. *Pinche*: scullion. No, whatever her life was to be, Katia would be no scullion.

ACKNOWLEDGMENTS

My gratitude to Johanna Castillo, literary agent, and to Tara Parsons, editor, for their enthusiasm and belief in my work, past, present, and future.

Also, with loving appreciation to Hediberto, who has been my constant during the writing of these stories.

Here ends Ana Castillo's
Doña Cleanwell Leaves Home.

The first edition of the book was printed and
bound at Lakeside Book Company
in Harrisonburg, Virginia, May 2023.

A NOTE ON THE TYPE

The text of this novel was set in Freight Text Pro,
a serif font family designed by Joshua Darden. This
typeface has twelve styles and was published by
Freight Collection. Aptly named for its suitability for
use across small and large sets of copy, it is a cleanly
designed font that feels both unique and familiar to
the reader at the same time.

HarperVia

An imprint dedicated to publishing international voices,
offering readers a chance to encounter other lives and other
points of view via the language of the imagination.